"A powerful novel whose unforgettable characters channel humanity's true superpowers: art and the act of creation."
— Elizabeth Hand, author of *Hokuloa Road*

"Sarah Pinsker plays genre like a favorite guitar, and I am in awe of her talents. How can a writer so new be so central, so necessary?"
— Andy Duncan, author of *An Agent of Utopia*

"An absorbing tale of a quiet, all-too-believable American dystopia in which a passion for music becomes the secretive, surprising seed of rebellion." — Linda Nagata, author of *The Last Good Man*

"A lively and hopeful look at how community and music and life goes on even in the middle of dark days and malevolent corporate shenanigans."
— Kelly Link, author of *White Cat, Black Dog*

"This book will help you survive the future . . . restored some of my faith in community, and I didn't even realize how much I needed this book right now." — Charlie Jane Anders, author of *Dreams Bigger Than Heartbreak*

"A deeply human song of queer found family and the tension between independence and belonging, thoughtful and raw like the best live music."
— Nicola Griffith, author of *Hild*

"An expertly drawn post-catastrophe world peopled by compassionately written characters." — Ann Leckie, author of *Provenance*

WE ARE SATELLITES

"Taut and elegant, carefully introspected and thoughtfully explored."
— *New York Times*

"A gripping, believable immersion in the day after tomorrow."
— *The Guardian*

"Like everything else she has written to date, *We Are Satellites* is highly recommended." — Charles de Lint, *The Magazine of Fantasy & Science Fiction*

★ "Pinsker's newest is a carefully crafted sci-fi web stretched over an intensely human core." — *Booklist* (starred review)

"Pinsker does an excellent job of presenting the turmoil of the implant impacts relationships between spouse and children, spouses with each other, siblings, the world, the haves and have nots, the disabled, the privileged. I found myself shaking my head at the choices the characters made, but on further reflection found myself wondering if I would react the same way." — LaShawn M. Wanak, *Lightspeed Magazine*

Lost Places

lost places

STORIES

Sarah
Pinsker

Small Beer Press
Easthampton, MA

Lost Places: Stories copyright © 2023 by Sarah Pinsker. All rights reserved. Page 273 is an extension of the copyright page.

Small Beer Press
150 Pleasant Street #306
Easthampton, MA 01027
smallbeerpress.com
weightlessbooks.com
bookmoonbooks.com
info@smallbeerpress.com

Distributed to the trade by Consortium.

Library of Congress Cataloging-in-Publication Data

Names: Pinsker, Sarah, author.
Title: Lost places : stories / Sarah Pinsker.
Description: First edition. | Easthampton, MA : Small Beer Press, [2023] |
    Summary: "A half-remembered children's TV show. A hotel that shouldn't
    exist. A mysterious ballad. A living flag. A group of girls goes
    camping. Nebula and Hugo Award-winning author Sarah Pinsker's second
    collection brings together her touchstones of music and memory, secret
    subversions and hidden messages"-- Provided by publisher.
Identifiers: LCCN 2022054098 (print) | LCCN 2022054099 (ebook) | ISBN
    9781618731999 (paperback) | ISBN 9781618732002 (ebook)
Classification: LCC PS3616.I579 L67 2023 (print) | LCC PS3616.I579
    (ebook) | DDC 813/.6--dc23
LC record available at https://lccn.loc.gov/2022054098
LC ebook record available at https://lccn.loc.gov/2022054099

First edition 1 2 3 4 5 6 7 8 9 0

Set in Centaur 12 pt.

Printed on 30% PCR recycled paper by the Versa Press in East Peoria, IL.
Cover illustration: Thomas Baldwin, *Airopaidia* (1786)

Contents

For the booksellers, the librarians, and the teachers,
in tough times and otherwise

Two Truths and a Lie

In his last years, Marco's older brother Denny had become one of those people whose possessions swallowed them entirely. The kind they made documentaries about, the kind people staged interventions for, the kind people made excuses not to visit, and who stopped going out, and who were spoken of in sighs and silences. Those were the things Stella thought about after Denny died, and those were the reasons why, after eyeing the four other people at the funeral, she offered to help Marco clean out the house.

"Are you sure?" Marco asked. "You barely even knew him. It's been thirty years since you saw him last."

Marco's husband, Justin, elbowed Marco in the ribs. "Take her up on it. I've got to get home tomorrow and you could use help."

"I don't mind. Denny was nice to me," Stella said, and then added, "But I'd be doing it to help you."

The first part was a lie, the second part true. Denny had been the weird older brother who was always there when their friends hung out at Marco's back in high school, always lurking with a notebook and a furtive expression. She remembered Marco going out of his way to try to include Denny, Marco's admiration wrapped in disappointment, his slow slide into embarrassment.

She and Marco had been good friends then, but she hadn't kept up with anyone from high school. She had no excuse; social media could reconnect just about anyone at any time. She wasn't sure what it said about her or them that nobody had tried to communicate.

On the first night of her visit with her parents, her mother had said, "Your friend Marco's brother died this week," and Stella had suddenly been overwhelmed with remorse for having let that particular friendship lapse. Even more so when she read the obituary her mother had clipped, and she realized Marco's parents had died a few years before. That was why she went to the funeral and that was why she volunteered.

"I'd like to help," she said.

Two days later, she arrived at the house wearing clothes from a bag her mother had never gotten around to donating: jeans decades out of style and dappled with paint, treadworn gym shoes, and a baggy, age-stretched T-shirt from the Tim Burton *Batman*. She wasn't self-conscious about the clothes—they made sense for deep cleaning—but there was something surreal about the combination of these particular clothes and this particular door.

"I can't believe you still have that T-shirt," Marco said when he stepped out onto the stoop. "Mine disintegrated. Do you remember we all skipped school to go to the first showing?"

"Yeah. I didn't even know my mom still had it. I thought she'd thrown it out years ago."

"Cool—and thanks for doing this. I told myself I wouldn't ask anybody, but if someone offered I'd take them up on it. Promise me you won't think less of me for the way this looks? Our parents gave him the house. I tried to help him when I visited, but he didn't really let me, and he made it clear if I pushed too hard I wouldn't be welcome anymore."

Stella nodded. "I promise."

He handed her a pair of latex gloves and a paper mask to cover her mouth and nose; she considered for the first time how bad it might be. She hadn't even really registered that he had squeezed through a cracked door and greeted her outside. The lawn was manicured, the flower beds mulched and weeded and ready for the spring that promised to erupt at any moment, if winter ever agreed to depart. The shutters sported fresh white paint.

Which was why she was surprised when Marco cracked the door again to enter, leaving only enough room for her to squeeze through as she followed. Something was piled behind the door. Also beside the door, in front of the door, and in every available space in the entranceway. A narrow path led forward to the kitchen, another into the living room, another upstairs.

"Oh," she said.

He glanced back at her. "It's not too late to back out. You didn't know what you were signing up for."

"I didn't," she admitted. "But it's okay. Do you have a game plan?"

"Dining room, living room, rec room, bedrooms, in that order. I have no clue how long any room will take, so whatever we get done is fine. Most of what you'll find is garbage, which can go into bags I'll take to the dumpster in the yard. Let me know if you see anything you think I might care about. We should probably work in the same room, anyhow, since I don't want either of us dying under a pile. That was all I thought about while I cleaned a path through the kitchen to get to the dumpster: If I get buried working in here alone, nobody will ever find me."

"Dining room it is, then." She tried to inject enthusiasm into her voice, or at least moral support.

It was strange seeing a house where she had spent so much time reduced to such a fallen state. She didn't think she'd have been able to say where a side table or a bookcase had stood, but there they were, in the deepest strata, and she remembered.

They'd met here to go to prom, ten of them. Marco's father had photographed the whole group together, only saying once, "In my day, people went to prom with dates," and promptly getting shushed by Marco's mother. Denny had sat on the stairs and watched them, omnipresent notebook in his hands. It hadn't felt weird until Marco told him to go upstairs, and then suddenly it had gone from just another family member watching the festivities to something more unsettling.

3

She and Marco went through the living room to the dining room. A massive table still dominated the room, though it was covered with glue sticks and paintbrushes and other art supplies. Every other surface in the room held towering piles, but the section demarcated by paint-smeared newspaper suggested Denny had actually used the table.

She smelled the kitchen from ten feet away. Her face must have shown it, because Marco said, "I'm serious. Don't go in there unless you have to. I've got all the windows open and three fans blowing but it's not enough. I thought we could start in here because it might actually be easiest. You can do the sideboard and the china cabinets and I'll work on clearing the table. Two categories: garbage and maybe-not-garbage, which includes personal stuff and anything you think might be valuable. Dying is shockingly expensive."

Stella didn't know if that referred to Denny's death—she didn't know how he'd died—or to the funeral, and she didn't want to ask. She wondered why Marco had chosen the impersonal job with no decisions involved, but when she came to one of his grandmother's porcelain teacups, broken by the weight of everything layered on top of it, she thought she understood. He didn't necessarily remember what was under here, but seeing it damaged would be harder than if Stella just threw it in a big black bag. The items would jog memories; their absence would not.

She also came to understand the purpose of the latex gloves. The piles held surprises. Papers layered on papers layered on toys and antiques, then, suddenly, mouse turds or a cat's hairball or the flattened tendril of some once-green plant or something moldering and indefinable. Denny had apparently smoked, too; every few layers, a full ashtray made an appearance. The papers were for the most part easy discards: the news and obituary sections of the local weekly newspaper, going back ten, fifteen, thirty-five years, some with articles cut out.

Here and there, she came across something that had survived: a silver platter, a resilient teapot, a framed photo. She placed those on the table in the space Marco had cleared. For a while it felt like she was just shifting the mess sideways, but eventually she began to recognize progress in the form of the furniture under the piles. When Marco finished, he dragged her garbage bags through the kitchen and out to the dumpster, then started sifting through the stuff she'd set aside. He labeled three boxes: "keep," "donate," and "sell." Some items took him longer than others; she decided not to ask how he made the choices. If he wanted to talk, he'd talk.

"Stop for lunch?" Marco asked when the table at last held only filled boxes.

Stella's stomach had started grumbling an hour before; she was more than happy to take a break. She reached instinctively for her phone to check the time, then stopped herself and peeled the gloves off the way she'd learned in first aid in high school, avoiding contamination. "I need to wash my hands."

"Do it at the deli on the corner. You don't want to get near any of these sinks."

The deli on the corner hadn't been there when they were kids. What *had* been? A real estate office or something else that hadn't registered in her teenage mind. Now it was a hipster re-creation of a deli, really, complete with order numbers from a wall dispenser. A butcher with a waxed mustache took their order.

"Did he go to school with us?" Stella whispered to Marco, watching the butcher.

He nodded. "Chris Bethel. He was in the class between us and Denny, except he had a different name back then."

In that moment, she remembered Chris Bethel, pre-transition, playing Viola in *Twelfth Night* like a person who knew what it was to be shipwrecked on a strange shore. Good for him.

While they waited, she ducked into the bathroom to scrub her hands. She smelled like the house now, and hoped nobody else noticed.

Marco had already claimed their sandwiches, in plastic baskets and waxed paper, and chosen a corner table away from the other customers. They took their first few bites without speaking. Marco hadn't said much all morning, and Stella had managed not to give in to her usual need to fill silences, but now she couldn't help it.

"Where do you live? And how long have you and Justin been together?"

"Outside Boston," he said. "And fifteen years. How about you?"

"Chicago. Divorced. One son, Cooper. I travel a lot. I work sales for a coffee distributor."

Even as she spoke, she hated that she'd said it. None of it was true. She had always done that, inventing things when she had no reason to lie, just because they sounded interesting, or because it gave her a thrill. If he had asked to see pictures of her nonexistent son Cooper, she'd have nothing to show. Not to mention she had no idea what a coffee distributor did.

Marco didn't seem to notice, or else he knew it wasn't true and filed it away as proof they had drifted apart for a reason. They finished their sandwiches in silence.

"Tackle the living room next?" Marco asked. "Or the rec room?"

"Rec room," she said. It was farther from the kitchen.

Farther from the kitchen, but the basement litter pans lent a different odor and trapped it in the windowless space. She sighed and tugged the mask up.

Marco did the same. "The weird thing is I haven't found a cat. I'm hoping maybe it was indoor-outdoor or something . . ."

Stella didn't know how to respond, so she said, "Hmm," and resolved to be extra careful when sticking her hands into anything.

The built-in bookshelves on the back wall held tubs and tubs of what looked like holiday decorations.

"What do you want to do with holiday stuff?" Stella pulled the nearest box forward on the shelf and peered inside. Halloween and Christmas, mostly, but all mixed together, so reindeer ornaments and spider lights negotiated a fragile peace.

"I'd love to say toss it, but I think we need to take everything out, in case."

"In case?"

He tossed her a sealed package to inspect. It held two droid ornaments, like R2-D2 but different colors. "Collector's item, mint condition. I found it a minute ago, under a big ball of tinsel and plastic reindeer. It's like this all over the house: valuable stuff hidden with the crap. A prize in every fucking box."

The size of the undertaking was slowly dawning on her. "How long are you here for?"

"I've got a good boss. She said I could work from here until I had all Denny's stuff in order. I was thinking a week, but it might be more like a month, given everything . . ."

"A month! We made good progress today, though . . ."

"You haven't seen upstairs. Or the garage. There's a lot, Stella. The dining room was probably the easiest other than the kitchen, which will be one hundred percent garbage."

"That's if he didn't stash more collectibles in the flour."

Marco blanched. "Oh god. How did I not think of that?"

Part of her wanted to offer to help again, but she didn't think she could stomach the stench for two days in a row, and she was supposed to be spending time with her parents, who already said she didn't come home enough. She wanted to offer, but she didn't want him to take her up on it. "I'll come back if I can."

He didn't respond, since that was obviously a lie. They returned to the task at hand: the ornaments, the decorations, the toys, the games, the stacks of DVDs and VHS tapes and records and CDs and cassettes, the prizes hidden not in every box, but in enough to make the effort worthwhile. Marco was right that the dining room had been easier. He'd decided to donate all the cassettes, DVDs, and videotapes, but said the vinyl might actually be worth something. She didn't know anything about records, so she categorized them as playable and not, removing each from its sleeve to examine for warp and scratches. It was tedious work.

It took two hours for her to find actual equipment Denny might have played any of the media on: a small television on an Ikea TV stand, a stereo and turntable on the floor, then another television behind the first.

It was an old set, built into a wooden cabinet that dwarfed the actual screen. She hadn't seen one like this in years; it reminded her of her grandparents. She tried to remember if it had been down here when they were kids.

Something about it—the wooden cabinet, or maybe the dial—made her ask, "Do you remember *The Uncle Bob Show*?"

Which of course he didn't, nobody did, she had made it up on the spot, like she often did.

Which was why it was so weird that Marco said, "Yeah! And the way he looked straight into the camera. It was like he saw me, specifically me. Scared me to death, but he said, 'Come back next week,' and I always did because I felt like he'd get upset otherwise."

As he said it, Stella remembered too. The way Uncle Bob looked straight into the camera, and not in a friendly Mr. Rogers way. Uncle Bob was the anti–Mr. Rogers. A cautionary uncle, not predatory, but not kind.

"It was a local show," she said aloud, testing for truth.

Marco nodded. "Filmed at the public broadcast station. Denny was in the audience a few times."

Stella pictured Denny as she had known him, a hulking older teen. Marco must have realized the disconnect, because he added, "I mean when he was little. Seven or eight, maybe? The first season? That would make us five. Yeah, that makes sense, since I was really jealous, but my mom said you had to be seven to go on it."

Stella resized the giant to a large boy. *Audience* didn't feel like exactly the right word, but she couldn't remember why.

Marco crossed the room to dig through the VHS tapes they'd discarded. "Here."

It took him a few minutes to connect the VCR to the newer television. The screen popped and crackled as he hit play.

The show started with an oddly familiar instrumental theme song. *The Uncle Bob Show* appeared in block letters, then the logo faded and the screen went black. A door opened, and Stella realized it wasn't dead-screen black but a matte black room. The studio was painted black, with no furniture except a single black wooden chair.

Children spilled through the door, running straight for the camera—no, running straight for the secret compartments in the floor, all filled with toys. In that environment, the colors of the toys and the children's clothes were shocking, delicious, welcoming, warm. Blocks, train sets, plastic animals. That was why *audience* had bothered her. They weren't an audience; they were half the show, half the camera's focus. After a chaotic moment where they sorted who got possession of what, they settled in to play.

Uncle Bob entered a few minutes later. He was younger than Stella expected, his hair dark and full, his long face unlined. He walked with a ramrod spine and a slight lean at the hips, his arms clasped behind him giving him the look of a flightless bird. He made his way to the chair, somehow avoiding the children at his feet even though he was already looking straight into the camera.

He sat. Stella had the eeriest feeling, even now, that his eyes focused on her. "How on earth did this guy get a TV show?"

"Right? That's Denny there." Marco paused the tape and pointed at a boy behind and to the right of the chair. Her mental image hadn't been far off; Denny was bigger than all the other kids. He had a train car in each hand, and was holding the left one out to a little girl. The image of him playing well with others surprised Stella; she'd figured he'd always been a loner. She opened her mouth to say that, then closed it again. It was fine for Marco to say whatever he wanted about his brother, but it might not be appropriate for her to bring it up.

Marco pressed play again. The girl took the train from Denny and smiled. In the foreground, Uncle Bob started telling a story. Stella had forgotten the storytelling, too. That was the whole show: children doing their thing, and Uncle Bob telling completely unrelated stories. He paid little attention to the kids, though they sometimes stopped playing to listen to him.

The story was weird. Something about a boy buried alive in a hillside—"planted," in his words—who took over the entire hillside, like a weed, and spread for miles around.

Stella shook her head. "That's fucked up. If I had a kid I wouldn't let them watch this. Nightmare city."

Marco gave her a look. "I thought you said you had a kid?"

"I mean if I'd had a kid back when this was on." She was usually more careful with the lying game. Why had she said she had a son, anyway? She'd be found out the second Marco ran into her parents.

It was a dumb game, really. She didn't even remember when she'd started playing it. College, maybe. The first chance she'd had to reinvent herself, so why not do it wholesale? The rules were simple: Never lie about something anyone could verify independently; never lose track of the lies; keep them consistent and believable. That was why in college she'd claimed she'd made the varsity volleyball team in high school, but injured her knee so spectacularly in practice she'd never been able to play any sport again, and she'd once flashed an AP physics class, and she'd auditioned for the *Jeopardy!* Teen Tournament but been cut when she accidentally said "fuck" to Alex Trebek. Then she just had to live up to her reputation as someone who'd lived so much by eighteen that she could coast on her former cool.

Uncle Bob's story was still going. "They dug me out of the hillside on my thirteenth birthday. It's good to divide rhizomes to give them room to grow."

"Did he say 'me'?"

"A lot of his stories went like that, Stella. They started out like fairy tales, but somewhere in the middle he shifted into first person. I don't know if he had a bad writer or what."

"And did he say 'rhizome'? Who says 'rhizome' to seven-year-olds?" Stella hit the stop button. "Okay. Back to work. I remember now. That's plenty."

Marco frowned. "We can keep working, but I'd like to keep this on in the background now that we've found it. It's nice to see Denny. That Denny, especially."

That Denny: Denny frozen in time, before he got weird.

Stella started on the boxes in the back, leaving the stuff near the television to Marco. Snippets of story drifted her way, about the boy's family, but much, much older than when they'd buried him. His brothers were fathers now, their children the nieces and nephews of the teenager they'd dug from the hillside. Then the oddly upbeat theme song twice in a row—that episode's end and another's beginning.

"Marco?" she asked. "How long did this run?"

"I dunno. A few years, at least."

"Did you ever go on it? Like Denny?"

"No. I . . . hmm. I guess by the time I'd have been old enough, Denny had started acting strange, and my parents liked putting us into activities we could both do at the same time."

They kept working. The next Uncle Bob story that drifted her way centered on a child who got lost. Stella kept waiting for it to turn into a familiar children's story, but it didn't. Just a kid who got lost and when she found her way home she realized she'd arrived back without her body, and her parents didn't even notice the difference.

"Enough," Stella said from across the room. "That was enough to give me nightmares, and I'm an adult. Fuck. Watch more after I leave if you want."

"Okay. Time to call it quits, anyway. You've been here like nine hours."

She didn't argue. She waited until they got out the front door to peel off the mask and gloves.

"It was good to hang out with you," she said.

"You, too. Look me up if you ever get to Boston."

She couldn't tell him to do the same with Chicago, so she said, "Will do." She realized she'd never asked what he did for a living, but it seemed like an awkward time. It wasn't until after she'd walked away that she realized he'd said goodbye as if she wasn't returning the next day. She definitely wasn't, especially if he kept binging that creepy show.

When she returned to her parents' house she made a beeline for the shower. After twenty minutes' scrubbing, she still couldn't shake the smell. She dumped the clothes in the garbage instead of the laundry and took the bag to the outside bin, where it could stink as much as it needed to stink.

Her parents were sitting on the screened porch out front, as they often did once the evenings got warm enough, both with glasses of iced tea on the wrought iron table between them as if it were already summer. Her mother had a magazine open on her lap—she still subscribed to all her scientific journals, though she'd retired years before—and her father was solving a math puzzle on his tablet, which Stella could tell by his intense concentration.

"That bad?" Her mother lifted an eyebrow at her as she returned from the garbage.

"That bad."

She went into the house and poured herself a glass to match her parents'. Something was roasting in the oven, and the kitchen was hot and smelled like onions and butter. She closed her eyes and pressed the glass against her forehead, letting the oven and the ice battle over her body temperature, then returned to sit on the much cooler porch, picking the empty chair with the better view of the dormant garden.

"Grab the cushion from the other chair if you're going to sit in that one," her father said.

She did as he suggested. "I don't see why you don't have cushions for both chairs. What if you have a couple over? Do they have to fight over who gets the comfortable seat versus who gets the view?"

He shrugged. "Nobody's complained."

They generally operated on a complaint system. Maybe that was where she'd gotten the habit of lies and exaggeration: She'd realized early that only extremes elicited a response.

"How did dinner look?" he asked.

"I didn't check. It smelled great, if that counts for anything."

He grunted, the sound both a denial and the effort of getting up, and went inside. Stella debated taking his chair, but it wasn't worth the scene. A wasp hovered near the screen and she watched it for a moment, glad it was on the other side.

"Hey, Ma, do you remember *The Uncle Bob Show*?"

"Of course." She closed her magazine and hummed something that sounded half like Uncle Bob's theme song and half like *The Partridge Family* theme. Stella hadn't noticed the similarity between the two tunes; it was a ridiculously cheery theme song for such a dark show.

"Who was that guy? Why did they give him a kids' show?"

"The public television station had funding trouble and dumped all the shows they had to pay for—we had to get cable for you to watch *Sesame Street* and *Mister Rogers' Neighborhood*. They had all these gaps to fill in their schedule, so anybody with a low budget idea could get on. That one lasted longer than most—four or five years, I think."

"And nobody said, 'That's some seriously weird shit'?"

"Oh, we all did, but someone at the station argued there were plenty of peace-and-love shows around, and some people like to be scared, and it's not like it was full of violence or sex, and just because a show had kids in it didn't mean it was a kids' show."

"They expected adults to watch? That's even weirder. What time was it on?"

"Oh, I don't remember. Saturday night? Saturday morning?"

Huh. Maybe he was more like those old monster movie hosts. "That's deeply strange, even for the eighties. And who was the guy playing Uncle Bob? I tried looking it up on IMDB, but there's no page. Not on Wikipedia either. Our entire world is fueled by nostalgia, but there's nothing on this show. Where's the online fan club, the community of collectors? Anything."

Her mother frowned, clearly still stuck on trying to dredge up a name. She shook her head. "Definitely Bob, a real Bob, but I can't remember his last name. He must've lived somewhere nearby, because I ran into him at the drugstore and the hardware store a few times while the show was on the air."

Stella tried to picture that strange man in a drugstore, looming behind her in line, telling her stories about the time he picked up photos from a vacation but when he looked at them, he was screaming in every photo. If he were telling that story on the show, he'd end it with, "and then you got home from the drugstore with your photos, but when you looked at them, you were screaming in every photo too." Great. Now she'd creeped herself out without his help.

"How did I not have nightmares?"

"We talked about that possibility—all the mothers—but you weren't disturbed. None of you kids ever complained. It was a nice break, to chat with the other moms while you all played in such a contained space."

There was a vast difference between "never complained" and "weren't disturbed" that Stella would have liked to unpack, but she fixated on a different detail. "Contained space—you mean while we watched TV, right?"

"No, dear. The studio. It looked much larger on television, but the cameras formed this nice ring around three sides, and you all understood you weren't supposed to leave during that half hour except for a bathroom emergency. You all played and we sat around and had coffee. It was the only time in my week when I didn't feel like I was supposed to be doing something else."

It took Stella a few seconds to realize the buzzing noise in her head wasn't the wasp on the screen. "What are you talking about? I was on the show?"

"Nearly every kid in town was on it at some point. Everyone except Marco, because his brother was acting up by the time you two were old enough, and Celeste pulled Denny and enrolled both boys in karate instead."

"But me? Ma, I don't remember that at all." The idea that she didn't know something about herself that others knew bothered her more than she could express. "You aren't making this up?"

"Why would I lie? I'm sure there are other things you don't remember. Getting lice in third grade?"

"You shaved my head. Of course I remember. The whole class got it, but I was the only one whose mother shaved her head."

"I didn't have time to comb through it, honey. Something more benign? Playing at Tamar Siegel's house?"

"Who's Tamar Siegel?"

"See? The Siegels moved to town for a year when you were in second grade. They had a jungle gym that you loved. You didn't think much of the kid, but you liked her yard and her dog. We got on well with her parents; I was sad when they left."

Stella flashed on a tall backyard slide and a golden retriever barking at her when she climbed the ladder and left it below. A memory she'd never have dredged up unprompted. Nothing special about it: a person whose face she couldn't recall, a backyard slide, an experience supplanted by other experiences. Generic kid, generic fun. A placeholder memory.

"Okay, I get that there are things that didn't stick with me, and things that I think I remember once you remind me, but it doesn't explain why I don't remember a blacked-out TV studio or giant cameras or a creepy host. You forget the things that don't stand out, sure, but this seems, I don't know, formative."

Her mother shrugged. "You're making a big deal of nothing."

"Nothing? Did you listen to his stories?"

"Fairy tales."

"Now I know you didn't listen. He was telling horror stories to seven-year-olds."

"Fairy tales *are* horror stories, and like I said, you didn't complain. You mostly played with the toys."

"What about the kids at home watching? The stories were the focus if you weren't in the studio."

"If they were as bad as you say, hopefully parents paid attention and watched with their children and whatever else the experts these days say comprises good parenting. You're looking through a prism of now, baby. Have you ever seen early *Sesame Street*? I remember a sketch where a puppet with no facial features goes to a human for 'little girl eyes.' You and your friends watched shows, and if they scared you, you turned them off. You played outside. You cut your Halloween candy in half to make sure there were no razor blades inside. If you want to tell me I'm a terrible parent for putting you on that show with your friends, feel free, but since it took you thirty-five years to bring this up, I'm going to assume it didn't wreck your life."

Her father rang the dinner gong inside the house, a custom her parents found charming and Stella had always considered overkill in a family as small as theirs. She and her mother stood. Their glasses were still mostly full, the melting ice having replaced what they'd sipped.

She continued thinking over dinner, while she related everything she and Marco had unearthed to her mildly curious parents, and after, while scrubbing the casserole dish. What her mother said was true: She hadn't been driven to therapy by the show. She didn't remember any nightmares. It just felt strange to be missing something so completely, not to mention the questions that arose about what else she could be missing if she could be missing that. It was an unpleasant feeling.

After dinner, while her parents watched some reality show, she pulled out a photo album from the early eighties. Her family hadn't been much for photographic documentation, so there was just the one, chronological and well labeled, commemorating Stella at the old school playground before they pulled it out and replaced it with safer equipment, at a zoo, at the Independence Day parade. It was true, she didn't recall those particular moments, but she believed she'd been there. *The Uncle Bob Show* felt different. The first time she'd uttered the show's name, she'd thought she'd made it up.

She texted Marco: "Did Denny have all the Uncle Bob episodes on tape or only the ones he was in? Thanks!" She added a smiley face then erased it before she hit send. It felt falsely cheery instead of appreciative. His brother had just died.

She settled on the couch beside her parents. While they watched TV, she surfed the web looking for information about *The Uncle Bob Show*, but found nothing. In the era of kittens with Twitter accounts and sandwiches with their own Instagrams and fandoms for every conceivable property, it seemed impossible for something to be so utterly missing.

Not that it deserved a fandom; she just figured everything had one. Where were the ironic logo T-shirts? Where was the episode wiki explaining what happened in every Uncle Bob story? Where were the "Whatever happened to?" articles? The tell-alls by the kids or the director or the camera operator? The easy answer was that it was such a terrible show, or such a small show, that nobody cared. She didn't care either; she just needed to know. Not the same thing.

The next morning, she drove out to the public television station on the south end of town. She'd passed it so many times, but until now she wouldn't have said she'd ever been inside. Nothing about the interior rang a bell either, though it looked like it had been redone fairly recently, with an airy design that managed to say both modern and trapped in time.

"Can I help you?" The receptionist's trifocals reflected her computer's spreadsheet back at Stella. A phone log by her right hand was covered with sketched faces; the sketches were excellent. Grace Hernandez, according to her name plaque.

Stella smiled. "I probably should have called, but I wondered if you have archives of shows produced here a long time ago? My mother wants a video of a show I was on as a kid and I didn't want her to have to come over here for nothing."

Even while she said it, she wondered why she had to lie. Wouldn't it have been just as easy to say she wanted to see it herself? She'd noticed an older receptionist and decided to play on her sympathies, but there was no reason to assume her own story wasn't compelling.

"Normally we'd have you fill out a request form, but it's a slow day. I can see if someone is here to help you." Grace picked up a phone and called one number, then disconnected and tried another. Someone answered, because she repeated Stella's story, then turned back to her. "He'll be out in a sec."

She gestured to a glass-and-wood waiting area, and Stella sat. A flat screen overhead played what Stella assumed was their station, on mute, and a few issues of a public media trade magazine called *Current* were piled neatly on the low table.

A small man—a little person? Was that the right term?—came around the corner into reception. He was probably around her age, but she would have remembered him if he'd gone to school with her.

"Hi," he said. "I'm Jeff Stills. Grace says you're looking for a show?"

"Yes, my mother—"

"Grace said. Let's see what we can do."

18

He handed her a laminated guest pass on a lanyard and waited while she put it on, then led her through a security door and down a long, low-ceilinged corridor, punctuated by framed stills from various shows. No Uncle Bob. "Have you been here before?"

"When I was a kid."

"Hmm. I'll bet it looks pretty different. This whole back area was redone around 2005, after the roof damage. Then the lobby about five years ago."

She hadn't had any twinges of familiarity, but at least that explained some of it. She'd forgotten about the blizzard that wrecked the roof; she'd been long gone by then.

"Hopefully whatever you're looking for wasn't among the stuff that got damaged by the storm. What *are* you looking for?"

"*The Uncle Bob Show.* Do you know it?"

"Only by name. I've seen the tapes on the shelf, but in the ten years I've been here, nobody has ever asked for a clip. Any good?"

"No." Stella didn't hesitate. "It's like those late-night horror hosts, Vampira or Elvira or whatever, except they forgot to run a movie and instead let the host blather on."

They came to a nondescript door. The low-ceilinged hallway had led her to expect low-ceilinged rooms, but the space they entered was more of a warehouse. A long desk cluttered with computers and various machinery occupied the front, and then the space opened into row upon row of metal shelving units. The aisles were wide enough to accommodate rolling ladders.

"We've been working on digitizing, but we have fifty years of material in here, and some stuff has priority."

"Is that what you do? Digitize?"

"Nah. We have interns for that. I catalogue new material as it comes in, and find stuff for people when they need clips. Mostly staff, but sometimes for networks, local news, researchers, that kind of thing."

"Sounds fun," Stella said. "How did you get into the field?"

"I majored in history, but never committed enough to any one topic for academic research. Ended up at library school, and eventually moved here. It is fun! I get a little bit of everything. Like today: a mystery show."

"Total mystery."

She followed him down the main aisle, then several aisles over, almost to the back wall. He pointed at some boxes above her head.

"Wow," she said. "Do you know where everything is without looking it up?"

"Well, it's alphabetical, so yeah, but also they're next to *Underground*, which I get a lot of requests for. Do you know what year you need?"

"1982? My mother couldn't remember exactly, but that's the year I turned seven."

Jeff disappeared and returned pushing a squeaking ladder along its track. He climbed up for the *"Uncle Bob Show* 1982" box. It looked like there were five years' worth, 1980 to 1985. She followed him back toward the door, where he pointed her to an office chair.

"We have strict protocols for handling media that hasn't been backed up yet. If you tell me which tapes you want to watch, I'll queue them up for you."

"Hmm. Well, my birthday is in July, so let's pick one in the last quarter of the year first, to see if I'm in there."

"You don't know if you are?"

She didn't want to admit she didn't remember. "I just don't know when."

He handed her a pair of padded headphones and rummaged in the box. She'd been expecting VHS tapes, but these looked like something else—Betamax, she guessed.

The show's format was such that she didn't have to watch much to figure out if she was in it or not. The title card came on, then the episode's children rushed in. She didn't see herself. She wondered again if this was a joke on her mother's part.

"Wait—what was the date on this one?"

Jeff studied the label on the box. "October ninth."

"I'm sorry. That's my mother's birthday. There's no way she stood around in a television studio that day. Maybe the next week?"

He ejected the tape and put it back in its box and put in another, but that one obviously had some kind of damage, all static.

"Third time's the charm," he said, going for the next tape. He seemed to believe it himself, because he dragged another chair over and plugged in a second pair of headphones. "Do you mind?"

She shook her head and rolled her chair slightly to the right to give him a better angle. The title card appeared.

"It's a good thing nobody knows about this show or they'd have been sued over this theme song," he said.

Stella didn't answer. She was busy watching the children. She recognized the first few kids: Lee Pool first, a blond beanpole; poor Dan Heller; Addie Chapel, whose mother had been everyone's pediatrician.

And then there she was, little Stella Gardiner, one of the last through the door. She wasn't used to competing for toys, so maybe she didn't know she needed to get in early, or maybe they were assigned an order behind the scenes. She'd thought seeing herself on screen would jog her memory, give her the studio or the stories or the backstage snacks, but she still had no recollection. She pointed at herself on the monitor for Jeff's benefit, to show they'd found her. He gave her a thumbs-up.

Little Stella seemed to know where she was going, even if she wasn't first to get there. Lee Pool already had the T. rex, but she wouldn't have cared. She'd liked the big dinosaurs, the bigger the better. She emerged from the toy pit with a matched pair. Brontosaurus, apatosaurus, whatever they called them these days. She could never wrap her head around something that large having existed. So yeah, the dinosaurs made sense—it was her, even if she still didn't remember it.

She carried the two dinosaurs toward the set's edge, where she collected some wooden trees and sat down. She was an only child, used to playing alone, and this clearly wasn't her first time in this space.

The camera lost her. The focus, of course, was on Uncle Bob. She had been watching herself and missed his entrance. He sat in his chair, children playing around him. Dan Heller zoomed around the set like a satellite in orbit, a model airplane in hand.

"Once upon a time there was a little boy who wanted to go fast." Uncle Bob started a story without waiting for anyone to pay attention.

"He liked everything fast. Cars, motorcycles, boats, airplanes. Bicycles were okay, but not the same thrill. When he rode in his father's car, he pretended they were racing the cars beside them. Sometimes they won, but mostly somebody quit the race. His father was not a fast driver. The little boy knew that if he drove, he'd win all the races. He wouldn't stop when he won, either. He'd keep going.

"He liked the sound of motors. He liked the way they rumbled deep enough to rattle his teeth in his head, and his bones beneath his skin; he liked the way they shut all the thinking out. He liked the smell of gasoline and the way it burned his nostrils. His family's neighbors had motorcycles they rode on weekends, and if he played in the front yard they'd sometimes let him sit on one with them before they roared away, leaving too much quiet behind. When they drove off, he tried to recreate the sound, making as much noise as possible until his father told him to be quiet, then to shut up, then 'For goodness sake, what does a man have to do to get some peace and quiet around here on a Saturday morning?'"

Dan paused his orbit and turned to face the storyteller. Two other kids had stopped to pay attention as well; Stella and the others continued playing on the periphery.

"The boy got his learner's permit on the very first day he was allowed. He skipped school for it rather than wait another second. He had saved his paper route money for driving lessons and a used motorbike. As soon as he had his full license, he did what he had always wanted to do: He drove as fast as he could down the highway, past all the cars, and then he kept driving forever. The end."

Uncle Bob shifted back in his chair as he finished. Dan watched him for a little longer, then launched himself again, circling the scattered toys and children faster than before.

Jeff sat back as well. "What kind of story was that?"

Stella frowned. "A deeply messed up one. That kid with the airplane—Dan Heller—drove off the interstate the summer after junior year. He was racing someone in the middle of the night and missed a curve."

"Oof. Quite the coincidence."

"Yeah . . ."

Uncle Bob started telling another story, this one about a vole living in a hole on a grassy hillside that started a conversation with the child sleeping in the hole next door.

"Do you want to watch the whole episode? Is this the one you need?"

"I think I need to look at a couple more?" She didn't know what she was looking for. "Sorry for putting you out. I don't mean to take up so much time."

"It's fine! This is interesting. The show is terrible, from any standpoint. The story was terrible, the production is terrible. I can't even decide if this whole shtick is campy bad or bad bad. Leaning toward the latter."

"I don't think there's anything redeeming," Stella said, her mind still on Dan Heller. Did his parents remember this story? "Can we look at the next one? October 30th?"

"Coming up." Jeff appeared to have forgotten she'd said she was looking for something specific, and she didn't remind him, since she still couldn't think of an appropriate detail.

Little Stella was second through the door this time, behind Tina, whose last name she didn't remember. She paused and looked out past a camera, probably looking for her mother, then kept moving when she realized more kids were coming through behind her. Head for the toys. Claim what's yours. Brontosaurus and T. rex and a blue whale. Whales were almost as cool as dinosaurs.

Tina had claimed a triceratops and looked like she wanted the brontosaurus. They sat down on the edge of the toy pit to negotiate. Uncle Bob watched them play, which gave Stella the eeriest feeling of being watched, even though she still felt like the kid on the screen wasn't her.

"So what was it like?" Jeff asked, but Stella didn't answer. Uncle Bob had started a story. He looked straight into the camera. This time it felt like he was truly looking straight at her. This was the one. She knew it.

"Once upon a time, there was a little girl who didn't know who she was. Many children don't know who they will be, and that's not unusual, but what was unusual in this case was that the girl was willing to trade who she was for who she could be, so she began to do just that. Little by little, she replaced herself with parts of other people she liked better. Parts of stories she wanted to live. Nobody lied like this girl. She believed her own stories so completely, she forgot which ones were true and which were false.

"If you've ever heard of a cuckoo bird, they lay their eggs in other birds' nests, so those birds are forced to raise them for their own. This girl was her own cuckoo, laying stories in her own head, and the heads of those around her, until even she couldn't remember which ones were true, or if there was anything left of her."

Uncle Bob went silent, watching the children play. After a minute, he started telling another story about the boy in the hill, and how happy he was whenever he had friends over to visit. That story ended, and a graphic appeared on the screen with an address for fan mail. Stella pulled a pen from her purse and wrote it down as the theme music played out.

"Are you sending him a letter?" The archivist had dropped his headphones and was watching her.

She shrugged. "Just curious."

"Is this the one, then?"

"The one?"

He frowned. "You said you wanted a copy for your mother."

"Yes! That would be lovely. This is the one she mentioned."

He pulled a DVD off a bulk spindle and rewound the tape. "You didn't say what it was like. Was he weird off camera too?"

"Yes," she said, though she didn't remember. "But he kept to himself. Just stayed in his dressing room until it was time to go on."

Jeff didn't reply, and something subtle changed about the way he interacted with her. What if there hadn't been a dressing room? He might know. When had she gotten so sloppy with her stories? Maybe it was because she was distracted. Her mother had told the truth: She'd been on a creepy TV show of which she had no memory. And what was it? Performance art? Storytelling? Fairy tales or horror? All of the above? She thanked Jeff and left.

She had just walked into her parents' house when Marco called. "Can you come back? There's something I need to show you."

She headed out to Denny's house. She paused on the step, realizing she was in nicer clothes this time. Hopefully she wouldn't be there long.

"Hey," she said when Marco answered the door. Even though she braced for the odor, it hit her hard.

He waved her in, talking as he navigated the narrow path he'd cleared up the stairs. "I thought I'd work on Denny's bedroom today, and, well . . ."

He held out an arm in the universal gesture of "go ahead," so she entered. The room had precarious ceiling-high stacks on every surface, including the floor and bed, piles everywhere except a path to an open walk-in closet. She stepped forward.

"What is that?"

"The word I came up with was 'shrine,' but I don't think that's right."

It was the sparest space in the house. She'd expected a dowel crammed end to end with clothes, straining under the weight, but the closet was empty except for—"shrine" was indeed the wrong word. This wasn't worship.

The most eye-catching piece, the thing she saw first, was a hand-painted Uncle Bob doll propped in the back corner. It looked like it had been someone else first—Vincent Price, maybe. Next to it stood a bobblehead and an action figure, both mutated from other characters, and one made of clay and plant matter, seemingly from scratch. Beside those, a black leather notebook, a pile of VHS tapes, and a single DVD. Tacked to the wall behind them, portraits of Uncle Bob in paint, in colored pencil, macaroni, photo collage, in, oh god, was that cat hair? And beside those, stills from the show printed on copier paper: Uncle Bob telling a story; Uncle Bob staring straight into the camera, an assortment of children. Her own still was toward the bottom right. Marco wasn't in any of them.

"That's the thing that guts me."

Stella turned, expecting to see Marco pointing to the art or the dolls, but she'd been too busy looking at those to notice the filthy pillow and blanket in the opposite corner. "He slept here?"

"It's the only place he could have." Marco's voice was strangled, like he was trying not to cry.

She didn't know what to say to make him feel better about his brother having lived liked this. She picked up the notebook and paged through it. Each page had a name block-printed on top, then a dense scrawl in black, then, in a different pen, something else. Not impossible to read, but difficult, writing crammed into every available inch, no space between words even. She remembered this notebook; it was the one teenage Denny always had on him.

"Take it," Marco said. "Take whatever you want. I can't do this anymore. I'm going home."

She took the notebook and the DVD, and squeezed Marco's arm, unsure whether he would want or accept a hug.

Her parents were out when she got back to their house, so she slipped the DVD into their machine. It didn't work. She took it upstairs and tried it in her mother's old desktop computer instead. The computer made a sound like a jet plane taking off, and opened a menu with one episode listed: March 13, 1980.

It started the same way all the other episodes had started. The kids, Uncle Bob. Denny was in this one; Stella had an easier time spotting him now that she knew who to look for. He went for the train set again, laying out wooden tracks alongside a kid Stella didn't recognize.

Uncle Bob started a story. "Once upon a time, there was a boy who grew very big very quickly. He felt like a giant when he stood next to his classmates. People stopped him in hallways and told him he was going to the wrong grade's room. His mother complained that she had to buy him new clothes constantly, and even though she did it with affection, he was too young to realize she didn't blame him. He felt terrible about it. Tried to hide that his shoes squeezed his toes or his pants were too short again.

"His parents' friends said, 'Somebody's going to be quite an athlete,' but he didn't feel like an athlete. More than that, he felt like he had grown so fast his head had been pushed out of his body, so he was constantly watching it from someplace just above. Messages he sent to his arms and legs took ages to get there. Everything felt small and breakable in his hands, so that when his best friend's dog had puppies he refused to hold them, though he loved when they climbed all over him.

"The boy had a little brother. His brother was everything he wasn't. Small, lithe, fearless. His mother told him to protect his brother, and he took that responsibility seriously. That was something that didn't take finesse. He could do that.

"Both boys got older, but their roles didn't change. The older brother watched his younger brother. When the smaller boy was bullied, his brother pummeled the bullies. When the younger brother made the high school varsity basketball team as a point guard his freshman year, his older brother made the team as center, even though he hated sports.

"Time passed. The older brother realized something strange. Every time he thought he had something of his own, it turned out it was his brother's. He blinked one day and lost two entire years. How was he the older brother, the one who got new clothes, who reached new grades first, and yet still always following? Even his own story had spun out to describe him in relation to his sibling.

"And then, one day, the boy realized he had nothing at all. He was his brother's giant shadow. He was a forward echo, a void. Nothing was his. All he could do was watch the world try to catch up with him, but he was always looking backward at it. All he could do—"

"No," said Denny.

Stella had forgotten the kids were there, even though they were on camera the entire time. Denny had stood and walked over to where Uncle Bob was telling the story. With Uncle Bob sitting, Denny was tall enough to look him in the eye.

For the first time, Uncle Bob turned away from the camera. He assessed Denny with an unsettling smile.

"No," Denny said again.

Now Uncle Bob glanced around as if he was no longer amused, as if someone needed to pull this child off his set. It wasn't a tantrum, though. Denny wasn't misbehaving, unless interrupting a story violated the rules.

Uncle Bob turned back to him. "How would you tell it?"

Denny looked less sure now.

"I didn't think so," said the host. "But maybe that's enough of that story. Unless you want to tell me how you think it ends?"

Denny shook his head.

"But you know?"

Denny didn't move.

"Maybe that's enough. We'll see. In any case, I have other stories to tell. We haven't checked in on my hill today."

Uncle Bob began to catch his audience up on the continuing adventure of the boy who'd been dug out of the hillside. The other children kept playing, and Denny? Denny looked straight into the camera, then walked off the set. He never came back. Stella didn't have any proof, but she was pretty sure this must have been the last episode Denny took part in. He looked like a kid who was done. His expression was remarkably similar to the one she'd just seen on Marco's face.

And what was that story? Unlike Dan Heller's driving story, unlike the one she'd started thinking of as her own, this one wasn't close to true. Sure, Denny had been a big kid, but neither he nor Marco played basketball. He never protected Marco from bullies. "Nothing was his" hardly fit the man whose house she'd cleaned.

Except that night, falling asleep, Stella couldn't help but think that when she compared what she knew of Denny with that story, it seemed like Denny had set out to prove the story untrue. What would a person do if told as a child that nothing was his? Collect all the things. Leave his little brother to fend for himself. Fight it on every level possible.

Was it a freak occurrence that Denny happened to be listening when Uncle Bob told that story? Why was she assuming the story was about him at all? Maybe it was coincidence. There was nothing connecting the children to the stories except her own sense that they were connected, and Denny's reaction on the day he quit.

She hadn't heard hers when Uncle Bob told it, but she'd internalized it nonetheless. How much was true? She wasn't a cuckoo bird. Her reinventions had never hurt anyone.

Marco called that night to ask if she wanted to grab one more meal before she left town, but she said she had too much to do before her flight. That was true, as was the fact that she didn't want to see him again. Didn't want to ask him if he'd watched the March 13 show. Didn't want to tell him his brother had consciously refused him protection.

She should have gone straight to the airport in the morning, but the fan mail address she'd written down was in the same direction, if she took the back way instead of the highway. Why a show like that might get fan mail was a question for another time. This was strictly a trip to satisfy her curiosity. She drove through town, then a couple of miles past, into the network of county roads.

The mailbox stood full, overflowing, a mat of moldering envelopes around its cement base. A weather-worn "For Sale" sign had sunk into the soft ground closer to the drainage ditch. Stella turned onto the long driveway, and only after she'd almost reached the house did it occur to her that if she'd looked at the mail, she might have found his surname.

The fields on either side of the lane were tangled with weeds that didn't look like they cared what season it was. The house, a tiny stone cottage, was equally weed-choked, but strangely familiar. If she owned this house, she'd never let it get like this, but it didn't look like it belonged to anyone anymore. She tried a story on for size: "While I was visiting my parents, I went for a drive in the country, and I found the most darling cottage. My parents are getting older, and I had the thought that I should move closer to them. The place needed a little work, so I got it for a song."

She liked that one.

Nobody answered when she knocked. The door was locked, and the windows were too dirty to see through, and she couldn't shake the feeling that if she looked through he'd be sitting there, staring straight at her, waiting.

She walked around back and found the hill.

It was a funny little hill, not entirely natural looking, but what did she know? The land behind the house sloped gently upward, then steeper, hard beneath the grass but not rocky. From the slope, the cottage looked even smaller, the fields wilder, tangled, like something from a fairy tale. The view, too, felt strangely familiar.

She knew nothing more about the man who called himself Uncle Bob, but as she walked into the grass she realized this must be the hill from his stories, the stories he told when he wasn't telling stories about the children. How did they go? She thought back to that first episode she'd watched in Denny's basement.

Once upon a time, there was a boy whose family planted him in a hillside, so that he took over the entire hillside, like a weed. They dug me out of the hillside on my thirteenth birthday. It's good to divide rhizomes to give them room to grow.

That story made her remember the notebook she'd taken from Denny's house, and she rummaged for it in her purse. The notebook was alphabetical, printed in a nearly microscopic hand other than the page headings, dense. She found one for Dan Heller. She couldn't decipher the whole story, but the first line was obviously *Once upon a time, there was a little boy who wanted to go fast.* She knew the rest. In blue pen, it said what she had said to Jeff the archivist: motorcycle wreck, alongside the date. That one was easy since she knew enough to fill in the parts she struggled to read. The others were trickier. There was no page for Marco, but Denny had made one for himself. It had Uncle Bob's shadow-brother story but no update at the bottom. Nothing at all for the years between.

Who else had been on the show? Lee Pool had a page. So did Addie Chapel, who as far as Stella knew had followed in her mother's footsteps and become a doctor. Chris Bethel, and beside him, Tina Bevins, the other dinosaur lover. If she spent enough time staring, maybe Denny's handwriting would decipher itself.

She was afraid to turn to her own page. She knew it had to be there, on the page before Dan Heller, but she couldn't bring herself to look, until she did. She expected this one, like Dan's, like Denny's own, to be easier to decipher because she knew how it would go.

October 30, 1982. Once upon a time, there was a little girl who didn't know who she was. Many children don't know who they will be, and that's not unusual, but what was unusual in this case was that the girl was willing to trade who she was for who she could be, so she began to do just that. Little by little, she replaced herself with parts of other people she liked better. Parts of stories she wanted to live. Nobody lied like this girl. She believed her own stories so completely, she forgot which ones were true and which were false.

If you've ever heard of a cuckoo bird, they lay their eggs in other birds' nests, so those birds are forced to raise them for their own. This girl was her own cuckoo, laying stories in her own head, and the heads of those around her, until even she couldn't remember which ones were true, or if there was anything left of her.

There was more. Another episode, maybe? She had no idea how many she'd been on, and her research had been shoddy. Maybe every story was serialized like the boy in the hill. It took her a while to make out the next bit.

November 20, 1982. Our cuckoo girl left the nest one day to spread her wings. When she returned, she didn't notice that nobody had missed her. She named a place where she had been, and they accepted it as truth. She made herself up, as she had always done, convincing even herself in the process. Everything was true, or true enough.

Below that, in blue pen, a strange assortment of updates from her life, as observed by Denny. Marco's eleventh birthday party, when she'd given him juggling balls. Graduation from middle school. The summer they'd both worked at the pool, and Marco'd gotten heatstroke and thrown up all the Kool-Aid they tried to put in him, Kool-Aid red, straight into the pool like a shark attack. The time she and Marco had tried making out on his bed, only he had started giggling, and she had gotten offended, and when she stood she tripped over a juggling ball and broke her toe. All the games their friends had played in Marco's basement: I've Never, even though they all knew what everyone else had done; Two Truths and a Lie, though they had all grown up together and knew every-thing about one another; Truth or Dare, though everyone was tired of truth, truth was terrifying, everyone chose dare, always. The *Batman* premiere. The prom amoeba, the friends who went together, all of whom she'd lost touch with. High school graduation. Con-crete memories, things she knew were as real as anything that had ever happened in her life. Denny shouldn't have known about some of these things, but now she pictured him there, somewhere, hold-ing this notebook, watching them, taking notes, always looking like he had something to say but he couldn't say it.

Below those stories he'd written: *Once there was a girl who got lost and when she found her way home she realized she'd arrived back without herself, and her parents didn't even notice the difference.* Which couldn't be her story at all; she hadn't been on the episodes he'd been on.

After graduation, he had no more updates on her. She paged forward, looking at the blue ink. Everyone had updates within the last year, everyone except for Denny, everyone who was still alive; the ones who weren't had death dates. Everyone except her. She tried to imagine what from her adult life she would have added, given the chance, or what an internet search on her name would provide, or what her parents would tell someone who asked what she was doing. Surely there was something. Parents were supposed to be your built-in hype machines.

She pulled out her phone to call Marco, but the battery was dead. Just as well, since she was suddenly afraid to try talking to anyone at all. She returned to the notebook and flipped toward the back. *U* for *Uncle Bob*.

Once upon a time, there was a boy whose family planted him in a hillside, so that he took over the entire hillside, like a weed. They dug me out of the hillside on my thirteenth birthday. It's good to divide rhizomes to give them room to grow.

This story was long, eight full pages in tiny script, with episode dates interspersed. At the end, in red ink, this address. She pictured Denny driving out here, exploring the cottage, looking up at the hill. If she ever talked to Marco again, she'd tell him that what he'd found in Denny's closet wasn't a shrine; it was Denny's attempt to conjure answers to something unanswerable.

She put the notebook back in her purse and kept walking. Three quarters of the way up the hill she came to a large patch where the grass had been churned up. She put her hand in the soil and it felt like the soil grasped her hand back.

Her parents said she didn't visit often enough, but now she couldn't remember ever having visited them before, or them visiting her. She couldn't remember if she'd ever left this town at all. She lived in Chicago, or did she? She'd told Marco as much, told him other things she knew not to be true, but what was true, then? What did she do for a living? If she left this hill and went to the airport, would she even have a reservation? If she caught her plane, would she find she had anything or anyone there at all? Where was there? She pulled her hand free and put it to her mouth: The soil tasted familiar.

"I walked down to the cottage that would be mine someday"— that felt nice, even if she wasn't sure she believed it—"and then past the cottage, through the town, and into my parents' house. They believed me when I said where I'd been. They fit me into their lives and only occasionally looked at me like they didn't quite know how I'd gotten there." That felt good. True. She sat in the dirt and leaned back on her hands, and felt the hill pressing back on them.

She could still leave: walk back to her rental car, drive to the airport, take the plane to the place where she surely had a career, a life, even if she couldn't quite recall it. She thought that until she looked back at where the rental car should have been and realized it wasn't there. She had no shoes on, and her feet were black with dirt, pebbled, scratched. She dug them into the soil, rooting with her toes.

How had Denny broken his story? He'd refused it. Whether his life was better or worse for it remained a different question. To break her story, she'd have to walk back down the hill and reconstruct herself the right way round. She thought of the cuckoo girl, the lost girl, the cuckoo girl, so many stories to keep straight.

The soil reached her forearms now, her calves. The top layer was sun-warmed, and underneath, a busy cool stillness made up of millions of insects, of the roots of the grass, of the rhizomes of the boy who had called this hillside home before she had. She'd walk back to town when she was ready, someday, maybe, but she was in no hurry. She'd heard worse stories than hers, and anyway, if she didn't like it she'd make a new one, a better one, a true one.

That Our Flag Was Still There

It would've been a normal day if the Flag hadn't up and died on us. Not even halfway through the shift, and she'd been up there on the platform, wide-eyed and smiling from the Stars and whispering to herself in the way Flags usually do, and then she got a funny look on her face. A moment later her vitals went all screwy.

"She's tanking!" I said, trying to control the panic in my voice. I'd trained for this scenario, but never encountered it in the five years I'd worked at the National Flag Center.

"Breathe," said Maggie Gregg, from the console beside me. "Can you get her under control?"

"I'm trying," I said, though I couldn't figure out the problem. I tried and failed to stabilize her chemically, then let Maggie deliver a series of jolts through the Flag's screensuit. It didn't work.

"We have to bring her down," Maggie said.

I looked over, surprised. Maggie's dark skin had gone pale. She'd been here twenty years. She had to know the protocol for a dead Flag. Even I knew it, though I'd never had to use it before, and she must have been through this at least once or twice. The Flag can't come down until sunset, or the visitors on the Mall would freak out, so we have to leave the dead one up there and trust the visitors can't tell a quiet living Flag from a dead one, and loop footage from earlier in the day, with the sky color-corrected to the current weather. I didn't respond, and she didn't say anything more.

We brought the Flag in at sunset, like always. It was harder than if she could've assisted in the transfer, but not too much harder, since most are pretty glassy after a day up on the platform. Removing the ink from someone whose liquids are pooling instead of pumping turned out to be tricky too, but we couldn't hand a body back to a family in that condition, with the skin settling red, white, and blue. I hope that doesn't come across as unpatriotic or disrespectful of the dead. I set the Colors draining the same as I would've on anyone.

I have two jobs: one, administer the Colors (under which falls monitoring and retiring the Colors, as well); two, administer and monitor the Stars. When the dead Flag came off the flagpole, I had the easy part. I felt worse for Maggie, who had to call the family. I did my part and watched Maggie do hers, and afterward offered to buy her a drink. To my surprise, she said yes. The first time she'd said yes in five years working together.

It took a while for us to finish the paperwork and make arrangements with the team who'd take the body home. By the time we left the Flag Center, the National Mall was empty except for the police-bot that chased us down to inform us the Mall was closed to visitors. It scanned our Center IDs, which were enough to appease it.

We didn't pass any people before we hit Chinatown, where the sidewalks got busy again. We hadn't discussed our destination, and I couldn't tell if she was leading or I was, so things got progressively slower and more aimless until finally I had enough and pointed up 7th.

"That one okay?" I pointed to the Pewter Spoon. "It's got a long happy hour."

In all the times I'd gone out with the other techs from work, Maggie had always said she had to get home. I didn't take it personally—she lived far away, and she had grandkids living with her—but I'd assumed that meant she hadn't spent time down here at all. I was surprised when she rejected my suggestion.

"Not that place. How about Forte?"

I'd never heard of Forte, but she was the one who'd had to call a family with bad news, so I agreed. She took me past the arena, under the bigscreen nightly Flag replay and the news tickers listing the day's top patriots, past the Friendship Arch. We walked faster than before, which told me I'd been right about neither of us leading earlier. Two blocks farther, around a corner, to a side door.

The place we stepped into was dark, with a utilitarian wooden bar down the room's length, and six tables against the opposite wall. Four customers sat along the bar: one talking to the bartender, two talking to each other, and one nursing a beer. No windows, no pictures. No screens anywhere. Nothing on the black walls at all, which is to say, the next thing I noticed was the absent Flag. Not over the bar, not on the back wall, nowhere.

"Don't say it, Lexi."

I shut my mouth. I'd offered a drink to a colleague. If she wanted to have that drink in a bar that broke the law, if she trusted me enough to take me to a place like this, she didn't want me pointing out the obvious.

"What are you drinking?" I asked instead, faking nonchalance.

She pointed to the last tap handle, a cheap local lager. I motioned the bartender for two, while Maggie shrugged off her coat and chose a table.

She raised her glass when I handed it to her. "To killing people and notifying their families by phone."

"Jesus." I sat without removing my jacket. "I can't drink to that."

"Sorry. It was an awful day. How about 'to another day closer to retirement'?"

We toasted, even though she was way closer to retirement than me.

"What is this place?" I asked.

"It's the only bar within walking distance where I can have a drink without having to watch the day's Flag reruns."

"Maggie," I lowered my voice. "It's *illegal* not to have a Flagscreen."

"I'm not stupid. I know that. But I'm not going to sit here and watch someone die for the second time today."

"Jesus," I said again. "We're not supposed to discuss that where anyone else can hear."

She had to know that too.

"Look, I know you believe in what we do—"

I had to interrupt. "You don't?"

"I don't know what I believe anymore, but I thought—when you offered to grab a drink with me this time I thought maybe you felt the same way I did. Like maybe this isn't how it's meant to be." She took a long drink. "Do you know what that husband said to me tonight? He didn't cry or yell or curse at me. He thanked me, Lex. He said 'the risk is worth the service.' Is it, though?"

"Of course. Nobody is forced to enter the Flag lottery."

She looked at me. "But how many understand there's a chance they won't survive it?"

"That's a tiny risk compared to the benefits. When did this happen last? She could've been hit by a car or gotten food poisoning, or slipped on ice, but those wouldn't leave her family with a lifetime stipend without a lot of litigation. They'll be fine. Think of the respect they'll get when people find out."

"Respect and an empty chair. I'm sure they're thrilled." She lifted her beer again. It was almost empty; I still hadn't touched mine beyond the sip when we toasted.

I stole a look at the other patrons. They were drinking in a bar without a Flag. Maybe we wouldn't get in trouble, but I couldn't risk losing my job or my own chance at being Flag someday.

"I'm sorry, Maggie. I know you had a rough day, and I wanted to commiserate, but I think maybe I need to get going. Next one's on me too, okay?"

On my way out, I paid for a third beer, wishing as my chip passed the reader that I carried cash, so there wouldn't be evidence I'd been here.

My Metro ride home took a full hour, thanks to a delay to remove a woman for complaining about the President without a free speech permit. For a moment I thought it was Maggie, though I'd left her at the bar, and she lived in a different direction. My local feed flashed the names and faces of the patriots in the next car who had turned the woman in, along with her name and transgression. We all applauded.

While the train sat, I watched the Flagscreen beside the system map. It was still early in the rerun; she hadn't died yet. She looked young and vibrant and healthy, her skin rippling in red, white, and blue, her screensuit too. Her eyes had that look from when the Stars drug kicks in: fever patriotism, pride, like she had waited her whole life for this moment, which she probably had. She kept repeating, "I am my country" and "beautiful, beautiful."

The autopsy would say what had gone wrong; an undiagnosed heart condition, I was guessing. I could still picture her face when she died: peaceful, happy, high. That led me to Maggie on the phone with the husband, the husband thanking her, the fact she'd found that more upsetting than crying. I wanted to understand.

My stop was the last on the line, and it was another ten minutes' walk from there. Sometimes I thumbed a ride in bad weather or close to curfew, but the night wasn't cold for January. As I left the Metro station, I stole a look up the Flagscreen above the entrance. She wouldn't die again for hours yet.

Pounding music greeted me through thin walls as I approached the apartment, courtesy of my louder roommate. When I flipped the foyer light switch, the Flagscreen came on full blast too. Usually we kept it muted, but a roommate must have turned up the volume.

I tried to catch the Flag's words now that she was talking. She hadn't spoken much at all, not in prep or on the platform. Hopefully she hadn't said anything unbefitting a flag in her last moments. I'd been watching her stats at that point, not her mouth. Nobody said anything negative while on Stars, though. Who could, feeling that good? I wished I knew what it felt like. Retired Flags always reported this perfect-day feeling, a lingering gladness, something to look back on and smile.

I considered what I'd do with the money and prestige if I ever got chosen. Get an apartment on my own, without roommates. Thicker walls. I'd keep my job, of course; the Flag payment wasn't enough money to go without work, just enough to live a little better for a while. Visit Charleston, let my parents get a little reflected glory. Someday, maybe.

Back at work the next day, Maggie didn't mention what had happened, and neither did I. The day's Flag was a talkative one, bridging our silence. A middle-aged white trucker from Dayton, as opposite the previous day's grad student as possible. She hadn't said much through the whole process, whereas this guy couldn't shut up.

"I had to buy white pants and a white shirt. I don't own anything white—I spill on myself the first time I wear it, and then I can never get it back to how it was. When I pulled the pants on this morning, I noticed a tiny smudge on the thigh, and spent fifteen minutes scrubbing. Almost made myself late, and I couldn't even call, since we're not supposed to carry anything but our ID. I didn't know which would be worse: the smudge or the lateness. I kept picturing some reserve waiting to take my place, all spotless and timely." He went quiet for a moment, and I realized he was waiting for reassurance.

"You did the right thing," I said, still concentrating on assembling my trays and lines. We got a lot of nervous talkers. "Better a tiny spot than arriving late. I can't even see it. In a minute I'm going to start the Colors. You'll feel a tiny jab."

He looked relieved. "I'd hate to get stuck back in the hopper. Do you even get re-entered if you blow your chance, or are you eliminated forever? Ow—

"Anyway, it's what, a one in three hundred fifty million chance of being chosen, minus the people who are too old or too young or need to opt out or whatever, or the however many thousand people who've been chosen already. I'm no mathematician, but the chance of my name going back in and then getting picked again?—I'll be damned."

That last was said gazing at his hand as the nano-ink spread out from the injection site.

I passed him the relay. "This goes around your wrist."

"Fitness band?"

"Similar. It sends us your vital signs, so we know how you're doing."

Maggie started her procedure next, while I checked that the nano-ink Colors and the relay conversed with each other and my monitor. Everything looked fine.

She held out the screensuit. "I'm going to need you to remove your clothes and put these on. You can change behind that curtain over there."

He looked surprised for the first time. "Why did I have to buy new white clothes if you're not going to have me wear them?"

"People get nervous if you tell them they're going to have to take their clothes off. More nervous than the needles or the nano. Better for you not to dwell on it. Didn't you feel proud today, marching in here in those crisp whites? They'll be waiting for you when you come down, and everyone will recognize you on your way back to your hotel tonight. There you go. I'll hand you the uniform and help if you need me to. This goes first. I know it looks like a diaper, but it's called a MAG. A Maximum Absorbency Garment, like astronauts use. Astronauts are cool, that's it. Now this one. The opening is in the back, like a hospital gown, but it'll close, I promise. I'll help you close it. It's delicate, so take your time. Don't tug."

It amazed me how her patter calmed them. Maggie helped him in that no-nonsense way she had, making it clear she wasn't touching him, she was making sure it was put on right. It wore like a not-quite-sheer body sleeve. Silky, but warmer than fleece in winter and cooler than cotton in summer. When she turned it on, the e-ink began its flag course, matching to the Colors in his skin.

"Cool!" he said, recovering from the indignity. "And soft. Can I buy this to wear around the house?"

We didn't have any mirrors or reflective surfaces in the room, a lab disguised in soothing spa colors. Flags got weirded out seeing their lumps and bumps in this setting; better to look at the recording we sent them home with, well-lit, color-corrected, filmed from a discreet distance. Still, this was always the moment where they stood a little taller and smiled, imagining what they'd look like up there, shining.

Maggie opened the next container. "These are special contact lenses to protect your eyes. It can get bright out there. Can you put them in, or do you want me to?"

The Flag frowned. "Would you mind? I'm not big on eye stuff. Always had perfect vision."

She washed her hands again, put on gloves, put the contacts in.

My turn. "The next thing I'm going to do is set up an IV line. It'll have two things connected to it: fluids, for if the monitors say you get dehydrated, and the Stars."

He stayed silent, but held out his arm for me to start the line. He had easy veins, close to the surface. As I stepped forward, he pulled his arm back. "Does anyone turn it down? I'm not much for drugs, to be honest. Smoked a little this or that in my day, but it's not my thing."

Before I could start my spiel, Maggie interrupted. "You don't have to take it if you don't want. It's not mandatory."

"No, it's not mandatory, but Stars enhances the experience." I glared at Maggie. "It's not addictive. It doesn't give you feelings you don't already have, but if you're feeling patriotic for doing your duty today, it's going to flood you with all those great emotions. If you're nervous, it'll calm you down. It'll make the day pass a little quicker, too. You may not think you need it, but trust me, it's a long day without it."

He nodded.

"Can you repeat that out loud?"

"Yes. I'll take the drug."

He'd already signed the consent forms and waivers, but verbal acknowledgment was required. It helped with something like the day before, I supposed, so if anyone reviewed the prep vid it would show we hadn't coerced her into anything.

"Here we go." I checked the levels on the pump and started it going. "Can you recite the Pledge of Allegiance for me?"

Stains spread at his armpits and chest as he began, but Danny Mtawarira could edit that out in post if the garment didn't dry fast enough. By the time he got to the Republic he was grinning and glassy.

"Here we go." Maggie took his hand; he followed her like a child.

"Flag walking," I said into my two-way as I followed them with the IV cart.

"Flag walking confirmed," came three more voices: installation, camera, post. Installation met us at the hall's end. It was their job to get him out there and secure him. Their job to hide the IV stand in the pole itself, and, once everything was settled, to raise the platform. I watched my monitor for the go light.

At sunrise, the anthem began to play, and the platform rose. The Flag wept as he ascended. I checked his levels to make sure I hadn't overdone the drug but he was just an emotional guy.

"This view," he shouted when the anthem ended. "Nobody mentioned the view!"

He gave a ragged, joyful scream. Not the most dignified Flag; he'd settle in a moment.

"Check me out, Granddad!"

Or not.

Given the Flag's age, I assumed his grandfather was deceased. His grandfather probably would've been surprised we had one daily human Flag now, instead of zillions of cloth ones and bumper stickers and hats and boxer shorts that devalued the symbol. That's what I'd learned, anyway, between school and job training. Somewhere in those in between years, a flag representing the people had become a Flag that was literally the people, with the right to say anything they wanted while they were up there.

I remembered my own excitement when I turned eighteen and got my automatic voter registration and Flag registration in the mail. It said I could opt out, but who would? A lifetime's stipend. A chance at a reckoning between yourself and your country, sixty feet in the air, overlooking the country's greatest monuments. The day my registration arrived, I considered the astronomical odds, and decided that if I'd likely never get chosen, the next best thing would be to work in the Flag Center and watch other people take their turn.

So here I was, watching a man talk to his dead grandfather, watching his body sort out endorphins and synthetic Stars and everything else, and wondering again how Maggie could complain about this glorious experience we got to make happen.

I looked over at her. She was frowning.

"You seeing a problem?" I asked.

She had one eye on the suit readout and one on the realtime screen. "Nah. It's not that. Are you listening to him?"

"I tuned him out, sorry. Thinking. Why? What'd he say?"

"He's chatting away. I—did you hear that thing he said in prep?"

"Which thing?" I tried to rewind the prep in my head, but nothing stood out.

"He still owes twenty thousand on the semi sitting in his driveway. The last company hiring human drivers shifted to self-driving, and they promised to retrain him, but they keep cancelling the trainings. That's what he should be saying up there. Not babbling."

"He can say whatever he wants. That's what's beautiful. A whole day to say anything he wants."

"Except he's drugged to his eyeballs and can't get those words back."

"His choice, Maggie. I did everything by the book." It didn't sound like an accusation, but it still felt like she was leaving me blame for something, between this and the day before.

"His choice, but when was the last time someone chose to go without Stars? Everyone talks it up, this amazing non-addictive high, and that's the thing getting people excited, instead of the chance to speak to the entire country."

"It would be a rough day without it, Mag. All those hours, the indignity, the diaper. They'd say whatever they wanted to say, and they'd still have an entire day to get through. We'd watch their stress levels rise without the ability to adjust them. They'd get hungry and thirsty, the IV would itch, they'd flinch when birds landed on them. This way they spend the day feeling amazing, and they go home knowing it was an amazing day."

She sighed. "I get what you're saying. It just seems like this isn't what was intended. How many even know they have the option to address people? When was the last time somebody did it?"

"The Flag and the Stars both came in at the same time. It's always been a choice."

"But was anyone ever encouraged to take the opportunity? It's a waste to do it for a high."

I was getting frustrated. "It's not just for a high. You know that. They get paid well. They get press when they go back home, so if there's something they didn't say up there, they can still say it if they want to."

"To their hometown news, if their hometown still has local news outlets, and if anyone's paying attention. That's not the same platform. And who knows what will make it to air?"

Neither of us was going to convince the other. I pretended I needed the bathroom and called for a tech to watch my monitors. She didn't say anything more when I returned.

The Flag made it through the day in the usual fashion. When he got back to us, he was quieter than he'd been in the morning. The drug was wearing off, and he'd worn his voice ragged singing through the afternoon. Still more talkative than most.

"That was quite a thing," he rasped. "Quite a thing."

"Yes, sir," I said as I drained the Colors. "You're a lucky man."

"A lucky man," he repeated. A lone tear rolled down his cheek.

"Are you okay, sir?"

"Yeah. I . . . you're right. I'm lucky. Lost my job a few months ago, when my company automated. Haven't been able to find any-place willing to let me and my old Kenworth haul anymore. This money's going to make a huge difference."

I shot Maggie a look that said "See?" but she was giving me the same look.

We didn't talk while he showered, and then we both busied our-selves checking him over one last time before the driver took him back to his hotel. I cleaned my station, and when I looked up, she was gone.

The next day was Friday, the start of our three-day weekend. The four-three-three-four schedule had always been a nice perk. On the longer weekends I sometimes drove home to see my family. The shorter breaks were good for relaxing, playing games, explor-ing the city. I tried to forget the argument with Maggie, since I still didn't entirely get it.

Monday morning, I headed back to work with a fresh head, but I was surprised to find Siya Peters from the opposite shift at Maggie's suit station.

"Maggie out sick?" I asked.

"I don't know," he said. "My supervisor asked me last week if I'd work an extra day today."

Weird that she hadn't said anything if she knew she'd be out. I tried to remember if she'd given any hint. Not that she had to, but we tended to mention it if we had something going on that broke the schedule.

I set up my station, prepping the Colors and the Stars. We were expected to arrive an hour before the day's Flag, rather than risking a train being late and us hitting the ground rushed. A rushed Flag was an anxious Flag.

Thirty minutes before sunrise, Ysabel opened the door from medical and ushered in the day's Flag: Maggie. Maggie was the Flag.

She crossed the room unsmiling and sat in my prep chair without waiting for me to tell her to do so. She wore painters' overalls and a spattered t-shirt: both had likely started out white. They technically met the standard, though I'd never seen anyone show up in such disarray.

"I didn't know," I said.

"I didn't tell you. Are you going to get started?"

Everything was upside down. I looked at my trays like I'd never seen them before. "Ah, sure. In a minute I'm going to start the Colors. You'll feel a tiny jab."

She presented her arm to me. I didn't usually get nerves, but this time I fumbled the syringe. I regathered myself to give a smooth injection.

We both watched as the Colors took over her skin, mingling her brown with red, white, and blue without losing it. "That's pretty cool from this perspective," she whispered.

"I've always thought it would be," I said.

Maggie looked over at her station, where Siya stood waiting. He smiled. "Do you want me to do the whole speech? I don't want to patronize but I don't want you to miss out if you want the full experience."

"I'd be disappointed if you didn't." Her eyes fixed beyond him at something on her desk.

"Okay, then." He held out the screensuit. "I'm going to need you to take off your clothes and put these on."

She took the suit from him and disappeared behind the curtain.

Siya gave me a panicked look before continuing. "You don't need me to engage in supportive conversation, do you? If you were anyone else, I'd tell you how to put on the MAG now, but I'm going to assume you know that, and I'd tell you the screensuit is delicate, and the opening is in the—"

Maggie emerged and turned her back to Siya, who sealed the suit, still looking discomfited. She stroked her hands down her sides once, but didn't look at herself the way most people did.

"I assume you'll put in your own contacts?" he asked, holding out the case. She nodded and took them from him.

My turn again. I found myself going rote because it was easier to say what I was used to than change it up. "The next thing I'm going to do is set up an IV. It'll have two things connected to it: fluids, for if the monitors say you get dehydrated, and the Stars."

"No," she said.

"Stars enhances the experience. It's not addictive. It doesn't give you—did you say no?"

"No," she said. "Yes to the fluids, no to the drug."

"Maggie. Don't be silly."

"My choice. No Stars."

"Why?"

"I've been telling you for days. If you don't know, you haven't been listening. What's the point of this if you sleep through it?"

"It's forty-two degrees, rainy, and windy. It's going to be awful up there."

"It's supposed to be hard, Lex. It's gone all wrong."

She didn't look like she would budge. "I have to ask one more time if you want the Stars. You have to say yes, ah, no for me."

"I did. I said no, and I'll say no again."

I started the fluids IV without the Stars, even though nobody in the entire time I'd been working there had ever said no before. It threw my rhythm off, so that I had to check every step of my procedure three times, afraid I had missed something. Without Stars, there was a lot less to do.

"Are you ready, Maggie?"

She pointed at a picture on her desk, two teenage boys and a younger one. "Have I ever told you about my oldest grandson?"

I glanced at the clock. Her prep had been quick. "No."

"He got beaten up four months ago by some 'patriots'"—she spat that word "—for saying he thought the curfew was unevenly enforced. Not even that he hated it, just that they kept waiting outside the youth center to catch kids who dawdled walking home. Beaten bloody for pointing out the truth because he said it outside the designated place and time, and the ones who attacked him got their names up in lights."

"I'm sorry." I didn't know what else to say. "We should get going."

Siya reached for her hand, but she pulled away. He shot me a look; we weren't used to an alert Flag.

I reached for my radio. "Flag walking."

"Flag walking, confirmed," came the response in triplicate.

I handed off the IV cart and returned to my station to watch. At sunrise, the anthem began to play, and the platform rose. Maggie stood tall, her jaw clenched. She didn't sing along.

In every home, in every business open this early around the country, Flagscreens played this tableau. Maggie was there with them, clear-eyed, biding her time as the anthem ended. She had a whole day to address them. Sunrise to sunset. If she pulled it off, our job might be very different from this day on. I'd never really considered what it meant to be a person who'd sacrifice her own comfort to say what she thought needed to be said. I leaned forward.

She looked straight into the camera.

"Wake up," she began. "It's time to wake up."

I Frequently Hear Music
in the Very Heart of Noise

"This green-gold city will embrace you /
Take you out of time and erase you /
And for one brief moment you will let her /
For one night only you'll be hers"
—Bess Morris, "For One Night Only," 1924

The Ambassador Billiard Parlor, the Aeolian Hall, Our Metropolitan Madness

Just before midnight on January 3, 1924, Ira Gershwin sat on a barstool at the Ambassador Billiard Parlor, reading the *New York Tribune's* amusements section while his brother George shot pool with Buddy DeSylva.

Ira called his brother's attention to an article entitled "What Is American Music?" In the piece, Paul Whiteman, the popular "King of Jazz," announced a February 12th concert featuring a George Gershwin jazz concerto and an Irving Berlin tone poem, neither of which yet existed.

We now take liberties with the script.

"Fuck," said George. "I told him I wasn't doing that show. He thinks I'm writing what, now?" He already had a musical comedy opening in three weeks' time. To compose and practice a new piece within five weeks would be impossible.

Imagine the phone call the next morning. Whiteman's desperation, having heard Vincent Lopez was planning a similar concert and might do it first. The King of Jazz deposed. Gershwin on the other end of the line, puffing a black cigar, bristling at the short turnaround for an event he'd already declined.

Whiteman somehow persuaded him it was a deadline worth meeting; George started writing two days later. "I had already done some work on the rhapsody. It was on the train, with its steely rhythms, its rattlety bang that is often so stimulating to a composer . . . I frequently hear music in the very heart of noise. And there I suddenly heard—and even saw on paper—the complete construction of the rhapsody, from beginning to end . . . I heard it as a sort of musical kaleidoscope of America—of our vast melting pot, of our unduplicated national pep, of our blues, our metropolitan madness."

He finished the piece in time for five days' rehearsal. *An Experiment in Modern Music* went off as announced, at the Aeolian Hall on West 43rd Street, built for the piano manufacturer of the same name. The building stood on the site occupied by the Latting Observatory during the 1853 World's Fair. At 315 feet, the observatory was the tallest structure in the city for the three years before it went up in flames, and helped inspire the Eiffel Tower. From its three viewing platforms, from its address midway between the Hudson and the East River, fifteen hundred fairgoers at a time saw all the way to Queens, Staten Island, and the New Jersey cliffs.

Picture all those visitors streaming upward, looking outward across the expanding city grid. Condense them, distill them, seed their amazement through the same space seventy years later, as the audience heard Gershwin's ode to collective metropolitan madness for the first time.

Before the concert, he changed the title from "American Rhapsody" to "Rhapsody in Blue." It was a tribute to the painting popularly known as *Whistler's Mother*, which is actually titled *Arrangement in Gray and Black*, and to another Whistler painting, *Nocturne in Green and Gold*. Everything in conversation.

The Plaza Hotel, Green and Gold

Sometime in the early twenties, a sober Scott Fitzgerald is said to have danced fully clothed through the Pulitzer Fountain at the Plaza Hotel. Another version of the apocryphal story says it was Scott and Zelda, both drunk. A 1922 show called *The Greenwich Village Follies* included a painted curtain depicting everyone who was anyone in the New York intellectual scene of the time, Zelda rising from a fountain at the center of the crowd.

Green and gold, gold and green, everywhere in *Gatsby*, a few years later. Daisy the golden girl, Gatsby's gold tie, old money versus new, the green light of the orgastic future. According to Plumb's *The Streets Where They Lived*, Fitzgerald, seeing the city as it was, "all blazing with green and gold lights, and the taxis and limousines streaming up and down Fifth Avenue, jumped in the Pulitzer Fountain just out of sheer joy."

Hilbert's Hotel

We step away from New York for a moment, to demonstrate a particularly New York thought experiment. In 1924, German mathematician David Hilbert gave a lecture hypothesizing that a fully occupied hotel with an infinite number of rooms might still accommodate additional guests. If you move the person in Room 1 to Room 2 and the person in Room 2 to Room 4 and every subsequent guest from room N to room 2N, you empty all the odd numbered rooms, making room for an infinite number of new guests.

———

Not Exactly Hilbert's Hotel

Scott Fitzgerald said of New York in 1919 that it "had all the iridescence of the beginning of the world."

If you move the hotel at #1 to #2, and the hotel at #2 to #4, and every subsequent hotel from its plot as in a variation on the problem above, the result is a lot of wobbly, unpinned hotels. Logic will only take you so far. Instead, create a hotel in between the others, right where people expect a hotel. Take all the time you need, and all the space. It's New York; you'll fill the rooms.

Give it all the things that make a hotel special. Make it very old, or very new. Give it secret passages and long corridors and dead ends. It must have a ballroom, and a welcoming lobby, and a bar, preferably a dim one, preferably with a secret trapdoor, and a restaurant that is just out of style, and a plaque or photograph that proves so-and-so dined here. Fill it with art, some of which may appear to move from time to time, and wasn't the figure in that portrait facing the other way? It may have a cat, sometimes, and a further idiosyncrasy or two about it: lobby acoustics that let someone on one end hear the conversation on the other, a mysterious button on the wall, a dead-end corridor, a ghost, a faulty elevator.

The Passenger Elevator

The same 1853 New York World's Fair that saw the construction of the Latting Observatory was also where Elisha Otis first debuted the safety elevator, in the Crystal Palace next door. His invention slowed the compartment's descent if a cable snapped, which had been the big concern about elevators until his dramatic demonstration. Prior to this invention, building heights were limited to a few stories, the wealthier living on the lowest floors.

The Hotel Ekphrastic

Composer Bess Morris had not ridden in an elevator prior to moving into the 12th floor suite at the Ekphrastic, her previous apartments having been walkups. The Ekphrastic's northeast elevator had a habit of stopping between floors. Most of the residents took pains to avoid that elevator, but she often waited for it specifically.

"All these stories, and we're nowhere," she remarked one night to the other people in the stuck elevator, her companion Judy Selig and the painter Charles Demuth. Demuth's painting *We Are Nowhere*, destroyed in a gallery fire three years later, was dedicated to Bess Morris, and Selig maintained that brief moment stuck in the elevator inspired two great works.

Selig said later, "We were headed out to see the Marx Brothers in *I'll Say She Is* at the Casino Theater, since I was between plays myself and eager to see what everyone had been talking about. Bess and Charles Demuth and I were halfway down to the lobby when the elevator stuck between floors, and Bess changed her mind about going out. Deem and I went on without her. That was the night she came up with 'For One Night Only.'"

The Hotel Shelton

Georgia O'Keeffe painted *Blue and Green Music* in her first years in New York City. She had "the idea that music could be translated into something for the eye," but she caught the city's hidden face as well: the angles and planes, the cacophony and the pockets of quiet, trees and buildings and shards of sky. They're in there if you look, even if she preferred Toscanini to jazz.

O'Keeffe and Alfred Stieglitz married in 1924 and moved to Suite 3003 on the Hotel Shelton's top floor. O'Keeffe had watched the skyscraper go up, the first in the neighborhood. It was cheaper than the first-class residential hotels, but still allowed them to live without the wasted time of a kitchen; they took their meals in the 16th floor cafeteria.

They had two small, low-ceilinged rooms, but the living room, which O'Keeffe used as her studio, had windows facing north and east. "I know it's unusual for an artist to want to work way up near the roof of a big hotel, in the heart of a roaring city, but I think that's just what the artist of today needs for stimulus," she said in an interview once. And in another interview: "I began talking about trying to paint New York. Of course, I was told that it was an impossible idea—even the men hadn't done too well with it."

She sometimes painted the city from her elevated perspective—Stieglitz took photos there too—but most of her skyscrapers are painted from a ground-level vantage. Look at *The Shelton with Sunspots, NY* (1926), the upper floors swallowed by sun. Or *Radiator Building—Night, New York* (1927), its forms precise as flowers, light beckoning from a hundred windows. *New York Night* is warm, lived in, even without human figures. It embodies O'Keeffe's theory that "one can't paint New York as it is, but rather as it is felt."

"As it is felt"—O'Keeffe was neither the first nor the last to try to tap that feeling in her medium of choice. See also prose and punk and poetry and jazz and photography. William Carlos Williams, who once wished he was a painter, wrote his poem "The Great Figure" after seeing—feeling—a fire engine clang and rumble through Manhattan on a rainy night. Charles Demuth's painting *I Saw the Figure 5 in Gold* translated that poem into oil, graphite, ink, and gold. Demuth translated his friend O'Keeffe into paint as well.

Two Square Blocks, Expanded

West 43rd and 44th Streets, between 5th and 7th Avenues, housed at various points in the twentieth century: the Algonquin Hotel, the shabby Hanover House, the Royalton Hotel, the Iroquois (where

James Dean lived because it was cheaper than the Algonquin), the Metropole, the Americana, the Coolidge, the Lambs Club, the Hotel Claridge, the Ekphrastic, the Astor, and the 44th Street Hotel, as well as the Belasco Theater and the Aeolian Hall, where Gershwin's "Rhapsody in Blue" debuted.

Expand another few blocks north and south and you can bring in the offices of the *New Yorker* and the *Smart Set*, the Hotel Knickerbocker, the New Amsterdam, the Lyric, any number of Broadway theaters, and Irving Berlin's place on 46th Street, where he wrote "Always," "Blue Skies," and "Puttin' on the Ritz."

Duke Ellington's band played down the nights at the seedy Hollywood Club, a few blocks up Broadway, and Bix Beiderbecke's Wolverines held court at the Cinderella Ballroom a few blocks down. When Hoagy Carmichael saw Beiderbecke play his cornet, he's reported to have said, "Just four notes . . . but he didn't blow them; he hit 'em like a mallet hits a chime." Beiderbecke lived in those same square blocks, Room 605 of the 44th Street Hotel, for a year in 1930.

The original Roseland Ballroom, on the second floor of 1658 Broadway, was where New York heard Louis Armstrong for the first time, in 1924, during his yearlong stint with the Fletcher Henderson Orchestra.

He started out nervous, nervous enough that his bandmate Howard Scott turned and told him, "Listen, just close your eyes and play what you feel in your body, in your heart, in your mind. Be yourself, that's all."

Later, Scott recounted that "they could hear him out in the street, and we were told that there were people passing by that stopped, listening to him." By the next night, word had spread, and the place was so packed they had to turn people away.

Ellington and his band went to hear Armstrong whenever they were able. Despite the proliferation of African American bands, most downtown venues were otherwise all white. The Roseland made a small exception: Black musicians were welcome to watch their peers play, if they stood in a specific area, out of the white patrons' view. Ellington wrote of hearing Armstrong play, "The guys had never heard anything just like it . . . there weren't the words coined for describing that kick." Howard Scott said that during that year, if you ran into a trumpet player with a bandage on his lip, it was likely because he'd split it trying to squeeze out Armstrong's high notes.

Run up and down the timeline, up and down that handful of blocks, and you'll overlay George Burns and Gracie Allen, Jack Benny (who was dating Gracie's roommate), Lenny Bruce and Toscanini, Jimmy Durante, Carmen Miranda, Maya Angelou, Charlie Chaplin, Spencer Tracy, Bert Lahr, Eugene O' Neill, the Astaires, the Marx Brothers ("Room Service? Send up a larger room."), Mary Pickford and Douglas Fairbanks, Audrey Hepburn, Billy Wilder, Tallulah Bankhead, Bess Morris and Judy Selig, James Dean, Ella Fitzgerald, Dorothy Parker and H.L. Mencken and the whole Algonquin crowd, Thurber and Guthrie and Gershwin. You'll overlay all the actors treading the boards of the Broadway theaters and the jazz musicians on their ballroom bandstands. Lucky Luciano will set up operations at the Claridge. Mobsters will shoot down gambler Herman Rosenthal on the sidewalk in front of the Metropole and escape in a gray Packard, the first known use of a getaway car, leading to a sensational trial and the execution of five men, as Fitzgerald described in *Gatsby*.

Expand outward in time and space. An infinite number of hotel rooms, holding an infinite number of hungry musicians and actors and writers. If we establish an infinite number of hotel rooms, perhaps we can also posit an infinite number of theaters and ballrooms, with an infinite number of guests, all aching for something about to begin. Enough to wake a city.

If a city wanted, it could dream a hotel into existence, and that hotel could dream a ballroom, and with that ballroom, a composer at a piano, as if she had always been, and with that composer a song, and with that song a band to play her work, and with that band, an audience. If a city wanted.

André Breton (Not a Hotel)

In 1924, the poet André Breton wrote in the first Surrealist manifesto that he believed "in the future resolution of these two states, dream and reality, which are seemingly so contradictory, into a kind of absolute reality, a surreality, if one may so speak."

The Hotel Ekphrastic

Among the many early twentieth century Manhattan hotels, the Ekphrastic stands out partly for its design, yes, Beaux-Arts grandeur mixed with classical elements, but also for the magnificent ballroom on the second floor. Partly, too, for the guests who called it home during the times when calling a hotel home was fashionable. Scott and Zelda stayed a single night there during their marriage's first year. They were kicked out for riding a bellman's cart through the plate glass front door.

The concert pianist Myra Hess stayed there in preparation for her American debut in 1922. She asked for a piano to be put in her rooms. The hotel purchased a Steinway Model L for her, the manufacturer's brand-new concert grand on a small scale. When Hess left, the piano was moved to the ballroom, since it was better than the one that had been in there.

Stage actress Judy Selig moved into the same suite two years later, along with her "companion," Bess Morris, by then working on Broadway as a rehearsal pianist; the two had met living in the new Webster Apartments the year before, and then found themselves working on the same show. Selig's star had risen quickly, but Morris had yet to sell any of her songs.

Morris discovered that the ballroom was left unlocked during the day, and began stealing hours there to compose. She loved that particular instrument so much she wrote to a college friend, "I will never be able to move out of this hotel, or if I do, I shall have to hide this piano among my bags. I'm writing a piece here that feels like everything I've ever wanted to do."

Morris may have believed she was sneaking into the ballroom, but most contemporary accounts suggest she was a known presence. H. L. Mencken wrote, "One of the secret highlights of the Ekphrastic's luncheon can only be discovered if one manages to get the table at the southeast corner of the dining room. There, an airshaft carries the exuberant melodies of a piano player in the shuttered ballroom above. Play on, mystery man. Make me forget the briny lobster."

The Old Hotel Knickerbocker, Hanover House, The Hotel Knickerbocker

Enrico Caruso lived in the original Hotel Knickerbocker on West 42nd Street, in a fourteen-room apartment on the ninth floor. On the day of the false armistice in 1918, as the incorrect story spread, as church bells and sirens clamored, as an anti-aircraft gun on the Equitable Building's roof fired blanks into the air, as stores and courts jammed with celebrants, Caruso stepped out on his corner balcony with an American flag and sang "The Star Spangled Banner" to the Times Square throngs.

Bess Morris was in the crowd that day, and wrote to a friend, "Picture that voice, from that balcony, cutting through the cheers. When we heard a little while later that the newspapers had been wrong, people started burning the papers. I got out of there quick, but I couldn't shake that beautiful tenor and the way it settled over us like a benediction, and a melody came to me that was entirely separate from the one he sang." Though it wasn't published until after her death, the melody she referred to was her song "Joy Rains Down."

Exactly one block north of the Knickerbocker, twenty-two years later, Woody Guthrie took a room in a fleabag residential hotel called Hanover House. Sick of hearing Kate Smith's popular version of "God Bless America," Guthrie lifted a Carter Family tune called "When the World's on Fire" and turned it into his response, "This Land Is Your Land."

Rewind the Knickerbocker again: after his first novel was published, Fitzgerald briefly took up residence there. On the day he left the hotel, he left the bathtub faucets running and flooded the room.

The Fitzgeralds moved into the Biltmore Hotel the same month, and were booted not long after. They relocated from there to the Commodore, where they reportedly once spent half an hour spinning the revolving door. Amidst all that they got married, and perhaps also splashed through the Pulitzer Fountain. The order doesn't really matter. The when of it doesn't matter to a waking city.

Tin Pan Alley, Seventh Street, Whitehall Hotel: I frequently hear music in the very heart of noise.

Picture a New York summer day in 1916, windows open on West 28th to catch whatever breeze could be caught. Picture the song pluggers in the top-floor rooms, young George Gershwin among them, demonstrating other people's songs on out-of-tune uprights to potential purchasers; as sweat rolled down their backs and their tunes joined others' tunes in disharmony, a dozen pianos like clanging pans to passersby.

Bess Morris, walking under those Tin Pan Alley windows on her first day at work in the office of Shapiro, Bernstein & Co. music publishing company, took inspiration from those clashing, crashing chords to compose her first known piece, "Overhead, the City Sings." She wrote it for four pianos, which immediately limited its utility as a performance piece. The song is all the more remarkable for the fact she was still living in a rooming house with no piano at the time. She wrote it in her head and picked it out in stolen moments at work when the players had gone home, but she can't possibly have ever heard all the parts together.

Gershwin was only fifteen when he got that job, high school dropout, youngest piano pounder in the street's employ, making fifteen dollars a week. It had been less than four years since his mother had bought a piano, hoisted through the window to their second story apartment on Second Avenue. He'd been the 7th Street rollerskating champion, a bit of a brawler, and on that first day he beat his older brother Ira to the keys.

In the twenties, the whole family moved to a five-story house on the Upper West Side: parents Rose and Morris, daughter Judy, sons Arthur, George, and Ira. When Ira married, he and his bride took over the fourth floor. The fifth floor was George's, but he also rented space at the Whitehall Hotel, three blocks away, when the family home got too hectic even for him. *I frequently hear music in the very heart of noise.*

After that, he took a penthouse overlooking the Hudson from Riverside Drive; Ira lived in the apartment next door. Friends and business partners came and went constantly. There were parties until the early morning, George at the piano, a Don Sebastian clamped between his teeth, highball on the sidebar.

Later still, George moved to the East Side, his last New York home, a fourteen-room apartment with the largest private bar in New York. Ira moved into the building across the street. The brothers had a direct telephone line installed between their apartments so they could write songs even across the enormous gulf of 72nd Street.

———

The Hotel Ekphrastic, the Hollywood Club, the Roseland Ballroom

Paul Whiteman dined at the Ekphrastic, as did Sam Lanin. Lanin's orchestra, one of the best white dance bands in the city, played the opposite bandstand from the Fletcher Henderson Orchestra at the Roseland, alternating sets. Lanin's band played waltzes and foxtrots, as Henderson's was supposed to, though the latter couldn't resist slipping in jazz, to the taxi dancers' confusion and the consternation of management.

Jazz scholars are generally confused on how the Bess Morris song "For One Night Only" slipped into their repertoires. It's unclear where any meeting might have taken place. Morris had shopped the song up and down Tin Pan Alley, with no interest from any of the publishing companies, even the one where she had worked a few years before. Did Lanin or Whiteman hear it through the Ekphrastic's airshaft? Whiteman frequented the Hollywood Club to hear Ellington's new band. Ellington admired Henderson's skills as a bandleader, so he might have been at the Roseland to hear Henderson and Lanin.

However it was transmitted, every band in town seemed to pick the song up within a single night in 1924. Lanin's version was sentimental, Whiteman's precise, Ellington's expansive, Henderson's grand. The version recorded by the Wolverines was short and staid; by all accounts it lacked energy, and Bix Beiderbecke had not yet managed to make his cornet sing on wax the way it did in person.

His live solos didn't have that problem. Fletcher Henderson wrote of Bix's "For One Night Only" solo, "He sat behind the beat at the start, lulling you into calm. Then he threw in a phrase right on the beat, tipped into the high register, and you were on your knees without knowing how you'd gotten there."

Edward Hopper painted his *New York Pavements* that year, his perspective tilted downward, in opposition to O'Keeffe's, which always craned for sky. Though he didn't paint *New York Ballroom* for another thirteen years, the seated dancer's expression of sated exhaustion captures precisely what Morris was going for when she wrote the lines, "My feet are done / but my heart is still dancing."

Further Studies in Overlap: The House of Genius

Number 61 Washington Square South at the turn of the century was a rooming house for artists, writers, and musicians. The third and fourth floor walls were decorated with murals and poetry by the residents, the landlady's second floor apartment full of art by past residents, some who became famous and some who didn't. At various times it hosted Willa Cather, Stephen Crane, Alan Seeger, Frank Norris, Adelina Patti (who once rehearsed her entire opera company in the parlor), O. Henry, and Eugene O' Neill, among others.

Further Studies in Overlap: The Barbizon Hotel

A women's residence from 1928 to 1981, the Barbizon at various times housed Grace Kelly, Candice Bergen, Liza Minnelli, Phylicia Rashad, Eudora Welty, and Sylvia Plath, who wrote *The Bell Jar* there.

Further Studies in Overlap: The Hotel Elysee

The Elysee was built in the twenties and became "a swank version of a theatrical boardinghouse," per *Life* magazine, housing Marlon Brando, Tennessee Williams (who died there), Sidney Poitier, Vladimir Horowitz, Harold Robbins, Helen Hayes, Joe DiMaggio, Vaclav Havel, Maria Callas, the Gish sisters, and Ava Gardner. Tallulah Bankhead lived at the Elysee for eighteen years, with a menagerie that included a mynah bird, a monkey, and a lion cub named Winston Churchill. After Truman defeated Dewey, she hosted a party there that lasted five days and five nights.

Further Studies in Overlap: The Hotel Chelsea

Let's not even get started.

Assorted Quotes to Exemplify a Phenomenon

"I don't see any boundaries between any of the art forms. I think they all interrelate completely."—David Bowie.

"There is a vitality, a life force, an energy, a quickening that is translated through you into action, and because there is only one of you in all time, this expression is unique. And if you block it, it will never exist through any other medium and will be lost."—Martha Graham.

"The signature of the city changes shape and is fleshed out as more and more people commit to the street. A magical transfer of power from the architectural to the human."—David Bowie.

Bowie and Iman purchased their first Manhattan home, an apartment at the Essex House Hotel, in 1992. He lived the rest of his life in the city, telling the *Times* he was a New Yorker and "I can't imagine living anywhere else."

"Would you mind calling up a little later after the light goes?" —Georgia O'Keeffe.

"At night it looks as though [the Shelton] reached to the stars, and searchlights that cut across the sky back of it do appear to carry messages to other worlds."—Henry McBride, visiting O'Keeffe's apartment.

"What does it mean to be a person in this city, if not that you're a part of the creation of something larger than yourself? That's what I keep trying to put into song, but it keeps eluding me."—Bess Morris, 1923.

". . . You get the full essence of Harlem in an air shaft. You hear fights, you smell dinner, you hear people making love. You hear intimate gossip floating down. You hear the radio. An air shaft is one great big loud-speaker. You see your neighbor's laundry. You hear the janitor's dogs. The man upstairs' aerial falls down and breaks your window. You smell coffee . . . One guy is cooking dried fish with rice and another guy's got a great big turkey . . . You hear people praying, fighting, snoring . . . I tried to put all that in 'Harlem Air Shaft.'"—Duke Ellington's Notes on *Harlem Air Shaft* (1940), from the *New Yorker,* July 1, 1944.

"New York is always hopeful. Always it believes that something good is about to come off, and it must hurry to meet it."—Dorothy Parker

The Hotel Ekphrastic

On this date in 1924, a crowd lined up beneath the Ekphrastic's arched entrance, eager to get into the ballroom. The New Amsterdam's stage was still known as the best ever built for dancing—the Astaires had said so—but the Ekphrastic had the better dance floor.

If you want, you can pick a different place where this happened. The New Amsterdam's roof garden nightclub, say, where the Follies' more risqué Midnight Frolic show took place, and where the ghost of Olive Thomas danced every night. Or the Belasco, with its state-of-the-art lighting and special effects and elevator stage, and a ghost of its own. The Roseland Ballroom, the sordid Hollywood Club. Take us uptown to the still-new Cotton Club, all rules relaxed, or Connie's Inn or Minton's Playhouse or the Lafayette. Hell, if you want to throw this party at Studio 54 or CBGB, that works too. Pick someplace glamorous or dangerous or both.

The band, that fucking band. Armstrong on trumpet and vocals, Beiderbecke on cornet, Charlie Parker and Coleman Hawkins on sax, Jelly Roll Morton and Eubie Blake fighting Gershwin for the piano, Duke Ellington leading the band. Moe Tucker glancing over her drums at Lou Reed every once in a while like she wasn't entirely sure how they got there, but she'd ride it out. Billie Holliday and Ma

Rainey and Paul Robeson and Debbie Harry trading off at the mic.

The band played all their own stuff, the songs they'd written and the ones they had yet to write. A dozen styles and sub-styles flamed into existence, stoked by the energy of possibility.

It doesn't matter who arrived when. The fact was, the moment Bess Morris first played "For One Night Only" to her empty ballroom, the only night she ever really played it, the entire world shifted sideways and gave you a seat in the room, or—if you had the chops—a spot in the band. The numbers don't approach infinity; shove over and there's room for another person on the stage, and time enough for them to play.

Everybody was there that night. The Fitzgeralds arrived with Zelda sitting on the taxi's roof and Scott ornamenting the hood. They invented a new dance, and convinced everyone to try it; the Astaires improved on it. Martha Graham did her own thing entirely. Ira sat on a barstool, watching. Eddie and Jo Hopper, Georgia O'Keeffe and Alfred Stieglitz, Charles Demuth and William Carlos Williams, Mary Pickford and Douglas Fairbanks, Jr., Bankhead and Brando, Williams and Capote.

Dorothy Parker and her vicious circle commandeered a prominent booth. Woody Guthrie and Leadbelly smuggled in their own stash of rye whiskey, even though nobody was paying at the bar. Countee Cullen, still an undergrad, swapped notes with Zora Neale Hurston, the sole black student at Barnard. All the Ramones leaned against the back wall, waiting for their set. Shirley Jackson and Stanley Hyman and Ralph Ellison hunched over drinks at a table in the back, each celebrating the release of their first books, none of which they'd write for a few years yet. David Bowie, the oldest person in the room, leaned on his elbows in the darkest corner, absorbed in the music and happy to be ignored. Leonard Cohen, simultaneously on the bandstand and whispering poetry into the ear of a woman in the corner, because he was just that smooth. Bess Morris bent closer to her piano, never looking up.

We don't need to list everyone. They were all in the room. Whoever it is you think is missing, fill in the name and they'll have been there. You were there too, even if you don't remember it. The room was hot but not too hot, the music loud but not too loud.

What people remembered afterward, if they remembered, was the tempo, the pulse, the band's white-hot urgency, the lights of the city at night, gold and green, blue and green, whirling bodies, the glint of a necklace catching light and sending it spinning. They wrote it, sang it, painted it, dreamed it, drank it, and invented it anew, talking across time for that one night only, before returning to their fleabags and luxury hotels and apartments to dream it off.

The Court Magician

The Boy Who Will Become Court Magician

The boy who will become court magician this time is not a cruel child. Not like the last one, or the one before her. He never stole money from Blind Carel's cup, or thrashed a smaller child for sweets, or kicked a dog. This boy is a market rat, which sets him apart from the last several, all from highborn or merchant families. This isn't about lineage, or even talent.

He watches the street magicians every day, with a hunger in his eyes that says he knows he could do what they do. He contemplates the tawdry illusions of the market square with more intensity than most, until he is marked for us by his own curiosity. Even then, even when he wanders booth to booth and corner to corner every day for a month, begging to learn, we don't take him.

At our behest, the Great Gretta takes him under her tutelage. She demonstrates the first sleight of hand. If he's disappointed to learn that her tricks aren't magic at all, he hides it well. When he returns to her the next day, it is clear he has practiced through the night. His eyes are marked by dark circles, his step lags, but he can do the trick she taught him, can do it as smoothly as she can, though admittedly she is not as Great as she once was.

He learns all her tricks, then begins to develop his own. He's a smart child. Understands intuitively that the trick is not enough. That the illusion is in what is said and what isn't said, the patter, the posture, the distractions with which he draws the mark's attention from

69

what he is actually doing. He gives himself a name for the first time, a magician's name, because he sees how that, too, is part of the act.

When he leaves Gretta to set out on his own, the only space granted to him is near the abattoir, a corner that had long gone unclaimed. Gretta's crowd follows him despite the stench and screams. Most of his routine is composed of street illusions, but there is one that seems impossible. He calls it the Sleeper's Lament. It takes me five weeks to figure out what he is doing in the trick; that's when we are sure he is the one.

"Would you like to learn real magic?" I send a palace guard to ask my question, dressed in her own clothes rather than her livery.

The boy snorts. "There's no such thing."

He has unraveled every illusion of every magician in the marketplace. None of them will speak with him because of it. He's been beaten twice on his way to his newly rented room, and robbed neither time. He's right to be suspicious.

She leans over and whispers the key to the boy's own trick in his ear, as I bade her do. As she bends, she lets my old diary fall from her pocket, revealing a glimpse of a trick he has never seen before: the Gilded Hand. He hands it back to her, and she thanks him for its safe return.

By now he's practiced at hiding his emotions, but I know what's at war within him. He doesn't believe my promise of real magic, but the Gilded Hand has already captivated him. He's already working it out as he pockets the coins that have accumulated in his dusty cap, places the cap upon his head, and follows her out of the marketplace.

"The palace?" he asks as we all near the servants' gate. "I thought you were from the Guild."

I whisper to my emissary, and she repeats my words. "The Guild is for magicians who feel the need to compete with each other. The Palace trains magicians who feel compelled to compete against themselves."

It's perhaps the truest thing I'll ever tell him. He sees only the guard.

The Young Man Who Will Become Court Magician

Alone except for the visits of his new tutor, he masters the complex illusions he is shown. He builds the Gilded Hand in our workshop, from only the glimpse I had let him see, then an entire Gilded Man of his own devising. Still tricks.

"I was promised real magic," he complains.

"You didn't believe in it," his tutor says.

"Show me something that seems like real magic, then."

When he utters those words, when he proves his hunger again, he is rewarded. His hands are bound in the Unbreakable Knot, and he is left to unbind them. His tutor demonstrates the Breath of Flowers, the Freestanding Bridge. He practices those until he figures out the illusions underpinning them.

"More trickery," he says. "Is magic only a trick I haven't figured out yet?"

He has to ask seven times. That is the rule. Only when he has asked for the seventh time. Only then is he told: If he is taught the true word, he has no choice but this path. He will not likely return to the streets, nor make a life in the theaters, entertaining the gentle-born. Does he want this?

Others have walked away at this point. They choose the stage, the street, the accolades they will get for performing tricks that are slightly more than tricks. This young man is hungry. The power is more valuable to him than the money or the fame. He stays.

"There is a word," his tutor tells him. "A word that you have the control to utter. It makes problems disappear."

"Problems?"

"The Regent's problems. There is also a price, which you will pay personally."

"May I ask what it is?"

"No."

He pauses, considers. Others have refused at this point. He does not.

What is the difference between a court magician and a street or stage magician? A court magician is a person who makes problems disappear. That is what he is taught.

There is no way to utter the word in practice. I leave it for him on paper, tell him it is his alone to use now. Remind him again there is a cost. He studies the word for long hours, then tears the page into strips and eats them.

On the day he agrees to wield the word, the Regent touches scepter to shoulder, and personally shows him to his new chambers.

"All of this is yours now," the Regent says. The Regent's words are careful, but the young court magician doesn't understand why. His new chambers are nicer than any place he has ever been. Later, when he sees how the Regent lives, he will understand that his own rooms are not opulent by the standards of those born to luxury, but at this moment, as he touches velvet for the first time, and silk; as he lays his head on his first pillow, atop a feather bed; he thinks for a moment that he is lucky.

He is not.

The Young Man Who Is Court Magician

The first time he says the word, he loses a finger. The smallest finger of his left hand. "Loses" because it is there, and then it is not. No blood, no pain. Sleight of hand. His attention had been on the word he was uttering, on the intention behind it, and the problem the Regent had asked him to erase. The problem, as relayed to him: A woman had taken to chanting names from beyond the castle wall, close enough to be heard through the Regent's window. The Court Magician concentrates only on erasing the chanting from existence, concentrates on silence, on an absence of litany. He closes his eyes and utters the word.

When he looks at his left hand again, he is surprised to see it has three fingers and a thumb, and smooth skin where the smallest finger should have been, as if it had never existed.

He marches down to the subterranean room where he'd learned his craft. The tutors are no longer there, so he asks his questions to the walls.

"Is this to be the cost every time? Is this what you meant? I only have so many fingers."

I don't answer.

He returns to his chambers disconcerted, perplexed. He replays the moment again and again in his mind, unsure if he had made a mistake in his magic, or even if it worked. He doesn't sleep that night, running the fingers of his right hand again and again over his left.

The Regent is pleased. The court magician has done his job well.

"The chanting has stopped?" the court magician asks, right hand touching left. He instinctively knows not to tell the Regent the price he paid.

"Our sleep was not disturbed last night."

"The woman is gone?"

The Regent shrugs. "The problem is gone."

The young man mulls this over when he returns to his own chambers. As I said, he had not been a cruel child. He is stricken now, unsure of whether his magic has silenced the woman, or erased her entirely.

While he had tricks to puzzle over, he didn't notice his isolation, but now he does.

"Who was the woman beyond the wall?" he asks the fleeing chambermaid.

"What were the names she recited?" he asks the guards at the servants' gate, who do not answer. When he tries to walk past them, they let him. He makes it only a few feet before he turns around again of his own accord.

He roams the palace and its grounds. Discovers hidden passageways, apothecaries, libraries. He spends hours pulling books from shelves, but finds nothing to explain his own situation.

He discovers a kitchen. "Am I a prisoner, then?"

The cooks and sculleries stare at him stone-faced until he backs out of the room.

He sits alone in his chambers. Wonders, as all court magicians do after their first act of true magic, if he should run away. I watch him closely as he goes through this motion. I've seen it before. He paces, talks to himself, weeps into his silk pillow. Is this his life now? Is it so wrong to want this? Is the cost worth it? What happened to the woman?

And then, as most do, he decides to stay. He likes the silk pillow, the regular meals. The woman was a nuisance. It was her fault for disturbing the Regent. She brought it on herself. In this way, he unburdens himself enough to sleep.

The Man Who Is Court Magician

By the time he has been at court for ten years, the court magician has lost three fingers, two toes, eight teeth, his favorite shoes, all memories of his mother except the knowledge she existed, his cat, and his household maid. He understands now why nobody in the kitchen would utter a word when he approached them.

The fingers are in some ways the worst part. Without them he struggles to do the sleight of hand tricks that pass the time, and to wield the tools that allow him to create new illusions for his own amusement. He tries not to think about the household maid, Tria, with whom he had fallen in love. She had known better than to speak with him, and he had thought she would be safe from him if he didn't advance on her. He was mistaken; the mere fact that he valued her was enough. After that, he left his rooms when the maids came, and turned his face to the corner when his meals were brought. The pages who summon him to the Regent's court make their announcements from behind his closed door, and are gone by the time he opens it.

He considers himself lucky, still, in a way. The Regent is rarely frivolous. Months pass between the Regent's requests. Years, sometimes. A difficult statute, a rebellious province, a potential usurper, all disappeared before they can cause problems. There have been no wars in his lifetime; he tells himself his body bears the cost of peace so others are spared. For a while this serves to console him.

The size of the problem varies, but the word is the same. The size of the problem varies, but the cost does not correspond. The cost is always someone or something important to the magician, a gap in his life that only he knows about. He recites them, sometimes, the things he has lost. A litany.

He begins to resent the Regent. Why sacrifice himself for the sake of a person who would not do the same for him, who never remarks on the changes in his appearance? The resentment itself is a curse. There is no risk of the Regent disappearing. That is not the price. That is not how this magic works.

He takes a new tactic. He loves. He walks through his chambers flooding himself with love for objects he never cared for before, hoping they'll be taken instead of his fingers. "How I adore this chair," he tells himself. "This is the finest chair I have ever sat in. Its cushion is the perfect shape."

Or "How have I never noticed this portrait before? The woman in this portrait is surely the greatest beauty I have ever seen. And how fine an artist, to capture her likeness."

His reasoning is good, but this is a double-edged sword. He convinces himself of his love for the chair. When it disappears, he feels he will never have a proper place to sit again. When the portrait disappears, he weeps for three losses: the portrait, the woman, and the artist, though he doesn't know who they are, or if they are yet living.

He thinks he may be going mad.

And yet, he appears in the Regent's court when called. He listens to the description of the Regent's latest vexation. He runs his tongue over the places his teeth had been, a new ritual to join the older ones. Touches the absences on his left hand with the absence on his right. Looks around his chambers to catalogue the items that remain. Utters the word, the cursed word, the word that is more powerful than any other, more demanding, more cruel. He keeps his eyes open, trying as always, to see the sleight of hand behind the power.

More than anything, he wants to understand how this works, to make it less than magic. He craves that moment where the trick behind the thing is revealed to him, where it can be stripped of power and made ordinary.

He blinks, only a blink, but when he opens his eyes, his field of vision is altered. He has lost his right eye. The mirror shows a smoothness where it had been, no socket. As if it never existed. He doesn't weep.

He tries to love the Regent as hard as he can. As hard as he loved his chair, his maid, his eye, his teeth, his fingers, his toes, the memories he knows he has lost. He draws pictures of the Regent, masturbates over them, sends love letters that I intercept. The magic isn't fooled.

All of this has happened before. I watch his familiar descent. The fingers, the toes, the hand, the arm, all unnecessary to his duty, though he does weep when he can no longer perform a simple card trick. He loses the memory of how the trick is performed before the last fingers.

His hearing is still acute. No matter what else he loses, the magic will never take his ability to hear the Regent's problem. It will never take his tongue, which he needs to utter the word, or the remaining teeth necessary to the utterance. If someone were to tell him these things, it would not be a reassurance.

For this one, the breaking point is not a person. Not some maid he has fixated upon, not the memory of a childhood love, nor the sleights of hand. For this one, the breaking point is the day he utters the word to disappear another woman calling up from beyond the wall.

"The names!" the regent says. "How am I supposed to sleep when she's reciting names under my window?"

"Is it the same woman from years ago?" the magician asks. If she can return, perhaps the word is misdirection after all. If she can find her voice again, perhaps nothing is lost for good.

"How should I know? It's a woman with a list and a grievance."

The magician tests his mouth, his remaining arm, with its two fingers and thumb. He loses nothing, he thinks, but when he goes to bed that night he realizes his pillow is gone.

It's a little thing. He could request another pillow in the morning, but somehow this matters. He feels sorry for himself. If he thinks about the people he has disappeared—the women outside the wall, the first woman, the entire population of the northeastern mountain province—he would collapse into dust.

I can tell he's done before he can. I'm watching him, as always, and I know, as I've known before. He cries himself out on his bed.

"Why?" he asks this time. He has always asked "how?" before.

Then, because I know he will never utter the word again, I speak to him directly for the first time. I whisper to him the secret: that it is powered by the unquenched desire to know what powers it, at whatever the cost. Only these children, these hungry youths, can wield it, and we wield them, for the brief time they allow us, this one longer than most. His desire to lay things bare was exceptional, even if he stopped short of where I did. I, no more than a whisper in a willing ear.

I wait to see what he will do: return to the marketplace to join Blind Carel and Gretta and the other, lesser magicians, the ones we pay to alert us when a new child lingers to watch; ask to stay and teach his successor, as his tutor did. He doesn't consider those options, and I remember again that I had once been struck by his lack of cruelty.

He leaves through the servants' gate, taking nothing with him. I listen for weeks for him to take up the mourners' litany, as some have done before him, but I should have known that wouldn't be his path either; his list of names is too short. If I had to guess, I would say he went looking for the things he lost, the things he banished, the pieces of himself he'd chipped off in service of someone else's problems; the place to which teeth and fingers and problems and provinces and maids and mourners and pillows all disappear.

There was a trick, he thinks. There is always a trick.

Everything Is Closed Today

Mae didn't see the news until after she got home. She'd managed to get a seat on the rush hour bus, which was always nice, but it had been crowded enough that she'd had to sit with her bag on her knees, and someone else's bag more or less on her knees too, which wasn't that woman's fault, but which hadn't given her any room to browse her phone. There'd been a murmur at one point, more people talking to each other than usual, but she hadn't caught the gist.

She'd looked out her window and people-watched, dog-watched, city-watched. A teenage boy kept up with the bus on his skateboard for a minute, pushing mongo, his front foot pushing and his back foot on the board. Terrible habit. She wasn't surprised when he hit a sidewalk crack and his board shot out in front of him.

She pressed the tape for her stop and managed to squeeze her way past everyone out onto the street, and then it was only a block's walk to their building. The skateboarder passed her, still chasing his board.

"You're pushing with the wrong foot!" she called to him.

He held up his middle finger and kept going. That had been what she expected, but at least she'd tried.

A couple of the building's teenagers were hanging out on the steps, both staring at one phone. She waved but they were engrossed and didn't wave back.

Dana had already made it home from work, a chicken box sitting unopened in the middle of their small table. She still wore her scrubs; usually she showered and changed as soon as she got home.

"Oh, thank goodness." She looked up from her tablet, her face pale. "You didn't answer."

"I didn't answer what?" Mae opened the box and snagged a wing. It was cold.

"Your phone. My text. The networks are all jammed. You haven't heard?"

"Heard what?"

Dana turned the tablet so Mae could see it. A bomb at a baseball matinee in California. The death toll a number she didn't want to contemplate.

"Oh, god," Mae said.

"There aren't many details, but they're saying stay put if you can, 'shelter in place,' there are other threats."

"In California?"

"The whole country. All tonight's games are cancelled. Concerts, movies. Malls are closing early. Planes are grounded. A curfew. They're saying to keep checking the news to see what else is closed."

"Oh, god," Mae said again. She closed her eyes, tried to remember whether anyone on the bus had said anything. The murmur she hadn't quite heard. The people on the street stopping as they looked at their phones, looking around, continuing on their way. The ones who looked like they wanted to say something. Things could be horrible but you still had to get home, get somewhere.

That number. Her brain caught up with it, tumbled it. All those people. All those people at the stadium, and then all those people waiting to get on planes, trying to get home, trying to get to loved ones who had been in the stadium, trying to—

"Ssh," said Dana, standing up and coming around the table, even though Mae hadn't spoken. "I know."

Someone had been in to put up the sign.

"The West Branch Library Will Be Closed Today."

Someone had taken the time to come in and type a sign. Some-one had taken the time to not only print the sign but to look for bright pink paper in the chaotic supply closet and change out the paper in the ancient copier, but not to call the other staff and tell them not to come in.

Mae tried the door anyway. It didn't open, of course. She tried the staff door on the side, then knocked, then knocked again. Sure, she thought. Don't tell the library assistant.

"Mrs. Peters came and left," said Ms. Sharon, the homeless woman who slept in the back alcove when the shelters were full. "She came in really early, let me use the bathroom while she did some stuff, and then she said the library's not opening today."

"Ah." Mae tried for noncommittal, like she had maybe known that and was just testing. She checked her phone again. Nothing.

Mae sighed and typed a message to Mrs. Peters. *We're not opening at all? I'm already here.*

Message not sent. Network unavailable.

Mae sighed again, then deleted the text. If hers wasn't getting through, who knew if Mrs. Peters had sent a message? She might have texted hours ago only to have it delayed by the system overload. Mae would look whiny if that were the case.

She wasn't whining, though. She had paid for a hack cab to work, shared it with a total stranger, because the buses weren't run-ning and the rideshare apps were overloaded and she didn't yet feel valuable enough at work to trust that she wouldn't be fired for being late, even on a day of special circumstances like this one. The cab had cost as much as half a day's work, and now she wouldn't even get paid at all.

"You heard, right?" Ms. Sharon asked, and for a moment Mae wasn't sure she meant whether Mae had heard her about Mrs. Peters, or the chaos of the day before, the stadium bomb, or the stuff that had happened overnight, the undetonated bomb found in a Pennsylvania hotel, the gunman barricaded at the bus station in Mississippi, ongoing, the bomb threats across the country, also ongoing. Whichever.

"I heard."

The walk home took two hours. Fewer people were out than usual, and those that were smiled thin smiles or nodded as they passed, some weird acknowledgment that the other was not the person who intended you harm, no matter the threats on the news. At least it was a nice day, the kind of sunny spring day that reminded you warmth existed in the world. A weird juxtaposition with everything else.

The girls from upstairs were on the steps watching something on a phone, one pair of earbuds split between them.

"No school?" she asked.

"Closed," said one.

When she got to their apartment, Mae tried to check what was going on, but couldn't get any sites to load, news or social media. She turned on the old radio her father had insisted she keep for emergencies, and tuned it to the news. Someone recited a long list of "threat closures": schools, colleges, courts, malls. The central library, but not the branches. Unless they'd messed up and thought the central library meant the whole system.

What wasn't being said was important too: how long would everything be closed? How serious were the threats? Was it one person making the threats or a network? It must be credible for all these closings, but there were no details about anything other than the stadium.

A series of texts came from Dana at nine p.m.—who knew when she'd actually sent them—saying she was probably stuck at the hospital overnight, people were getting drunk and stupid, and there were more suicide attempts than usual, and the ER was a madhouse, and some nurses hadn't been able to get in because they couldn't find babysitters for their kids on short notice.

Love you, good luck, Mae responded, hoping Dana would see it eventually. She put the phone down, then picked it up again and texted Mrs. Peters. It was a little late to message the boss, but not TOO too late, and better to know now.

Will we be open tomorrow? I didn't see our branch listed in the closings.

An hour later, a response. *Closed.*

Shit. She thought of her paycheck short two days' work. What if it stretched into three days? Four?

She checked the clock again. It wasn't ten yet. The first and second calls got weird tones, but her third try got through.

"Mrs. Peters?" she asked when the other woman answered. She'd never called her boss on the phone before; they'd only ever spoken in the library and via text when they were snow delayed.

"What is it, Mae?" She sounded tired, but not like she'd been asleep.

Mae wished she hadn't called. "Um, I was wondering if you know anything you can tell me. I saw the main branch on the news, not ours. Why are we closed?"

"They don't want any public computers available."

"Can't we open but leave the computers off?" Mae pictured all the people who used the computers: the grocery-orderers, the homework-doers, the job seekers. She'd be one of the job seekers if they didn't open soon. She loved working at the library, but she couldn't afford to not-work at the library. "We're a library. Don't we have a responsibility to be open?"

"We have a responsibility to keep our customers safe. Sometimes that means opening, sometimes that means closing. I promise, we'll open as soon as they say the threat is past."

Mae knew a dismissal when she heard one. She thanked her supervisor and hung up. So that was that. Closed until they opened again. Never mind that she was three quarters time, that she only got paid for the hours she worked. Never mind the kids who used them as a safe haven during the hours between the school day's end and their parents returning from work—school was out, anyway. Never mind the job hunters, or Ms. Sharon needing a bathroom, or the cancelled computer classes, or the volunteer tax prep, or any of the million other reasons people used the library.

Those were the reasons she was working there. She wanted to go to library school, to be the kind of librarian who made sure a branch did everything for its neighborhood that the community didn't have. It would be one thing to take out giant loans to become a corporate lawyer or a plastic surgeon, but it seemed like a bad idea to go into debt for a public librarian's salary no matter how much she wanted it. She'd been putting money aside for it for ages; she'd be dipping into that soon if she didn't get more hours.

The worry outweighed the fear for her; maybe it was the other way around for Mrs. Peters and the other people making decisions. Maybe they knew something that made the threat less nebulous, less distant. As it was, the lack of information and stalled websites scared her far more than the bomb threats.

Dana crawled into bed at seven a.m., damp from the shower. "Do you need to get up for work?" she whispered.

Mae grunted no, though she was actually awake behind closed eyelids. Her body was used to getting up at this time, even with nothing to get up for. She lay in bed for a few minutes more, listening to Dana's breathing change, then rolled over to check her phone. Remembered the sites were down and tried the radio instead, where nothing new was being reported, but the list of shuttered facilities had grown.

When she went to make coffee, she realized she'd forgotten to pick some up the day before. She'd been too busy cultivating annoyance over traveling all the way to work for nothing. She always used snow days as an excuse to stay in pajamas; now she had an urge and an excuse to get out. She dressed and left a note for Dana.

This was her usual hour for catching the bus, but the streets were emptier than usual. A few people sleepily walked dogs—they gave their usual familiar-stranger waves, though more strained looking than usual. More suspicious. No speeding cars using her street as an alternate route to downtown, no crowd at the bus stop.

Why did this feel different from a weather closure? She'd lived through blizzards that had stopped the city in its tracks, introduced snow-baffled silences to the normally busy roads. Life-interrupting hurricanes had become more common too. Dana always worked through them, since hospital life went on.

The closure list went far beyond any snow day. Movie theaters usually managed to open in everything but the worst blizzards. Malls, too. Then there was the clear blue sky, the first warmth, the do-somethingness of spring. She wished she knew what to do.

The grocery store was closed. A sign on the door said "you can still order online and we will deliver," with their online service's logo printed large. That was all well and good for the people doing full grocery runs—it was free over $25—but Mae wasn't about to pay $10 extra for a pound of coffee, assuming the grocery sites were faring better than news and social media. And what about the seniors who came into her library for her to help them order groceries to be delivered? They didn't have smartphones; the delivery fee was waived if you used the library program.

The convenience store on the corner didn't have any bulk coffee beans. She bought a quart of iced coffee to carry them through the next few days, because it worked out cheaper than getting individual cups. Still more than the supermarket bags, on a week where every penny was going to count. The man behind her in line clutched two small packages of diapers, and the woman ahead of her a tiny bag of sugar and a tiny box of tampons, at the price of convenience.

Dana was still asleep, so Mae poured herself some coffee and sat down to math out the month's bills. She ran the numbers for three days off work, then a week. They wouldn't close things for more than a week, would they? Dana made a good salary, but a week without Mae's pay was the most their budget allowed without dipping into savings, and she knew she was luckier than most to have managed to save at all.

She started trying random websites to see what was available and what wasn't. Grocery sites were up, and online retailers, and streaming services. All the big social media sites were either offline or too slow to be worth anything. It didn't make any sense. There shouldn't be any reason for one to work and not the other, unless there was also some weirdly specific cyber-attack happening. What she wanted most was information from other people, not just the calm radio voices.

It was a twilight zone of a week. Perfect sunny days, quiet streets, no work but nothing open. Mae stayed in, watching the news, while Dana reported back to the hospital a few blocks away. When they'd moved into this apartment two years ago, Mae hadn't yet had the library job, so they'd picked the location to be close to Dana's work. With the buses down, that turned out to have been a great decision; a thing they couldn't have anticipated that worked out in their favor.

Mae wondered how many other people were stuck doing what she was doing: checking the news, worrying, counting pennies, counting again. She'd been too young to understand the last time the country was rocked like this, but none of the accounts mentioned the deep sense of powerlessness she was fighting. They didn't want blood donors. They didn't want anyone doing anything at all. Stay home, good citizens. Never mind that you won't have a home if the stores and theaters and libraries and schools don't open again, that rental offices would still expect rent and banks would still expect mortgage payments. How long could they possibly expect people to put up with this? The news kept reporting threats. Where were the stories about ordinary people struggling? Where was the resistance to this becoming the new normal? She sent out a group chat to friends to see if anybody knew of protests. Nobody responded, and she wasn't sure if the message had even gone out.

On the third day, she babysat a toddler on the second floor whose parents still had jobs to go to. She brought some old paperbacks down to the lobby and made a sign that said "Free Library."

On the fourth day, she wished she had a dog, and put up a sign in the lobby offering her services as a dog walker, with little tabs for people to pull off with her phone number. People with dogs had routines they had to follow no matter what. The dog needed feeding, expected walks at regular intervals. Nothing felt normal. She watched a movie online, expecting the same stutter and lag as the news sites, but finding none; even that was odd. She tried to find info about the extended outages and found nothing there either. Ads everywhere offered discounted memberships to various streaming and delivery services.

On the fifth day, she went downstairs to see if anyone had pulled her dog walking tabs, but nobody had. She sighed. She didn't need a dog to take a walk, she supposed. She should get some exercise.

The girls from upstairs were on the steps again, watching a phone.

"Hey," she said, and they waved.

It was another beautiful spring day, perfect walking weather, disconcertingly quiet. When she got back, the two girls were arguing.

"We've already seen that one," said the older one.

"We've seen them all," said the other.

She tried to remember their names. Lily and Kima? No, Kimi, she was pretty sure.

"Kimi?"

The older girl looked up.

She was going to make sure that they knew about the library's app, that they could rent shows and movies for free, but as she opened her mouth, she found herself asking something else instead. "Have you ever skateboarded?"

Kimi shook her head.

"Want me to show you how? It'll kill a few hours if you're bored."

Kimi looked like she was going to say no. Her sister nudged her, and she shrugged.

Mae smiled. "I'll be right back."

Mae ran up to the apartment to get the storage locker key, then down to the basement. Mae had wanted to donate the skateboards, so Dana had hidden them in the back of the locker; Mae knew they were there, and could've tossed them at any point, but if Dana hadn't wanted to part with them yet, it wasn't Mae's job to trash them. Now they were coming in handy! Finding the helmets and pads took a little longer. They smelled funky but didn't look actively gross. There was no bloodstain on her board to hint at the last time she'd been on it. None on the helmet because she'd been stupid that day and hadn't worn it.

The girls still sat on the steps; she'd half-expected them to be gone. They eyed the gear skeptically.

"You can choose whether you want to wear the pads. Helmets are non-negotiable," she said. "I don't want anyone getting brain damage because of me."

She thought they might refuse, but they reached for the helmets.

"Great!" She waited while they adjusted. Kimi's hair was bigger than Mae's, so the fit wasn't too bad.

Lily reached for Dana's skateboard.

"Not so fast," Mae said. "Basics first. I'm going to show you how to stand. Your front foot is for balance, your back foot is for steering."

"My feet are right next to each other," Lily said. Her sister giggled.

Mae laughed too. "Okay, fair enough. Let's start from there. If you take turns pushing each other from behind—not hard—while your feet are right next to each other, you can see which foot you put forward first, and that'll tell you which foot should be in front on the skateboard."

They took a minute shoving each other, maybe a little harder than she'd intended, despite her warning.

"Okay, you both put your left foot forward, so that's the one that'll be in front. That's a regular stance."

"Now can we get on?"

"Yeah, but just on the grass over there." She pointed to the narrow grassy strip below the ground floor windows.

"We're riding on grass?"

"You're standing on grass. I'll show you."

Mae handed Dana's board to Lily and carried her own over to the grass. She demonstrated where she wanted their feet. "Just stand on it and get used to balancing. Try shifting your weight around, toe, heel, whatever. Get used to standing without it rolling."

"I thought you said no riding without a helmet."

"I did. This isn't riding. It's standing still on grass."

She gave her board to Kimi and stepped back. The two girls spent a few minutes doing as she'd said. Kimi kept pulling out her phone to text; Mae figured if she could text and balance it was probably a good sign. After a bit, both girls started getting silly.

"Look at me," Lily said, balancing on her back wheels. She toppled a second later.

Mae offered a hand. "That's why you're on grass. It's fine to try that, but it might take a little while to get good at it."

A girl emerged from the building next door and stood back, watching. Mae smiled at her. "I only have two boards. You can join us if they're willing to take turns."

"My brother has one," she said. "I'll be right back."

She disappeared into her building and returned with a beat-up board. No helmet. No helmet would be okay for this first day, while they were on the grass, but after that she'd have to insist. After that? Apparently she was already anticipating a next day.

The new girl was Joni, from Lily's class. Two more girls showed up a few minutes later, and Kimi walked over to whisper to them and point at Mae, then approach.

"I told my friends to come over. Is that okay?"

Mae nodded. They'd have to take turns with the boards and helmets.

She started over again with Joni and the two newest girls, Fatima and Tamsin, showing them how to stand. Kimi and Lily gave pointers like they were old hands.

By evening, all five girls could balance and stand on the grass without the board flying out from under them, and she'd started showing them how to foot brake, and nobody had landed badly.

"If there's no school tomorrow can we do this again?" Fatima asked.

Mae nodded. "If we find more helmets." It would be one thing if she was another kid, or if they were adults, but an adult teaching kids had some responsibility to keep them safe. Plus she couldn't afford to get sued.

Dana got home at a reasonable hour for the first time since everything had gone screwy. Mae made mac and cheese while Dana showered. She left the bathroom open so they could still talk. "The union rep had been in California and had to drive back. When he saw the hours we'd been working he threw a fit, so I have a whole two days off whether I want them or not. What've you been up to?"

"I, ah, you know those girls who hang out on the stoop? I started teaching them to skateboard."

The water came on. "Really? I thought you—argh, cold! Ice cold!—I thought you were never going to touch one again."

Mae's hand went to her head, fingers tracing the scar beneath her hair. "I dunno. Everyone's walking around like they're accepting that everything is closed forever, and I figured if we're going to get killed any second I might as well skateboard again."

"Good logic there, babe. I'm not going to stop you! I miss it myself. And not everyone is accepting it. People are organizing. Vigils. Protests. I've treated a few people coming in from protests that got broken up by police. They're out there—you just haven't gone looking."

"If they're that hard to find, the people organizing them can't be doing that good a job."

"It's not their fault communication's all messed up." Dana emerged from the bathroom, drying her hair in a towel. "We're so used to everything being at our fingertips we've forgotten how to spread information the old-fashioned way."

"What's the old-fashioned way? Telegraph?"

Dana disappeared into the bedroom and returned in pajamas. She reached for a bowl and answered as if there'd been no pause. "I dunno. I do know about one meeting tonight, if you want to go. This guy told me about it while I stitched his eyebrow."

"Isn't there a curfew?"

"Curfew's at ten, meeting's at eight. It's not far. I'd have to put on real clothes again, but we could make it."

Mae recognized the generosity of the offer of post-shower clothes after all those work days in a row. "I'd love to."

The café was a twenty-minute walk, a tiny independent bookstore café with a classroom in the back, where the meeting was already underway. A man with a rubber duck bandage above his left eye, presumably Dana's patient, sat chatting with a dozen people in folding chairs.

They stood in the back and listened to plans for a major protest, warnings that no permits were being given, so any march or rally that wasn't on private property would be an illegal one. Someone asked what the goal of marching would be, which launched a spirited discussion of protest with goals versus protest for protest's sake. Then there were the big problems: how to get the word out, how to get the crowds that would make protest safer, how to communicate within the operation itself if text messages were still delayed and phones unreliable.

Mae was cheered by the fact the group recognized those flaws in their plan. They appeared to know what they were doing. She liked the idea of a protest, something to focus people on the questions at hand instead of the extended, unwanted vacation. She liked, too, that they voiced some of her own concerns: that it didn't make sense for communication to be interrupted for this long, or for news to be so hard to find and distraction so easy.

"There's something seriously wrong on a national level," someone said. "But I think the answers will probably be local."

When the planning meeting broke up, Dana introduced Mae to her patient, who said his name was Duck—hence his bandage choice. Someone tapped her on the shoulder, and she realized her old friend Nora had been sitting in front of them through the meeting.

"You still not skating?" Nora asked.

"Nah. Can't afford it." Mae didn't need to show Nora her wrists or her head; Nora had been there.

Dana put an arm over her shoulder. "It's not the skating we can't afford. It's the falling."

"Nah," said Mae. "It's the *landing*. And the work I missed in rehab."

Nora laughed. "If you say so. We miss you at the park."

Mae was about to mention the girls from that morning, but someone else came over to chat with Nora, and they were introduced, and the conversation drifted.

Walking back, Dana laced her fingers around Mae's. "Did that help?"

"I think so. I'm glad someone's doing something, even if it's logistically challenging."

They walked home on empty streets that felt far less safe than the usual bustle.

The next day, Mae woke to laughter below the bedroom window. She looked down to see seven girls on the steps. Lily was shoving one of her friends from behind, which Mae hoped was to see which foot she favored.

"Where are you going?" Dana asked from the bed. "Nothing's open."

"I've got a class to teach. Come downstairs if you want to help when you wake up."

She grabbed the boards and helmets and headed downstairs. Seven girls, four boards, three helmets. She'd have to fix that.

They went over what they'd learned the day before, and that day's girls taught the new ones how to stand and balance.

"Why are you doing this?" a new girl asked.

"It's something to do," Mae said, which was as good an answer as any. Then she felt bad, because these girls didn't need cynicism. "I love skateboarding, and I hate that everyone has somehow been convinced that the safest thing to do is sit around doing nothing, and I hate seeing people look bored."

"My mom says if you're bored, you're boring."

"That seems a little unfair. I'd say if you're bored you should look around for an opportunity to learn something. There's always something to learn."

Dana came out of the building. She stood on the top step and surveyed the scene.

"Hey, everyone, you're in luck," Mae said. "It's time for a demonstration. Kimi, give that helmet and board to Dana."

Dana held out her hands, and the girl brought it up to her.

"Is she going to ride down the steps?" Lily whispered. "That's *advanced.*"

Mae grinned and stood back. She'd always been okay, but Dana was a skater who surveyed any space and immediately knew how she'd ride it. She rolled down the stairs then did a few basic tricks. Stuff that looked impressive but wasn't discouraging for a beginner. The next building's stairs had a railing that gave her a chance to show off a little.

"Are we going to be able to do that, Ms. Mae?"

"Maybe. I was never able to do that last one."

Dana returned with the board and helmet. "I've got an errand to run. Back in a while!"

"Can we learn to do that railing thing next?" Lily kicked up her heels in imitation.

"Nope. Next we learn how to fall."

The girls giggled, clearly thinking she was joking.

"I'm going to show you how to land so you don't hurt yourselves if you fall. This is serious stuff." She thought about showing them the scars on her wrists and head, but she didn't actually want to scare them off.

Dana returned around noon with arms full of battered boards and less battered helmets, enough for all the girls. They had still been falling—it turned out they liked falling—but scrambled to call dibs.

"Should we order them pizza?" Dana whispered.

Mae shook her head regretfully, the dollars spinning in her head.

The next day, with enough helmets and boards for everyone, they all walked two blocks to the empty middle school parking lot.

"Is there anyone here whose parents would object to you leaving the block?" It had occurred to her that she didn't know where these girls were and weren't allowed to go. It was one thing when they showed up at her door, another when she led them somewhere. "If anyone asks, you all decided to take a walk, right? We're not kidnapping you?"

"Ms. Mae." Kimi's voice dripped with scorn. "We're fourteen."

"And thirteen," said Lily. "And we walk this alone every day when there's school."

Dana laughed at the exchange.

The lot had been repaved in the not-too-distant past, and proved to be a safe enough practice ground. The two sets of pads had been divvied up among the girls, so that two had elbow protection, two wrist, and so on. Lily, the boldest skater among them, had taken none. Within an hour her leggings were shredded, as were her knees, but she didn't seem bothered. They'd brought wet wipes and antiseptic and adhesive bandages, and the presence of Dana the on-site nurse reassured Mae, even if she couldn't help anticipating the screech of an unexpected car, the deep thud of head meeting pavement.

"Relax," Dana whispered. "They'll be okay."

She tried to relax. If the world was ending, at least they'd have brought a few more girl skaters into the world. At least it kept everyone entertained.

The skies opened around midnight, and the rain continued into the morning. Dana had to return to work, and after checking to see if the library was open yet, Mae burrowed into the covers to sleep late. Until the pounding on the door.

"You're late," said Kimi.

Mae yawned. "How did you even know which door is mine?"

"We didn't. We knocked on all of them. There are some grouchy people in this building."

"We can't skateboard in the rain."

"We need to do *something*," Kimi said, as if it was on Mae.

The funny thing was, she felt like it really was on her. She went down to the lobby. Her books were still in the corner. No; hers were gone, but other books had replaced them. Nice.

There were ten girls now, all looking at her, except one who was thumbing a paperback. How did they keep multiplying? What would they be doing if she hadn't offered them something to do? She wished the library was open. An art project? She didn't have any materials.

"How many of you are worried about your parents right now? Worried about how much they're worried about bills, that kind of thing?"

A couple raised their hands.

"And how many of you want to be back in school?"

Different hands.

"And do you know why jobs and schools are closed right now?"

"It's dangerous?"

"Well, they say it's dangerous, but we don't know. We don't know if there's something to be scared about, or if someone wants us to be scared. Are you scared?"

Heads moved in various directions. Some were, some weren't.

She tried another. "What are some questions we could be asking?"

"How are we supposed to do year-end exams if we aren't learning anything?"

"Are they going to keep us into summer because we're missing school now?"

They built on each other. "Is there really someone threatening our school? How can they threaten all the schools at once?"

"We already had to risk people shooting at the malls and stores and school and stuff. How is this any different?"

"Who's in charge of deciding?"

"If my mom doesn't work she doesn't get paid, but it's not her fault. Shouldn't the management company take that into account?"

"And we have to eat! How are we going to pay for food?"

Mae's heart went out to these kids. This was a lot to be thinking about as an adult, let alone a fourteen-year-old. "Okay, so next question. What can we do about it?"

They all looked at her, waiting. "It depends on which one you want to tackle, right?"

The conversation paused as Mr. Snow from the third floor made his slow way through the lobby, a paper bag holding a pint of milk from the convenience store in his shaking hand.

"All of them," said Fatima, when he had gone upstairs. "They all matter."

Joni shook her head. "The rental office. Straight up. My mom says they charge a huge late fee, and if you already can't afford your rent, you can't afford the late fee either. They could waive the late fees but they won't. All the other stuff gets harder if we evicted."

The kid was right. She'd spoken with enough homeless library visitors to know how much harder everything got once you lost your home. "Okay, then. Let's see. Their office is only a couple of blocks away." The same company managed all three buildings on the block, and Mae assumed most of these kids came from these three buildings or the rowhouses around the corner.

"What do we do?"

Mae didn't really know. "Ask nicely, I think."

The rain still fell steadily, and other than one girl with a polka-dotted umbrella and rubber boots, they were all underdressed for it, Mae included. The walk left them soaked.

Starsign Management had its office in a storefront on the ground floor of yet another apartment building, this one larger and more modern than those a few blocks away. The building was recessed from the street, with a well-maintained entry plaza. It would be a decent skateboarding spot on a nicer day.

The office itself had an awning, a small kindness Mae was grateful for, and a wooden front door displaying two laminated signs, one reading "$50 lost key fee" and the other "by appointment only." A phone number was listed below each. She hadn't remembered the "by appointment" part. Was that sign here when she'd dropped her rent check last month? Maybe they weren't the first to stop in to plead a case.

"Who wants to do the honors?" Mae asked, pointing.

Kimi pulled out her phone and entered the number. "Hi, my name is Kimi Porter, I'd like to talk to you about an apartment. Yes. I can be there in a few minutes. Ten o'clock would be fine. Thanks."

When she disconnected, the others copied her in their own best phone voices, giggling. Mae wondered if the receptionist could hear them over the rain; as she remembered it, the front desk was only a few feet inside the door.

At ten, they rang the doorbell. The receptionist buzzed them in. She didn't hide her surprise at a gaggle of dripping teenagers and one dripping librarian. "We don't rent to students," she said.

"We're not looking to rent. We're already your tenants," said Mae.

"We have an appointment," said Lily in an awful British accent, settling herself in the nearest chair. The others followed her lead, sitting on the floor or leaning against the wall after the chairs were taken.

"Nicely," Mae whispered.

Kimi leaned forward. "My name is Kimi Porter and this is my sister Lily. We live in the 152 building. Our mom is a cashier at Fresh Fare. Except they don't need cashiers right now because the store is closed, so she hasn't had a shift all week."

The receptionist smiled. "I'm not sure what you expect me to do about that. We have one half-time handyperson position open. She should come in person if she wants to apply."

"That's not the issue. She's got a job, but if this paycheck is short, she won't be able to pay the whole rent. If she doesn't pay the whole rent, you charge a fee, and then we're playing catchup, like when she had back surgery and didn't get paid."

The receptionist turned to Mae to answer. "It's in the lease—"

"Talk to Kimi, ma'am. She's the one talking to you." Mae had expected to talk, but these kids had things to say. There was nothing for her to add.

"Kimi, the lease had specific terms. Your parents signed the lease. I can't help . . ."

"Sure you can," said Joni. "You can choose to enforce those terms. You can also choose to offer a grace period or not enforce while all this is going on."

The receptionist frowned. "I don't have that power. I can talk to the manager, but she isn't really big on exceptions. I'll pass your concerns along for you, Miss Porter."

"For all of us?" asked Fatima. "It's not just their family. Everybody's hurting."

"For everyone. Now, if you can excuse me? I have another appointment waiting." There was nobody else in the office.

Lily opened her mouth, and Mae interrupted before anyone said anything. "Thank you for meeting with us, and thanks for considering it. Is there a manager we could follow up with?"

The woman opened a drawer and rustled for a business card, which she handed to Mae. "Can I get one too?" asked Kimi. "I'd like to follow up with a manager too."

The rain was still falling, though not as hard as earlier. The girls made it out the door before erupting. "That woman didn't listen at all!"

"She didn't care!"

"What was the point of doing that if she wasn't going to listen?"

Mae fished for positives. "Now we have the manager's number, and now we know their messed up no-exceptions policy, so we know what we're up against."

"What does that help?"

"We can write letters, right? To the manager, to the news outlets, to the school board, to"—she wracked her brain for civics class memories—"to city council reps and state government reps."

"Letters? That's all?"

"What do you mean write a letter?"

"How will that help?"

"Letters—"

"Can't we do something real?"

"Letters are real."

They were almost back to the apartment building. The other girls could have peeled off to their doors, but they all followed Mae into the lobby. One of the borrowed skateboards leaned in the corner near the mailboxes.

"Letters are real but they aren't enough, Ms. Mae. Isn't there something else we can do?"

Lily dropped the board and climbed on.

"A protest," Mae said. "On wheels."

"That's more like it," said Kimi.

"We have to do it right, so we don't make things worse. Permits. Letters. So people know why we're doing it. Otherwise it's just a bunch of kids skating, and you could get in trouble."

"Lily's always in trouble."

"I am not! Anyway, that's not what she means."

"What does she mean?"

"I don't know, but Miss Mae will show us."

She still didn't know how she'd wound up in this position.

They looked up how to get a demonstration permit, but it turned out the city wasn't giving any out. No demonstrations, legal or otherwise. She'd forgotten that from the meeting the other night.

"Letters," Mae said again, not admitting that it was only slightly better than nothing. She needed to come up with something real and useful for them to do while those letters worked their slow way through the system. What had they said at that meeting? Solutions would be local.

Payday Friday came and went, a meager check with only the period's first three days worked. The library was still closed, so Mae poured all her energy into her growing girl gang. Mornings, they wrote letters and emails. Afternoons, they skateboarded.

A couple of the girls were cautious. Lily was completely fearless. Joni was more careful, and Mae could tell she was practicing at home. There were twelve girls now. Twelve girls who had somehow decided that this was the way they would spend their days.

"What are you doing?" Dana asked that night.

"I don't know. I don't know how this happened, but they're good kids, and they need something to do."

"And you need something too . . ."

"Maybe. I want to do more for them."

"You're doing a lot, Mae. You're teaching them how to skate, and how to be civically engaged."

"Neither of which will help if they get evicted. I wish there was a way to help them. And to help us, for that matter. I hate that I can't contribute anything right now. I don't even know what to make for dinner—we're out of everything."

Dana stood to rummage in the cupboard. "Whoa. We're in serious need of groceries. At least we need enough to get over the $25 hump."

Mae stared at her.

"What?"

"I know a thing we can do!"

"Yeah?"

"Everyone's buying stuff from the convenience store because they can't afford the delivery fee online, right?"

"Right."

"So what if we talk to everyone on the block and take orders? We can lump them all together for one big order, then deliver."

"You want to knock on all those doors?"

"No, but I'll bet the girls will. They can deliver too. Tips with regular grocery prices will still be cheaper than the corner store or the delivery fee."

"Huh . . ." said Dana. "That's not all, you know."

"What do you mean?"

"I think you might have solved a problem for the protest organizers too . . ."

Mae thought about it for a moment. "Oh. Communication!"

"A few girls on skateboards, maybe a few on bikes, acting as pages, passing information along. If the cops catch them, they look like teenagers goofing off. You don't think they'd think they were being used?"

"Are you kidding? They've been dying for something useful to do."

Once it had been said, for the first time since everything had changed, she couldn't wait for the next morning. They liked the idea even more than she had expected.

"We can be the pony express," Lily said. She held Mae's old board like she was itching to ride.

Joni ticked more off on her fingers. "And human text messages. And chat systems. And news sites. We can shout headlines like those kids in old movies."

"We can MAKE the news," said Kimi. "What if we skate outside the rental office and the TV news place with signs saying 'Starsign Management wants to evict my family.' We can take off if they call the cops, but maybe they won't like the publicity . . ."

These kids, Mae thought. She didn't know when the library would open, or if they could really stop the evictions and late fees, but she had a tiny free library to maintain, a human grocery app to instigate, protests to plan, and a skater girl gang information superhighway ready to deploy. There was so much to do.

Left the Century to Sit Unmoved

The pond only looks bottomless.

Clambering up the moss-slick stones beside the waterfall, finding purchase with cramping toes and fingers, if I chance a look back over my shoulder, the pond is a moonblack sky even on a sunny summer's day. It absorbs light. I push back off the narrow ledge, as hard as I can, always feet first, hoping I miss the rocks, hoping I don't overshoot the middle, hoping I won't lose my bathing suit on the way back up because Otis and Kat are here too, and I'd become a legend in all the wrong ways.

When I'm in the water, plunging, sinking, one hand dragging my sagging waistband back to something approximating my waist, wondering why I let Kat convince me to buy this suit in the first place, I let myself drop as deep as I possibly can. I trail my toes in the silt, and there is silt, and some kind of tough grass that wraps long fingers around my calves, and silt and grass mean there is a bottom. If I open my eyes, if I ignore the grit, I might catch a glimpse of trout silvering between the grasses. Or a water snake, black in the blackness.

That's all universal to everyone jumping, I think, except maybe the bit about the suit. And except maybe the next bit, where I come up gasping, and immediately go under again as Otis crashes in on top of me.

"Jerk!" I say when we've both surfaced. "One at a time! That's the rule!"

"They aren't rules, Shay," Kat says from the shore. She's spread a large towel over the flattest boulder, and she's sitting at the center reading a paperback with both covers missing. "They're superstitions."

"Easy for you to say, chicken." Otis skims his hand across the water, sending a plume her way that dies before it touches her. She doesn't even flinch. I make a mental note: cool is in not flinching. Cool is in keeping your resolve not to jump, even when your boyfriend calls you "chicken." If I have any cool at all, it comes from the fact that I jumped before either of them. I didn't even do it to impress them. No peer pressure here.

Anyway, Kat's not wrong. They are superstitions. Everyone in town follows them, except when they don't.

The rules:

1. One person at a time, so everyone can see if the pond is hungry.
2. No skinny-dipping, so your friends will know if you were taken or you just drowned. (Clothes don't get taken.)
3. Don't jump if anyone depends on you.
4. Saying "one more jump" is just tempting fate.
5. Jump, don't dive. The pond prefers divers.
6. Don't jump alone.

Number three has variations. Some say it's more like "don't jump when you're in love." Others say the rule is "the pool can't take you if you're truly in love," in which case Otis is actually being romantic. That's what he claims. He loves Kat, and she loves him back. He always jumps anyway, just once, not usually on me. She's never jumped. When he gets out, she always slugs him in the arm before kissing him.

I'm maybe in love with both of them, or maybe just in love with the way they are around each other. I want to be the arm-puncher or the arm-punchee or the punch itself, or the plume of water that knows better than to drench Kat while she's holding a book. I want to believe they are superstitions, not rules, even though Kendra Butcher and Grant Pryor jumped together and vanished without a trace. I was there that day, though I wasn't ready to jump yet myself at the time.

The thing about the rules is they don't change anything at all. The pond doesn't follow any rules. They're just things people made up and passed down to make us feel better about our chances. To remind us what's at stake. Something to cling to when we're telling somebody's parents and they're nodding like, of course, this is the risk we all take, and they shouldn't have jumped together.

People break the rules all the time. My brother Nick used to jump alone. When he disappeared, three years ago, his old Buick Century was found at the far end of the dirt lot where people park to hike down here if they come by car instead of by bike.

"Maybe he went hitchhiking," my mother said. "Maybe he'll be back."

Nick had done that before, too, going off for days without telling us where he was headed. But he hadn't tried to thumb a ride since he bought the car, and anyway nobody would hitchhike from that particular spot, since the only cars there were coming from or going back to our own town. It didn't make any sense for his car to be there unless he'd jumped.

We left the Century to sit unmoved. The spare key, the one that didn't disappear with Nick, lives in a bowl of coins near our front door. It used to be on top, but it gradually drowned in pennies and dimes. I know it's in there, but there's no use digging it out. I might have been able to drive the car away at the beginning, but I don't know where I'd have taken it. Since then, vines have grown over it and punched their way in through the windows. Somebody stole the hubcaps, and the tires have all gone flat and given in to rot. I think there's a raccoon living in the backseat. It's not Nick's anymore, not anybody's. Just a thing caught up in the slow process of transforming into another thing.

I can't say what happens when the pond takes a person. Only what we've all seen. Someone climbs the waterfall, pushes off the wall. The same way we all do. Same arc, same splash, but they never surface. There's no struggle, no roiling water, no sign anything was disturbed. A swimsuit will come floating up, which is why the old joke that the pond doesn't like synthetic fabrics. And we never see that friend/sibling/mother again. I've seen it happen twice with my own eyes. Kendra and Grant, both from my homeroom.

The bottom has been dredged at various points, once at my mother's request and my family's expense. People have gone in with scuba gear. They found a rubber boot, a bicycle, a picnic table. House keys and cell phones and car keys, though not Nick's. No bodies, no bones, no brothers.

There's always somebody who grew up here coming back to study it, only they realize quickly there's nothing to study. Set up a video camera and you could wait forever, and even if you caught someone as they disappeared, you've got nothing to show afterward. No proof it wasn't photographic trickery. No after to the before.

My father isn't one of the ones who came back to study it, but he's one of the few who came back. He says when he was a teenager, only boys jumped. The girls all sunned themselves on the flat boulder the way Kat does. Otis says he's heard the same; his mother's first and last jump was on her fortieth birthday. She and two friends drove out with a cooler full of pre-mixed margaritas to celebrate. I think that's why Otis prefers the "truly in love" version of the third rule, the version centered on romance, not responsibility. It used to bother him a lot that she took the chance, even if she did come back. He hasn't spoken about it since we started jumping.

My own mother isn't from here. She doesn't understand at all. She's the one who forced the town to put up a fence, so that now we have to climb over. She's the one who insisted Nick's car stay in the lot instead of taking it home for me. She closed the door on Nick's bedroom and left it untouched, just in case he comes back. Unlike the Buick, the bedroom has mostly stayed intact. Content the way it is, maybe, or on a slower journey.

I sneak in sometimes to go through Nick's stuff. I choose one area to explore each time, so if I find something I can pretend he meant me to find it at that very moment. The first fall he was gone, I discovered his copy of *Twelfth Night* right before my English mid-term, with useful notes on every page. Another time, an issue of *Penthouse*, which cleared up some questions my parents weren't ready to answer and I hadn't yet worked up the nerve to research. Two years ago, I found a notebook filled with drawings of imaginary carnivorous plants. There was a folded page in the middle, and on it, in his block lettering:

Why We Jump

We jump because we have to.
We jump because we can.
We jump because we dare ourselves.
We jump because we're lonely.
We jump because we want to be alone.
We jump because once you're up there's really no other good way down.
We jump because otherwise we'll never do anything that matters.
We jump because we want to fly, just for a moment.
We jump because everything is better afterward: beer, breathing, sandwiches, sex.
We jump because the water is clear and deep.
We jump because there are so few things in life that can't be explained away.
We jump because we want to know what happens when the pond takes somebody.
We jump because we don't want that somebody to be

us, or maybe we do.

We jump because otherwise we will never know who we are.

We jump because we want to know what else there is to be.

We jump because we don't want to be the kind of person who wouldn't.

We jump because each of us knows we are the invincible center of the world.

We jump because we want to be

We jump because

I can't tell if those last two lines are unfinished or how he meant them. I don't know if his "we" is meant to speak for everybody or just himself. I'm pretty sure I was meant to find this right when I did, right when the word "why" had started unmooring me. Nick's multiple becauses couldn't all be true, not all the time, but I liked the fact they couldn't be pinned down. They weren't answers. They were anchors.

I made my first jump the week after I found the note, dragging my friends along so I wouldn't chicken out. Just one jump, I promised. I didn't say: I want to do something that matters. I want everything to be better afterward, beer and breathing and sandwiches even if sex is not on the menu yet.

I can't say everything was better afterward, but I learned on the first jump that fear and relief are two forms of the same compound, like ice and water. The terror that built in my muscles and bones as I climbed the waterfall, as I pushed off, as I let go, it all bubbled out when I came up for air.

"What are you laughing at?" Kat called to me.

I just laughed and laughed, treading water. When we came back the next week, Otis jumped for the first time. Since then we've come out here at least once a week if the weather is at all conducive. It's not a decision on anyone's part. It's what we do. I'm happy to be part of this small "we" as well as the larger "we" that I think my brother was talking about, the "we" of everyone who has ever jumped or considered jumping.

I've added a few of my own ideas to my brother's list, speaking only for myself. I jump because I don't understand. I jump because something that is impossible shouldn't also be something that is true. I jump because Ms. Remlinger taught us about conservation of mass and conservation of energy, and a brother is not something that can become nothing.

Some people say when somebody's taken they're spat out somewhere else, clean and naked and ready to live a different life. Some people think they're reborn as babies elsewhere. I don't find either idea all that appealing.

I don't imagine the people who are taken die or are reborn. I think they're transformed, but I don't know into what. Rainbow trout, black snake, water molecules. Is that different than dying? To become part of this beautiful pond, to receive the waterfall, to be surrounded always by rock and pine and birch and sky? A quick change. Quicker than my brother's room turning to dust, or the Buick becoming forest. People can change much faster than things can, if they're given the chance.

"Are you done?" Otis calls to me. He's standing over Kat, dripping on her. She scoots away with mock annoyance.

"One more jump," I say.

They both give me a look. I return my bravest grin.

I say "I love you" as I jackknife, not loud enough for either of them to hear me. Break the glassy surface. I'm not a fish or a snake or a baby on the other side of the world. The sky is impossibly blue, and the water is impossibly black. There have never been any rules.

Escape from Caring Seasons

The doctor was a nice young man, and Zora hated him. Hated the way he settled in the second chair beside Anya's bed like a friend. Hated that he didn't pull the privacy curtain between Anya's bed and nosy Eleanor Grimm's, when Eleanor was only pretending to sleep. Hated the way he directed everything he said toward Zora, the person in the chair, instead of Anya, the person he was talking about.

"Just because she can't talk right now doesn't mean she can't understand you," Zora told him. "She hears you fine."

". . . where was I?" He reoriented, but didn't apologize.

"You were telling us you weren't ready to let Anya leave yet."

He nodded. "Right."

"Even though her vital signs are all stable, and she's been meeting her rehab goals, other than speech. You're not making sense."

He smiled, which added to his patronizing impression. This was no time to smile. "I'm sorry if you think it doesn't make sense. The algorithm is quite accurate. If it says the risk of your wife leaving the hospital is too great, then I'm powerless to do anything."

Anya grunted, an angry sound, and Zora squeezed her hand. "But you're a doctor. Can't you override an algorithm if you disagree? We'll be fine with a hospital bed and a home health aide. This community's purpose is to keep people in their homes."

"I can override if I'm prepared to defend my action before our medical board, but what if your wife has another stroke after I release her against DOC findings? I'm not willing to take that risk."

Zora's wrist chip pulsed a blood pressure warning. The chip was supposed to cue her to take calming breaths, but this time she slapped at it; she was upset for good reason, and willing to lose a few Keep Your Cool points. "But what if somebody entered something wrong, so your program is interpreting inaccurate data? What about the psychology of healing at home?"

"I can look over the data one more time to make sure nothing looks wrong, but most evaluative tools report directly in order to cut user error risk." He held up placating hands. "Lives have been saved by the DOC program. It takes everything into account. If it says Ms. Stein should stay in the hospital another month—"

"You said week."

"Either way. If it says she'd be better off under observation, I'd advise you to pay attention."

"Can she go home against your wishes?"

"Sure, but you won't get your hospital bed or your home health aide, and you'd be billed for any complications that occur while she's under your care. I strongly advise you not to do that." It was the first time he sounded sincere.

A tear ran down Anya's cheek. She wiped it away with the back of her better hand.

"I'm sorry this upsets you," the doctor said in non-apology.

"She's not sad," Zora said. "She's angry. We moved to this community to be together as long as possible. Medical can get to us in minutes. It's not right to keep her in the hospital when she'd probably recover faster in our home, which I can see out the window, by the way."

He was the one human in the command chain, and he wasn't wired to listen. He repeated his spiel as if she hadn't spoken. She wanted him chastened, distraught, willing to fight the system on their behalf, but he didn't look at all diminished.

"I'm sorry, love," Zora said when he left.

Anya picked up the tablet on her lap and painstakingly spelled: GET ME OUT. She tapped each word for emphasis, her pale face flushing. Anger made her look healthier than she had in weeks.

"I will, love."

The nurse's station was unoccupied, but Zora passed room after room with names and charts on the door: Amelia Setzer, Wilf Ringgold, Bonnie Sola, their friends and neighbors. Were they all here out of necessity, or because an algorithm decided they had to stay? Maybe the next time she returned she'd do a survey. For now, she had a mission. "GET ME OUT."

She tried knocking on the hospital ombudsman's door, but nobody answered. The rest of the hospital administrative system worked remotely, so she resorted to leaving messages.

When nobody on the hospital floors would listen, she tried the new complex administrator. Zora had known all the administrators before the complex's sale overseas; odd now to walk through the offices and not recognize names on the doors. New activity coordinator, new facilities director, new librarian.

The business offices were all on the first floor, so Zora was surprised when the new receptionist directed her back up to the eighth for the administrator, Mrs. Ilyin. Sadie Ng rode the elevator with her.

"Gotta get those reps in." Sadie pressed the button for the gym on ten. "If I do two more days in a row I get the Iron Warrior badge. I'm working on getting enough points for a new bathing suit."

"I'm not familiar with that badge."

"Part of the new batch introduced last month. Anya's been in hospital, right? You must've missed it."

Zora nodded. "Good luck."

Their phones both chimed at once, but neither bothered to look. Social Butterfly points were easy to come by.

The door to Suite 805 opened as she approached. Inside, nobody. The faint odor of paint. A large walnut desk, three leather chairs, a screen on one dark blue wall, another all window. Zora looked out over the community garden and beyond to the stream, the woods, the wall hidden beneath the trees. An administrator working from this room could forget this place was about people.

"How can I help you, Ms. Stein?"

Zora turned to find the wall screen had activated. Wherever Mrs. Ilyin worked, it wasn't here. Her image was enormous. Meant to intimidate, perhaps, but Zora wasn't easily intimidated.

"The whole point of integrating hospital and supplemented home living is to keep people in their homes," Zora said. "And to get people back into their homes as soon as possible."

"We're trying to do that, Ms. Stein." Mrs. Ilyin's giant face smiled, like the infuriating doctor.

"You're not. Something is wrong with this system if I can't take Anya home right now. She'd be fine at home."

"Are you a doctor?"

"No, but she's not on any monitors, it's been a month since her stroke, and we live five hundred feet from the hospital. She'll be more rested sleeping in her own bed, looking out her own window, eating my food."

Mrs. Ilyin's expression didn't change. "I'm sure you think so, Ms. Stein, but the algorithm wouldn't demand she stay without reason."

"That may be, but there's something wrong if no human can explain why it's making this decision."

Zora's wrist buzzed another blood pressure warning, and she slapped it again in frustration. She wasn't getting anywhere regarding Anya. "This room isn't supposed to be an office. It's designed to be a yoga studio. This view isn't meant to be yours."

Mrs. Ilyin's smile wavered for the first time. "Why do you say that?"

"Because I was on the team that designed Caring Seasons, back when we called it Brighter Futures. This should be a community view, not a personal one. How did you end up in here?"

"When we bought your development, we repurposed the space. Uses change. Now if that's all?"

It was, Zora supposed. Nothing had gone as planned. She'd been so excited about Caring Seasons—as designed—that they'd taken spots on the waiting list as part of her consultation fee. When they'd moved in, it had still felt like the right decision. It was only in the last year, since the sale, that things had started to fray. Little changes at first: increased automation, new bureaucracy; nothing that had raised alarms. Now a remote administrator stealing a yoga studio. Now an algorithm keeping Anya from coming home.

"It's not often I'm at a loss for what to do," she told Anya.

"I KNOW," Anya wrote.

"I can't tell whether nobody will listen because we're wrong, or nobody will listen because we're old."

"Old," said Eleanor Grimm from the next bed. "I've been asking to go home for days but they're afraid I'll fall again."

Zora didn't like when Eleanor butted in, but she agreed this time. So did Anya.

"OLD," Anya wrote. "KEEP TRYING."

Zora reached out to their lawyer next, their old friend Norman Lloyd, but the call wouldn't connect. Neither would a call to their daughter, Jordan. She tried a pizza place back in Boston whose number she still had memorized, then hung up when it went through.

"Your stress levels are higher than usual," said their house AI from the speaker embedded in the kitchen counter. "May I brew you some herbal tea?"

"Of course they are, and yes," said Zora.

The hot water dispenser gurgled and spat into a cup. "Congratulations. You've earned another point toward your Healthy Decisions badge!"

"Go away, Mrs. Landingham." They'd named their AI after an old TV character. It was useful, but Anya had always hated the feeling somebody else lived with them, and now Zora understood why. She missed Anya's voice and wanted her home; anyone else was an intrusion.

"Mrs. L, why are my phone calls not going through?"

"You recently completed a call to Pizza Wow," said the AI.

"And the calls before that?"

"I have no information on that subject."

Zora collected her mug and stepped outside. Nick Castro waved from his porch next door, and she walked over to sit beside him. "Have you been having any trouble making phone calls?"

They'd been neighbors for ten years now, so she didn't feel bad asking a question without preface.

"No, sorry. Why?"

"May I use your phone?"

He spoke to the porch. "Jeeves, call——?"

Zora showed him Norman's number, and Nick repeated it aloud.

His AI responded. "I'm sorry, that call cannot be completed at this time."

Nick cocked his head. "What's going on?"

"Try this one." She recited Jordan's number.

Nothing. A moment later her phone buzzed and she grabbed for it, hoping Jordan had called back, but it was only a Being Neighborly point coming through.

"What's going on?" Nick asked again.

She opened her mouth to explain, and then shut it again. If she said she thought the phone wasn't letting her complete outside calls, she'd sound paranoid. Worse, the AI would hear. Who knew what it would do if it decided she was delusional.

"I'll explain later," she said, getting up to leave.

Her front door opened at a flick of her wrist. She sat at the kitchen counter and composed a message to Jordan, but after sending it, had the uneasy realization she had no way of knowing whether it had been delivered. Jordan lived in Portland and visited twice a year, but they didn't talk on a schedule. How long until she noticed she hadn't heard from her mothers?

"Mrs. L, is there any reason you'd prevent me from completing a phone call?"

"If it was bad for your health."

Damn. What were they thinking? That hadn't been part of the plan. "Mrs. L, Is there any way for me to override that protocol?"

"I'm afraid I don't have an answer to that question."

Once upon a time, she'd had access to the code underpinning the development's tech; coding hadn't been her specialty, but the language they'd used wasn't foreign to her. Or hadn't been. She had to give up after a couple of attempts; her login no longer worked.

"Mrs. L, call the police," Zora said.

There was a brief silence, then a human voice. "Caring Seasons Emergency Services. Is this a police or medical emergency?"

"Just testing. Mrs. L, hang up." Maybe she was paranoid, or maybe the system didn't want her complaining. Either way, she was more determined than ever to get Anya back.

21:30
Patient: A. Stein
Location: Hospital #743
Status: NREM Stage 3
HR: 105 bpm

Patient: Z. Stein
Location: Cottage #114 BR 1
Status: NREM Stage 1
HR: 128 bpm

22:00
Patient: A. Stein
Location: Hospital #743
Status: NREM Stage 2
HR: 110 bpm

Patient: Z. Stein
Location: Bathroom
Status: Awake/sitting.
HR: 130 bpm
Toilet activated.
Analysis:
Achieved Urine Good Health badge!

22:30
Patient: A. Stein
Location: Hospital #743
Status: REM Sleep
HR: 110 bpm

Patient: Z. Stein
Location: Cottage 114 BR 1
Status: NREM Stage 1
HR: 128 bpm

23:00
Patient: A. Stein
Location: Hospital #743
Status: NREM Stage 2
HR: 111 bpm

Patient: Z. Stein
Location: Cottage 114 BR 1
Status: NREM Stage 1
HR: 131 bpm

———

ALERT
23:11

Patient: Z. Stein
Location: Bathroom
Status: Awake/standing
HR: 140 bpm
ALERT

ALERT
23:12

Patient: Z. Stein
Location: Bathroom
Status: Awake/standing
HR: 149 bpm
ALERT

ALERT
23:13

Patient: Z. Stein
Location: Bathroom
Status: Awake/standing
HR: 157 bpm
ALERT

ALERT
23:14

Patient: Z. Stein
Location: Bathroom
Status: Awake/standing
HR: 170 bpm
ALERT

ALERT
23:15

Patient: Z. Stein
Location: Bathroom
Status: Error
Status: ProneError
HR: Error
ALERT

Zora cut the spy out of her wrist. The cutting wasn't the hard part: her arthritis pain-blockers took the edge off. Scraping the chip out wasn't any worse than that one spot during her egret tattoo where the artist had crossed bone.

No, the harder part was keeping her hand from shaking as she went at her own wrist with their sharpest paring knife, sterilized as best she could. There were no cameras in the bathroom, out of respect for their privacy, but the mics and chip snooped as well as any eye.

She knew she only had a few minutes. The alert would start when the trauma spiked her blood pressure, and continue as she wadded the spy in tissue and buried it in the wastebasket so it could no longer read her. A thought flitted past: what would happen to all her points and badges? Who cared. Medical would arrive in minutes. Get out; ask silly questions later.

"Ms. Stein, do you need medical assistance? Please say yes or no."

"No, I'm fine." She kept her voice controlled.

The bathroom mirror was the most condescending of the appliances. Okay, maybe not, but she resented it more than the others, with its rewards for proper tooth brushing and moisturizing, like she was a child. They'd overstepped with the mirror; that hadn't been in her design.

"Ms. Stein, your chip is giving anomalous readings. Medical is on its way. Estimated arrival 23:21. Don't move if you're injured."

She used the same knife that had excised the spy to cut the window screen. She'd overridden the security warning and left the window open before bed. It was 72 outside, the same temperature as the house, so that shouldn't have rung any further alarms once she'd acknowledged the break-in risk. They didn't consider break*outs*. If she exited the front door they'd know, but management probably assumed they were all too frail to leave through a window.

She was still capable. She couldn't figure out how their dream retirement situation had wound up as this pleasantly creepy Stepford senior village, but the time had come to bust out. She'd figure out how to rescue Anya once she'd freed herself. Anya would understand.

The knife left blood spatter on the white tile floor and the lintel. No time to wipe it off. She pushed the screen out, then tossed her purse and all their pillows. The stepstool they used to reach the higher cupboards got her high enough; she whispered a prayer for solid bones and climbed through.

It wasn't a big drop. The bushes under the window broke her fall, and the pillows minimized their damage. Some scratches on her arms to add to the bleeding wrist, but nothing worth noticing. Before extricating herself, she reached up and closed the window. With any luck, they'd assume she couldn't have gone out this way.

The bathroom window faced the walking path circling the village, and beyond that, the wall. As far as she knew, the lampposts along the path didn't have cameras; if they did, that couldn't be helped. Her safest bet was to stay within the tree line.

She slipped into the trees' shadows, outside the lamplight, hugging close to the big oaks but careful to avoid stumbling over their roots. It wouldn't do to hurt herself now that she'd freed herself from the spy that could call help.

Headlights. She held her breath, her hand going to her wrist automatically, even though they weren't looking for her yet. Medical pulling up at the house. They'd knock, then override the lock.

She needed to move before they started searching. She wasn't quick, but she wasn't slow either. She still walked four miles a day, and she was fit for her age, as all the Urine Good Health and Eating Right and Heart-Happy badges attested.

From this distance, the houses all looked peaceful. Fourteen cul-de-sacs around the central complex of rec center/apartment building/hospital, store, pool, community garden. The most pleasant prison, this prison she had accidentally created.

The prison not built to be a prison, because prisons didn't have rivers running through them. Rivers that had to pass under the wall.

She took off her clothes and wadded them into the collapsible shopping bag she kept in her purse. She'd kept the purse light: cash, untrackable; first aid for her bleeding wrist; tissues; protein bars. She didn't have a throwing arm anymore, but the purse and clothes sailed over the narrow wall without catching on top. So did both shoes. If she'd given any thought at all to going back, she'd committed to following through now. Wanderers were assigned drone escorts whenever they walked out their front door. Getting caught as a Wanderer *and* naked would be even worse. No, this was it.

Anya had always been the one to test water before stepping in; Zora believed in jumping first. The anticipation was always worse than the plunge. She wasn't sure this was deep enough for a plunge, so she waded in. Cold, but better a cold stream than a warm one. Less bacteria to worry about with her bleeding wrist. It woke her up more too, which was good. This would be a long night.

To her ankles, to her knees, to her thighs, to her waist. Not ice cold, but cold enough to raise goose bumps on a spring night. When had she last gone skinny-dipping? Thirty years? Forty? Too long.

She had to duck underwater to get through the wall cutout. Why hadn't they considered a grating? It had never been discussed. Nobody would go to this effort to get into a compound of old people and their last personal treasures.

The riverbank outside the wall was steeper and slicker, or else it seemed so as she clawed her way up it. She grabbed a root and hoisted herself the last few feet, landing in an undignified heap.

The bag of clothing had unfurled. Her blouse lay on the ground, not far from her cardigan and slacks. Her socks were still knotted together, both shoes nearby, adorning a bush like practical orthotic Christmas ornaments. Her brassiere had snagged on a branch, too high to shake down. If she had to lose an item of clothing, that was the best one, she supposed. Better to walk braless than pantsless or shoeless.

She found her purse under a rhododendron, and pulled out some tissues to dab away water and mud. A damp outer layer wouldn't kill her. So far, so good.

It had been so long since she had been outside the wall, not counting the occasional field trip to a museum or concert. Groups didn't count. It had been so long since she'd been outside the wall on her own agenda. When they'd stopped venturing out on their own, it was only because everything they needed existed in the community.

And it was perfect for Anya! Great that they could still live together, still share a bed, until now, and get help within minutes. Twice, the biometrics had called medical to help Anya before Zora even realized she needed help. Those had been scary moments, startled from sleep by strangers who knew Anya's situation better than she did.

A full moon filtered through the branches. By her estimate, she was two hundred feet off the main road, down in the ravine. The woods followed the stream, parallel to the road but far below it, for a half-mile, before intersecting a looped hiking trail. At that point, one arm picked up alongside the stream, while the other headed up toward the road in a long series of switchbacks. If she continued along the stream for another mile, she could climb a steeper path out where it crossed under the road and the woods thinned out. They'd hopefully not think to look for her that far away. People underestimated old women all the time. Maybe, for once, that could work to her advantage.

On the walking loop she averaged a seventeen-minute mile, but the woods demanded a slower approach. If she tripped over a root and injured herself, nobody would look for her here. The same underestimation that let her make her slow escape could also mean her death.

She didn't have her watch or her cell phone, since either could be used for tracking, so she had no idea how long she'd walked. Zora followed the stream, using the moonlight reflecting off the water as her guide.

She was almost to the spot where she hoped the stream and road met, when something buzzed above the trees, a bat or an owl perhaps. It buzzed by again. Whirred. She whipped her head around, and spotted it over the stream, rotors gleaming. A drone, no bigger than a sparrow.

She didn't think it had spotted her yet, but she couldn't be sure. Couldn't be sure, either, if it was a village drone. She had no idea of their range, and she thought maybe they were larger. She looked for a rock, wondering if she still had the aim she'd had as a child. Her clothes had made it over the wall, but that was more about trajectory than accuracy.

"Are you Zara Stein?" The voice was young, distorted by the tiny, tinny speaker. Zora strained to hear.

"No." If it didn't have her name right, maybe it wasn't from the village. She kept walking.

The drone followed her.

"Are you sure? Zara—sorry, Zora Stein, age 82, height five feet ten inches, weight 170 pounds, white hair, brown eyes, last seen at 11:15 PM at Caring Seasons of Tall Pines, which, by the way, is the world's most terrible name for a rest home. It sounds like a bad translation."

It wasn't a rest home, but it was a bad translation, though Zora wasn't about to say so. She hated the name change.

"We'll get used to it," Anya had said. "It's not like the name matters. It's our home."

Anya had been right, of course. What mattered was they lived together in their own cozy cottage, with their own plot in the community garden, a favorite table in the café, friends nearby.

"So that isn't you?" The drone sounded skeptical. It hovered above her head.

"Sorry. Not me. If I see her, I'll tell her you're looking for her. Good night."

She walked on, hoping the drone wouldn't follow. It followed.

"It's just that I think you're her," the drone said. "I already searched all the roads within a two-mile radius of Caring Seasons of Tall Pines, and you're the only person out walking tonight. It's hard to estimate height, but you look like you're the right age."

Zora eyed the drone. If she managed to grab it without getting sliced by rotors, she might be able to drown it in the stream. But what if it was armed? Or the operator knew the last known coordinates and called her in anyway?

She sighed. "If I say that's me—I'm not saying it is—can you wait to report me until I explain?"

The drone dipped closer. Zora reached out a casual hand, but it bobbed out of reach.

"I guess." She heard the frown in the voice. "Do you promise you're not in any immediate bodily danger? If you're injured, I'll have to doctor my logs so they don't see I talked with you before reporting. If you've been kidnapped or hurt and I didn't report, I'd get in trouble."

"I wasn't kidnapped, and I'm not hurt. No immediate danger."

The drone backed off.

Zora stopped walking, to encourage the operator to listen to her instead of making an immediate call. A large, flat rock jutted out over the stream, and she sat down. "If you're not from Caring Seasons, did they hire out?"

"No. I'm independent."

"Independent? You're obviously looking for me. You knew my name."

"Missing Vulnerable Person report."

"I'm not a 'vulnerable person'! And I'm not missing. I left."

"It says 'Likely wandered away from home. No threat to tracker. Treat as lost and confused.' You don't look lost or confused, if you don't mind my saying so."

"I'll take that as a compliment." Zora gave a half-smile, before realizing she was smiling at a sparrow-sized helicopter as if it were a person. She rearranged her face to a neutral expression.

"You should. Most of the 'vulnerable people' I find are muttering to themselves, or crying, or sleeping. You're muddy but you look like you know where you're going."

"I do, and you're keeping me from getting there. So if you wouldn't mind?"

"Mind what? I still need to report back."

Zora sighed. "Why? I told you I'm not missing. I'm my own guardian. If I want to take a walk in the woods, that's my business."

"Look, I hear you, but how do I know this isn't a lucid moment for someone who doesn't have many? I need to make this call. I don't know why I haven't done it already. I'm losing points for every minute we talk."

"Points?" Zora studied the drone in the moonlight. It must have an infrared camera, since it wasn't running a headlight. She didn't know too much about drone design, but it looked like a custom job. She wished it had a face, though she supposed that would be even weirder.

"I'm waiting for an answer," she said when she didn't get one. She tossed a pebble into the stream, and trailed fingers around the rock feeling for more.

"You sound like a teacher. Were you a teacher?"

"I lectured on environmental gerontology."

"I have no idea what that is."

"The study of old people and the places they—we—live. Ironically enough."

"That's a job?"

Zora frowned and slipped her cardigan off. It was a little cooler than when she'd left the house, but still pleasant. "You still haven't answered my question. I've answered yours. What did you mean by 'losing points'?"

"Have you heard of SloothIt?"

"No, sorry." She stood up, stretching.

"It's an app. You can play it from anywhere, but it works best in communities where there aren't enough law enforcement officers to go around, where they're understaffed, or whatever, like here. Anybody can play the basic level. You don't need a drone, just a phone or tablet or whatever. You get points for finding missing people, pets, stolen cars. You can spot people who are wanted for crimes too, but you're not allowed to approach them, you know? And when you have ten thousand points, if you're eighteen, you can level up to being allowed to follow people instead of just calling in tips. That's if you have a drone."

The voice gained enthusiasm. The drone dipped as if she were gesturing while she talked. "If you get ten thousand points in *that* one, and if you have no criminal record, and you've got first aid and CPR certification so you'll recognize injuries, you can level up to SloothIt Pro and actually get paid bounties for all the stuff you were doing for free before! And when you get to a certain score with *that*, you can level up to ProPlus, where you're basically a contractor, and you don't have to compete for—"

The drone's voice—the operator's voice—died as Zora's cardigan hit it.

"I'm sorry," Zora said. "I'm not points in a game."

She bashed it three times with the rock she'd picked up, until its rotors stopped beating under her fingers. Then she held the whole bundle underwater, and left the drone weighted down and tangled in her wet sweater on the rock.

She felt a bit sorry for the thing. No, for its operator. It had looked homemade. That was someone's hard work she'd destroyed. Not her fault. They'd come after her; they had to accept the job's risks.

Obviously, the operator would report her current location based on where they lost contact with their drone. She had to get as far as possible, and quickly. If the police came into the woods, which way would they arrive from? They'd probably drive to the trailhead parking lot, far above her. That couldn't be more than a quarter mile at this point, maybe a little more with the switchbacks, but she wasn't beating anybody to anywhere. And if they didn't find her here, they'd follow her up the other trail and catch her before she reached the bridge.

The only way to stay hidden was to cross the river and climb the steeper, trailless slope on the opposite side. She couldn't remember what was at the top, but if she clambered up to whatever road or subdivision lay on that side, then hid somewhere other than the woods while they looked for her here, she'd probably be better off. Maybe someplace with less open air.

If one mercenary had found her, others could too. She pictured a drone-filled sky, all searching for her in a grid pattern, shooting each other down for the right to report her. Not that civilian drones were supposed to have guns, but she hadn't thought they were allowed to go around looking for people either, so who knew anymore. The idea of people running around turning each other in for game points chilled her, too, but she didn't have time to mull it over. Keep moving.

The stream was rocky and shallow here. She removed her socks, shoes, and pants again to keep them from getting wet. She imagined the little drone bobbing alongside her, asking her why she took off her pants instead of rolling up the legs, and didn't she know people were watching? She shook the thought from her head and picked her way across the moss-slick rocks.

Was it her imagination, or was there a light bobbing down the slope on the side she'd just left? She pulled her pants and shoes back on. The ground underfoot was soft with fallen leaves and smelled like mulch. The trees were a mix of old growth and new. She aimed for the new, walking at angles to avoid the steepest parts, steadying herself on the sturdiest saplings. If she fell here, they'd never find her.

Anya would worry something had happened to Zora, but would anybody listen to her? Worse, nobody would be alerted to the problems she'd escaped to warn about. Anya would be stuck in the hospital forever. That was what drove Zora as she made her slow way up the hillside. She had to get somewhere. She had to fix this.

Approaching the ridge, she skirted tall wooden fences until she found an unfenced yard abutting the parkland. On another night she'd have paused to admire the view. If Anya were here with her, they'd make guesses at the house's value, and who lived inside, and how they moved through the rooms. This wild yard blended into the woods, a stilted deck cantilevered out over the space. Another night, she might have wondered if the residents sky-watched or woods-watched. Tonight she just hoped they were sound sleepers, without perimeter alarms or drones or dogs.

The last meters were the hardest, the soil beneath the deck sandy and loose, with no trees to hold. She avoided the deck supports, in case they were alarmed, though she almost risked drinking from the spigot on the side of the house. Maybe if she had guarantee it was potable, but she'd risked enough tonight. She reached the street above and fought the urge to collapse onto the dewy grass. Keep going.

Zora vaguely recalled this subdivision's existence, but she had no clue how it fit into any map. If she kept the ravine-backed houses on her right, she hoped she'd find her way to a main road. Nothing to do but keep walking.

"Wow!" said a voice beside her. "You're still going."

Zora spun around, but didn't see anyone. With nothing to drink and no sleep and all that exertion, it figured she'd start hallucinating.

"You killed Tiny."

Zora looked around again, more carefully this time. The drone hovered at forehead height, beyond reach. It was larger than the earlier one, more cumbersome.

"Is there anything left of her? My drone?"

"I don't know," Zora said. "I left her—it—wrapped in my sweater."

"I know about the sweater. I only got any points at all because your sweater was there where I said you'd been. Clue points, not recovery points. Not enough to make up for if I have to rebuild Tiny. And how am I supposed to get her?"

"I don't see how that's my problem."

"You killed her."

"You were going to turn me in. You did turn me in. I'm sorry I had to smash your drone, and I hope you can rebuild. Please leave me alone now." Absurd: she was apologizing to a drone about another drone. She started walking again.

"You're heading toward a cul-de-sac."

Zora squinted up ahead. She hadn't considered cul-de-sacs. "Why tell me that?"

"They'll find you faster if you're on a main road when I call. You're a missing person, not a criminal. Why don't you want to be found? I've found other missing people from that place before, but they'd wandered away. I didn't realize how badly you didn't want them to catch up with you until you killed Tiny."

"I wish you'd stop saying killed. And why would I have left if I didn't want them to catch up with me?"

"That isn't an answer."

Tell this person? Zora had no phone, and a hole in her wrist that marked her as self-destructive. She'd lost her bra up a tree and her sweater to a drone-murder. The sweat she'd worked up climbing from the ravine had dried on her skin and chilled her. She'd kill for water. If this road twisted it could be hours before she found her way to a main artery, and she'd still not be anywhere.

"I've met your drones," Zora said. "Introduce yourself, and I'll tell you why I'm out here."

The drone sighed and bobbed along beside her as Zora back-tracked to the last intersection. She considered asking if this road was better. It was wider, so maybe this was the through-street.

"My name is Gina."

"And . . . ?"

"You *are* a teacher, aren't you." Not a question. "I get points for finding lost people. I'm 253 points from leveling up to where I get paid actual money for doing this—203 points. I got fifty points for your sweater."

"Who's looking for me?"

"I don't know," the drone said. "You're still on our list. Too early for police. So it's still Sloothers and whoever reported you to the app to begin with. They're anxious to get you home, I guess."

"That place isn't home."

"Sorry?"

"We live there, but it isn't home. I thought it was, but it's a mistake. That's why I left. I want to talk to my lawyer, I want to talk to the newspaper. There's bad stuff going on."

"Why not let me tell the police, then? I can put a beacon out right now."

"They're going to treat me like a lost old woman, like somebody who needs to be talked down to but not someone who gets heard."

"I don't understand. What's the emergency?"

"The village is blocking my calls. Monitoring emails. Anything I say that even hints at the problems we're having never makes it out."

"What? Whoa. Are you sure?"

"Of course I'm sure," Zora snapped. "Do you think I'd be out here on this jailbreak if I had other options? See? Nobody listens."

"Okay, okay. I'm listening. I'm sorry. Take a right at the stop sign, if you're trying to leave this neighborhood. It's a maze. Why are they blocking your calls? I still don't understand. And why do you live there if it's so bad?"

Zora sighed. "It wasn't bad at the beginning. I helped design it."

"Wait, what?"

"I told you, my field is environmental gerontology. I signed on as a consultant on the development. It's meant to be the perfect environment for seniors. Cottages for those who can still live independently. Assisted living and hospital for those who can't live on their own anymore. Grounds to keep people active. Neighbors, great activities. AI monitoring. Incentives for healthy living and socializing. On paper, it's perfect. Everyone who worked on it included a stipulation that we be reserved spots to retire there ourselves. Then it was sold last year, and the new company, well, let's say they cut some corners."

"What corners?"

"Why do you care? You're keeping me talking so I won't notice when they swoop in to take me back."

"I haven't called again yet."

"Why not? You'll get all your points."

"You've got me curious now. I missed the first time bonus, anyhow. The second one won't be for another hour. So what corners are they cutting?"

"For starters, my house won't let me phone my daughter or my lawyer because it decided the calls were causing stress."

"So that's why you're out here?"

"That's why I'm out here, yes, but that's not the only problem. They track everything."

"Track everything?"

"It was supposed to be a health benefit. Monitoring. But it's constant, and now they're using it against us." She held up her wrist. The cut had stopped and started bleeding a few times already, and now just oozed. Dried blood stained her forearm. "They measure everything: sleep, urine, calorie intake. They track how we move around the house, if we're active enough, if we're too aimless. It's more intrusive than it was supposed to be."

"Huh."

"Then they dismissed most of the human staff. Onboarded a new program called 'DOC'—I don't even know what it stands for—that synthesizes all the data coming in. Nothing matters but numbers anymore. And Anya's numbers aren't right, so now they say she can't come home. She'd be fine in the house. We take care of each other."

"Don't you have the right to choose? To stay in the house?"

"They say if her numbers work, and they don't right now." Zora fought tears. She wouldn't cry at a drone. "It should be our choice."

"Was the monitoring program part of your design?"

Zora shook her head. "Not like that. The chip for home entry made sense, so nobody had to worry about losing keys. It can be loaded with money, so you don't have to turn around if you get to the café and realize you forgot your wallet. The badges and points really work, like your Slooth program, I guess, but deciding if somebody gets to go home or not based on numbers makes no sense. There are some things that need a human touch. We didn't mean for algorithms to make major life decisions."

"Maybe algorithms make better life decisions. No emotions involved; just cold, hard facts."

"Says you. You're a bounty hunter with a drone."

"I'm not a bounty hunter. I've already shown you I can make decisions based on emotion. If there weren't a person behind this drone you'd already be on your way back to Big Brother. There are other Slooths who give their drones AIs. Takes out all the fun if you ask me, but they get results. If you don't need to stop for sleep you can get way more points. You're lucky you ran into me."

"You're right. I'm sorry."

"Duck."

"What?"

"Get behind that tree on your right. There's another drone coming."

Zora did as told, and watched as a clunky quad-copter made its way down the street. It was louder than the one trailing her, a headlight sweeping in front of it as it flew. It came from the direction they were traveling, and headed down the road toward where they'd come from.

"Okay, safe."

"Thanks," said Zora.

"You're welcome. That was Tagg007. He's at 18,000 points, and he wouldn't have cared one bit to hear your story before calling you in. Just saying."

"I said thank you."

"I'm making sure you understand. I'm listening. I want to help."

Zora looked at the machine bobbing in the air beside her. There were no expressions to read, no ways to measure sincerity. It had hidden her from the other drone, but that was still obviously self-interest. Nobody had dragged her back yet, and while she had no idea how much time had elapsed, she had a feeling it was enough for them to have caught up with her by now. Maybe she could trust this person.

"You want to help, for real? Or you want to help me get to a main road so they can pick me up faster, like you said earlier?"

The speaker crackled in what approximated a drone sigh. "I want to help. At least I got a few points for giving them a clue. I can get you out of this neighborhood, and maybe keep others from finding you for a while. For what good that'll do. I'm still not sure what you think you can accomplish. Why didn't you bring a phone to call your lawyer as soon as you got outside the wall?"

"I was afraid they'd track my phone."

"Good point. So what's the plan?"

Zora considered. "Find me a pay phone so I can call Norman? I don't know what to do from there, but at least that's a start."

"What's a pay phone?"

"Never mind. Hmm."

They walked in silence for a minute. No, Zora walked; the drone kept pace.

"Look . . . I'm going to need to switch batteries soon in any case. If you can make it to my place, you can use my phone."

"Really?"

"Really. It's another mile by road. Any chance you can walk faster? I've got eight minutes' battery left."

"I couldn't have done an eight-minute mile when I was twenty, let alone now."

"Right. Hm. It's way shorter if I go over the rooftops. What if I leave you here, bring Junior home, swap out the battery, and come back for you? You'd need to hide from the other Slooths. I'll be back in ten minutes, more or less."

Before Zora answered, the drone spoke again. "I've got to go. Hovering next to you and talking drains me fast. I don't have a third drone to send out if this one dies."

The drone flitted away over the houses. Zora listened until its whir faded. She knew the general direction it had traveled in, but who knew how many twisty roads and cul-de-sacs lay in between. Or how many Slooth drones that wouldn't stop to listen to her. The next yard had a low stone border. She sat down on the wall, as still as possible. If she heard a drone, she'd hide behind it, but for now she sat.

It felt like hours passed. The slab sent cold up through her bones, and got harder by the second. She rehearsed what she wanted to say to Norman. Hoped he'd answer his phone if a strange number called at this hour.

Twice lights swept past and she crouched behind the wall. One was a car, the other a drone like the one that had passed earlier.

When the friendly drone returned, relief surged through her. Relief, at this dubious rescuer.

"You're still here!"

"You came back," Zora said.

"I promised I would."

"You aren't exactly a reliable source."

"Fair enough. Are you ready to walk a little further?"

Zora stretched her legs. "I'll be honest. Everything is starting to hurt. I don't have too much more in me, but I can make it one more slow mile."

The slow mile took everything she had left. By the time they arrived at a bland sandstone ranch, only the shooting pains in her hips kept her awake.

"Around the back," said the drone.

It didn't look like a murderer's house. If she'd had any concern, the time to escape would have been while the drone had disappeared for its battery change, anyway. She followed a wide walk around to the back door, which swung open.

"Come in." A voice from inside, echoed by the drone.

The drone flitted in like a bird and alit on a cluttered counter, sweeping papers away with rotor chop. She followed it into a small one-room apartment, galley kitchen on the left, where the drone had settled, a bed divided from a workstation by a single tall bookcase on the right.

"Don't mind the mess." No drone echo this time.

Zora looked up to find the voice's source, then down, as a woman came around the bookcase in a wheelchair.

"Nice to meet you in person," the woman said. "I'm Gina."

"Zora."

Gina was young, though Zora wasn't good at assessing age anymore. Younger than Jordan, older than the undergrads she'd taught.

"Let me guess: I'm not what you expected?"

"I didn't know what to expect. This explains why you said 'how am I supposed to get Tiny back.' I didn't understand why you wouldn't climb down to get it—her."

"Yeah. I think I got lucky there. Her GPS says they took her with them when they took your sweater, so I'll be able to claim her from someplace that doesn't involve hiking. Anyway, you probably need to sit. You must be exhausted."

Zora tried to rally. "A bathroom first, then water, then my phone call, then I'll sit."

"Priorities. I get it. The bathroom is over there."

The door had been removed to clear room for the wheelchair, but Zora was beyond privacy. She didn't use grab bars at the house, because the bathroom mirror always suggested she use them, and she hated the bathroom mirror. Tonight she grabbed, afraid she wouldn't get back up again otherwise. When she came back out, Gina handed her a glass and a cell phone, then disappeared into the galley.

Zora guzzled the water, the best thing she had ever tasted. The phone still felt like a trap, but it was too late to worry.

Bless him, he answered, at four-thirty in the morning. "Norman, this is Zora Stein. Anya has been hospitalized against our wishes, and I can't get her out."

His voice on the other end radiated warmth and concern, instantly alert. She didn't realize how worried she'd been that he wouldn't believe her until she heard him swearing under his breath, punctuated by lawyerly phrases. She breathed a sigh of relief. If she was at home, Mrs. L would be throwing all the calming tea at her by now.

Gina wheeled back in a moment after she'd hung up. She'd probably been listening, but that was okay.

"Thank you," Zora said.

"No problem. Being trapped in a situation is terrible. I've been there too."

"Been there, but not anymore?"

"Working on it. I sell drones online. If I can get to the paid Sloothit levels I'll be golden."

"I'm sorry you're losing points on me."

Gina shrugged. "There'll be others."

"Is it easy?"

"Not the easiest. I'm limited by how far from here my drones can go and get back on their batteries. I'm working on making them more efficient, but the more power, the heavier the battery, the harder the rotors have to work . . . it's a vicious cycle. I get enough cases, anyway."

An idea crept into Zora's tired brain. "Who puts the cases in the system?"

"There's a portal. Anybody can, but you can't find somebody or something you called in, or your own immediate family. If I called in my landlord as missing from upstairs, and then 'found' her, I'd be frozen out for a month."

"What if you called in a missing person from Caring Seasons?"

"You, you mean?"

"No. My wife and the others who've been put in the hospital against their will. What if we called them in?"

Gina's face twisted in contemplation, like she was sizing up a problem just beyond her view. "Can you imagine if we called the press to report all the local Slooths converging on Caring Seasons?"

Zora imagined. She pictured twenty Tinys and Juniors batting against the hospital floor windows, flying through the front door and up to the rooms to check on people. Operators behind the drones, asking questions and listening the way an algorithm couldn't. It was hilarious to think their AI doctor problem could be solved by a drone army, but she was tired, and it didn't seem that far outside the realm of possibility anymore. The sun would be up soon, and everything already felt a little brighter, like the life they had planned for was still within reach.

A Better Way of Saying

1915 was the year I got hired to shout the movies. The silent movies, you say now, but back then they were the only ones, so we didn't need "silent" on the front.

They weren't silent anyway, not really. Bess Morris, who lived in the room next to ours, played the piano along with the film at the Rivington, either following a cue sheet or improvising for the movies that arrived without. She was a few years older than me, my sister's friend. I was in love with Bess—a cliché, I know—and she didn't ever give me a single look, also maybe a cliché, though she was the one who had recommended me and Golde for the job when the couple who had been doing it moved to Buffalo. More precisely, she recommended Golde, and Golde said I had to do it with her, because otherwise she'd be telling love stories with some strange man. Better to tell them with her brother, even if I was only thirteen.

A lot of the audience couldn't read, you see, or else couldn't read English, so on Bess's recommendation, Yosef Lansky invited me and Golde to shout the title cards for one night on a trial basis. I'd read the men and she'd read the women. We had a megaphone that we passed back and forth. Have you ever tried acting through a megaphone? That's why even if the job didn't have a name, I just remember us as the shouters. Lansky would remind us to leave the acting to the actors anyway, if we got too artistic in our interpretations. I pays you to shout, Lansky said. So we shouted.

Our first movie, Theda Bara's *A Fool There Was*, definitely stretched the sibling relationship, with its famous "kiss me, my fool" and hellcat this and devil that. We were both surprised by the turns the film took, and we did our best with the racy material. I don't remember if Golde ever talked about this in any of her interviews, but this is where she got her start with acting. Before she became Judy Selig, she was my big sister Golde, shouting movies at her brother through a megaphone.

The other thing about shouting the title cards was that it gave the audience permission to shout back. It surprised me on the first night.

"Innocence breakfasts," I read. For that first film I read the narration as well as the men.

"What did he say?" asked someone from the back as the title card gave way to a scene of a little girl sitting down at a formally set table, a doll in the seat beside her. "It makes no sense. What does that mean? In Yiddish?"

"Dus maydele est frishtik," someone else responded from the room's dark fringe. Others joined in. "He didn't say 'dus maydele.' He said something else. What did he say?" "When he says 'innocence' he means dos meydele. Dos meydele didn't do nothing wrong." Whoever said that spoke in the Litvish dialect, though from their voices I guessed most in the room were Galitsianers like me and Golde. "Why didn't he say that? And what is 'breakfasts?' I know breakfast. You eat it. It's not a thing you do." "Maybe like 'breaks fast'?" "Babies don't have to fast."

I'd had enough. Into the megaphone, I said, "You can see she's about to eat. She doesn't know what's going on, she's playing like she's grown, so it calls her innocent, like 'imshildike maydele.'"

The scene was only thirty seconds long, and it took the whole thirty seconds to silence the crowd. I shouted the next card, the blessedly straightforward line "The next morning," then a moment later, Lansky grabbed my arm and pulled me aside. "I pays you to shout," he whispered. "Let them figure it out. It'll help them learn English as good as you."

Chastened, I let them litigate the remaining lines for themselves. My English was good because our parents had insisted. They were both educated people, worn down already by what New York had failed to offer them, but not too tired to teach us what school didn't. They made sure Golde and I read and wrote and spoke fluent English and Yiddish, read us fairy stories in both of those languages, in German, in French. They said we would thank them later, and I don't remember if we did, but I hope so. I'm sure they knew we couldn't have done the things we did without their foundation, but that's for another day. That first night, after I was told not to explain, we shouted our lines, and I bit my tongue.

At the end of the evening, paying us out, Lansky said, "You both did well, so the job is yours if you want it. Even if your voice breaks. You just gotta not talk back."

"He understands." Golde gave me a look. "He won't do it again."

"I promise," I said. I wanted the job.

That's how my movie career started, such as it was, the same year as Douglas Fairbanks's. I tell you this first to make sure you understand that by the time I found myself in the same room as Fairbanks seven years later, I had been his voice a dozen times at least.

I wasn't even supposed to be there that day; I was a stand-in, nothing more, per my friend Lenny's strict instructions. Doing a favor for him. I'd long since quit the Rivington by then, having hung on for only two months after Golde left for real acting—two months during which I shouted opposite a woman whose loudest voice was a whisper, and whose breath left our shared megaphone smelling like cabbage. After that, I sold tickets at the Grand by night, and in the day I got a few cents for calling in stories from our neighborhood to the *Evening World:* so-and-so of Broome Street getting hit by a truck or firefighters getting called to a house on Orchard or the mayor buying egg creams for everyone at Auster's one afternoon, all of which went in the paper without my name, and without me writing a single line.

What I wanted most was to write for the movies. To write better lines than the ones I'd shouted, and to craft them from the start. To create, instead of edit. A few years before, I'd even taken the 125th Street ferry across the Hudson to Fort Lee to offer my services at the studios set up there.

"There's a job for me in writing," I told the Fox gateman with confidence, but all I got for my trouble was a walk-on as a hooligan kid; I've never even figured out what movie I appeared in. Then the studios all moved out to California, taking my screenwriting dream with them. After that disappointment, I'd started to think I wanted to write for the papers instead, but I had no idea how to get there, either. Calling in stories was the farthest I'd gotten so far.

So there's no way I would have ever been invited to the Fairbanks press event, except that Lenny Mandel and I were both late to Yom Kippur services the morning before, and wound up in the crowd clustered outside the open windows instead of inside the shul. With no prayer books and pavement beneath our feet, it was easy to get distracted, and the conversation turned to his dilemma.

His dilemma: the World Series was starting Wednesday, Giants versus Yanks, and it was going to be the first time they broadcast it to radio, and the midtown hotels were full of tourists, and a whole bunch of reporters got pulled out of their designated areas and sent elsewhere to observe the excitement. Then a couple of the boys traded places, and they traded with others, and Lenny had convinced someone to let him go watch Bullet Joe work out his pitching arm on Tuesday, but in order to do that, he still needed another reporter to take his place at this promotion for Fairbanks's *Robin Hood*.

"Let me do it," I suggested.

He shook his head. "My editor did not in fact give me permission to go watch the workout. It's gotta be someone who writes for the *World*."

"Does it?" I sensed opportunity. "Technically I work for them, even if I don't write. And you said yourself most of the guys there will be standing in for others, and that you were only going as a favor to another guy because everyone's trying to get onto baseball for this week. This'll be easy enough. Let me be you."

He wavered. "You can't even open your mouth, you understand. I know you have opinions about movies, but you can only listen. Other guys will ask questions, and you write down their questions and the answers. After, you call it in with my name. If anything goes wrong, you lie and say you're there for the *Herald*."

Lenny didn't have a byline either, but he'd climbed several rungs above me on the ladder of success at that point. Yom Kippur felt like a good day to agree to a mutual favor: he got his baseball and I got an opportunity. A small deception too, sure, but one that didn't harm anyone.

The next day, I walked into the Ritz-Carlton trying not to look like I belonged on a tenement beat, like I wasn't a kid out of a tenement myself, like I'd ever been in a place that grand. It didn't help that everyone in the lobby looked like a banker—there was in fact a ten-thousand-banker convention in town, though I didn't know it at the time. I tried my best to blend into the furniture.

I'd never been in a hotel, and I'd never ridden in an elevator. I stepped on with two other men, one of whom gave the floor number I was going to, so I hid behind them and tried to figure out if they were real newspapermen or impostors like me. Their suits were less worn, but they both stood silent as we rode. The elevator was operated by a boy who couldn't be older than I'd been when I started movie shouting. His uniform was impeccable, but at least two sizes too big; it made me feel better about my own fraying cuffs.

The other two men got off before me and I followed them. The room we entered was overstuffed with people and furniture. I'd arrived ten minutes early, which meant ten minutes of silent jockeying for position. I wanted to find a wall to fade into, but paintings hung on every inch, just as every other surface was occupied, ornamented, adorned: a sword rested in an armchair, a model airplane on a trunk, feathered arrows on a table, a feast spread across another table, a collection of longbows in the corner. The other men and I positioned ourselves in a tight cluster, elbows in, notebooks out, around an empty sofa. A telephone rang insistently in the corner and we all ignored it, shifting from foot to foot as we sank into the plush carpet.

At the appointed hour, Douglas Fairbanks and Mary Pickford emerged from their private apartments and took their seats. She wore her hair up, though she usually had it down in the movies, and she carried what I imagined was the scent of flowers that bloomed in fairy tale gardens. He was tan, darker than any other in the room, and vibrated with energy, like stillness took an active effort. He'd shaved the pointed beard from the *Robin Hood* posters, though the mustache that remained was dashing.

The telephone rang again as he turned to sit, and for a second he forgot his smile. I felt a sudden kinship with him; not any presumption he knew my life or I knew his, but a sense we both were playing roles that depended on convincing everyone around us of how we were exactly where we belonged. Not that anyone paid a moment's attention to me, with the king and queen of the movies in the room; they were the sun we were all there to orbit.

"You look tired, Doug," a photographer called to him. Teasing, maybe; I didn't see it.

"That's from performing trapeze stunts on the luggage racks all the way across the country," Mary Pickford joked, poking her husband in his solid-looking ribs. "The trains cheered when we got off because they could finally get some rest."

"No, that was you cheering to be back in New York again. Civilization! The land of shopping and shows." When Fairbanks spoke, I realized I'd never heard his voice before; it suited him well enough.

Everyone laughed, and there were other questions, and other answers, and I did my best to do as I'd been told, to stay silent, to take notes on everything I saw and heard. I tried not to look at the food on the table; it being the day after Yom Kippur, I had woken with the particular holy hunger that follows a fast day. All that food and nobody eating it, but it wasn't mine to touch and I didn't know the rules, so I pretended I was watching a movie, with food no more touchable than the stars. If Lenny had been Lansky, he would have been in my ear with "I pays you to observe. Leave the food for them."

Some reporter pointed to the longbows resting in the corner and asked if they were for show. What I learned later, but didn't ken to at the time, was that whoever asked had to have known the effect of his question. Fairbanks took it as a personal affront. Why, didn't we know he had done all the film's stunts himself? He'd taken to archery as naturally as he'd taken to swordsmanship for *The Mark of Zorro* and *The Three Musketeers*. He was an excellent marksman now. In fact, he'd show us.

Which was how we wound up on the Ritz-Carlton's roof, Fairbanks and his press man and Allen Dwan, the director, the only other person who'd been introduced by name, and the whole herd of us, photographers hungering for the perfect shot, real reporters looking for the quote that would win them inches in the crowded columns, fakes like me hanging back so nobody realized our deception.

It was a perfect October day. I remember that much. The roof, the sun, the breeze, the temperature not too hot or too cold. Perfect baseball weather too, and I wondered if Lenny was enjoying himself out at the Polo Grounds, and if the weather would stay that nice for the whole week.

Fairbanks wanted to climb onto the roof's edge to recreate the crouch from the poster, but Dwan talked him out of it. He puffed out his chest and then raised the longbow and took aim at some invisible point in the city. The photographers crowded around and took aim themselves.

In the one photo I ever saw of the moment, the great actor, in his bespoke suit, with his bespoke, antique-looking bow, straddles a cornice far above the city, an expanse of sky and rooftops behind him, Manhattan Bridge in the distance. His left arm is straight and strong, his bowstring drawn and arrow nocked, a modern day Robin Hood. There is a slight upward tilt to everything: his posture, his arrow, his bow. The photo matches my memory, though it is grainy and renders the beautiful day similarly gray.

In Frank Case's version, the one in his memoir, his friend Doug proceeded to drop arrows on the neighboring rooftops with great accuracy, but Case also implied in his story that this happened at his hotel, the Algonquin. Was he even there? I wouldn't have recognized him at the time. His version is closer to true than Dwan's, though both men defanged the anecdote in their telling, and took liberties with the few facts that can be agreed upon. Truth degrades over time.

This is where I should tell you what—who—Fairbanks's arrow pierced. You can look it up if you need to jump ahead, but a story is not an arrow's flight, and mine loops back to the Rivington. December 1915, and Golde and I had been working there for nearly the full year by then. We had a patter down, as well as an unspoken agreement dating to the second night of *A Fool There Was* that we would both read all the romantic lines in the direction of Bess's piano rather than each other. We'd learned not to let the audience responses rattle us, to shout what we needed to shout and not editorialize.

By December, Golde knew she wanted to be an actress. She did what was expected of her, the shouting, but she varied the inflections, interpreting a character as tortured in one showing and unrepentant in another. If Lansky noticed he didn't mention it, or it didn't fall outside his expectations of us.

Actors, like my sister, have a way of keeping it interesting for show after show. I was never an actor. I found each movie entrancing in the first few showings, but after a while my mind started looking for new entertainment. If my sister's challenge was "how can I read this differently?" mine was "how would I improve this?" I started looking for scenes I'd cut, scenes I'd add, different ways of getting the same information across. All of which bled over into my own lines, because once you start looking at that sort of thing, you can't help but ask which lines you would change. "Innocence breakfasts," for starters, though I didn't begin considering how it might be improved until months after *A Fool There Was.*

The good titles stayed good. We shouted them over and over and they didn't get old. But some. The ones that irritated me got worse with each night. On the walk home, Golde would ask what was bothering me, and I'd recite back the ugly and awkward, and my suggestions for making them better. Telling her helped, but the bad lines bruised like pebbles I couldn't remove from my shoe. I had no options but to say them.

Which is how we came to December and *Double Trouble.* Not the first Fairbanks film, but the first I remember, for good reason. He played a nebbishy, sweaty-looking fellow named Florian Amidon, and a second personality who emerged Jekyll-and-Hyde-style after Amidon was hit over the head in a train station.

It was entertaining enough, but the titles started bad and got worse. "The pace that kills," I shouted into the megaphone. It felt sideways to what was happening, melodramatic. If you want to say he'd exhausted himself through work, say that. The audience agreed, arguing out the line's meaning.

"The pace began to tell, and he was voted a vacation." Voted a vacation? Vacations were foreign to everyone in the room, but even so, the idea that it was something to be voted on made no sense at all.

The title after the mugging included an editor's note: "Aphasia is a mental condition, vouched for by all our best novelists and dramatists." Why was that necessary? It followed "For five years after this unfortunate occurrence, Florian's life was a blank to him," but it pulled the viewer from the narrative, in my opinion, by reminding them of the writers in the very moment they should have been losing themselves in the story. The acting was fine, the film well enough made, but I could barely stand to utter the words.

One chilly night—I don't remember the date, but I remember my teeth chattering, and my fingers numb where they held the megaphone, my other hand deep in my coat pocket—I had enough. Lansky had said not to talk back, but he'd never said anything about changing lines. I didn't even see him; he'd probably retreated to the projector room to warm up.

When we got to the first of the title cards that offended me, I read "The pace that kills," as written.

"What's that supposed to mean?" Someone in the crowd yelled.

"He works hard, unlike you, schnorrer," came a response.

I kept my mouth shut, but it grew harder. The cold was getting to me, or the writing, or the crowd. I dreaded the audience debate over the next line. Which is why, when it arrived a minute later, instead of saying "The pace began to tell, and he was voted a vacation," I said "He worked until he got sick, so they gave him a vacation." Simple, to the point, but not inelegant.

I expected a glare from my sister, but she didn't comment on the change I'd made. No Lansky appeared at my elbow to whisper "I pays you to shout." I expected someone else in the audience who could read to ask why I'd changed it, but nobody said anything. Nobody talked back, either; my plain line had satisfied them for that particular scene. Everyone in the room understood hard work and exhaustion, except maybe whoever had been called a schnorrer.

Lansky said nothing about it when he paid us out for the evening, so I guessed nobody had complained to him. On the walk home, I waited for Golde or Bess to mention it, but they huddled against each other, against the cold, and left me to my thoughts.

Which made it even stranger when, the next night, as I prepared to return to "The pace began to tell, and he was voted a vacation," the card read "He worked until he got sick, so they gave him a vacation." I stumbled over the line—my own line—and someone in the darkness laughed at me.

I looked over at my sister for her reaction, and she grabbed the megaphone from me and shouted my next line, which I had forgotten to read in my surprise. "Judge Blodgett headed the town's delegation to see him off." So I got teased on the way home for my distraction, for forgetting to read, but neither Golde nor Bess said anything about the line I had edited, which stayed changed the next night, and the next. I began to think maybe I'd imagined changing it.

At the fourth show afterward, I spoke the original line instead. Immediately, the confused clamor I remembered from before my edit arose, but nobody complained that I wasn't reading the lines as written. I worked up the nerve to ask Golde afterward if she had noticed anything different about what I had done.

"Your voice only cracked once," she said.

I let the original line stand, but after that, when a new show started its run, I always found some way to test this strange ability. A line here, a line there, always for better, in my opinion. Edits worked, but not entirely new directions. Once I tried reciting the first lines of the Jabberwocky poem into some romantic scene; it didn't take. Golde looked over at me like I had lost my mind, and afterward, Lansky held back half my pay for the night and said, "I pays you to shout what they wrote."

From then on, I concentrated on editing titles that I believed were truly improved for my interference. By the end of most runs, I couldn't even remember what I had changed anymore. Once or twice I spent an afternoon and a hard-earned seven cents at another theater to watch a movie I already knew by heart, in order to see if they used the original titles or the ones I'd overwritten.

Always mine: once I said them they stuck. I had no way of knowing how it worked, whether they rippled out from me or changed instantaneously.

Some of the films are gone now, disintegrated or burned; lost to time. You know some of my lines, even if you don't know they're mine, and other than those I've admitted to here, you don't know which they are. I met the writers of many of them over the years, and even they didn't seem to realize a change has been made. Myself, I've forgotten more than I remember.

This small and strange ability I had only lasted as long as my movie shouting job. I tested it in other places every once in a while, rephrasing a newspaper headline in hope it might rearrange itself, or whispering an altered line from the audience of another theater. That one time I took the ferry to New Jersey, I spent a week beforehand crafting the perfect line. "There's a job for me in writing," I said at the Fox gate, speaking my hope into existence, visualizing the words as printed as a title card in my mind.

It didn't take.

It had to be some combination of me and the megaphone and the title cards, or me and the megaphone and the Rivington, or something else, but whatever that something else was, it disappeared when Golde and I walked away from that theater. I got other jobs, the ones I told you about, others not worth mentioning, but none where I managed even that smallest magic, except for once.

I didn't have a nickel for the train when I left the hotel; even if I had money, I think I would have walked. It took me a good hour or so. I needed the time to try to sort out what had happened, whether everything in my missing notebook could be brought to memory, and what exactly I was going to tell Lenny. Fairbanks met with reporters at his hotel, then took everyone to the roof, where—what happened? I wished I knew any of the other newspapermen there to ask them, but like I said, I wasn't supposed to talk to anyone, and anyway, they were all strangers to me, and anyway, I left quickly after the second arrow flew.

Lenny caught up with me later that evening as I walked to the theater for my real job. "Did you call in the Fairbanks bit?"

I nodded. A lie, my first of the new year if you didn't count pretending to be him at the hotel. My hope was that between the baseball and whatever else had transpired over the day, there'd be enough news for Lenny to assume the paper had simply run out of room. A non-event, unworthy of column space. He looked at me like he expected me to tell him how it had gone. I waited him out, and after a minute he started talking about Bullet Joe's fastball and where he put the Yankees' chances.

The next day, I scrounged two cents each for the *Herald* and the *Tribune*, eager to read how their reporters had written up the event. The *Herald* had a story on the third page, "Mysterious Arrow Hits Man on Fifth Avenue." What was mysterious about it? A fellow from the *Herald* stood next to me when that arrow flew! I kept going, and on page fourteen found, "Fairbanks Here with Mustache but Minus Beard," which quoted Pickford at length but made no mention of the rooftop.

The *Tribune* had "Furrier Punctured by Arrow; Fairbanks Denies Practice Stunt."

"That archery yarn was a press agent story that unfortunately coincides with the accident to the injured man," the picture star's representative declared. "Mr. Fairbanks was not on the hotel roof this afternoon and he did not fire any arrows." That one baffled me too, with reporters from every newspaper up there on the roof, or at least real photographers standing alongside all of us pretending to be reporters.

Someone else at the *Evening World* put the two together. I hadn't bothered to buy the *World*, assuming they had no story without my call, but Lenny appeared in my ticket line mashing page three against the window to show me the headline "Police Trace Responsibility for Arrow that Hit Seligman."

"This wasn't worth mentioning?"

I shrugged. "They encouraged us not to write about it while they sorted it out."

Lenny looked at me with pure disappointment, like I had completely misunderstood the brief he'd given me; he never asked me to stand in for him again, and soon after, the *World* stopped paying me for news.

The story as the various papers had it over the next few days, the part I wasn't present for: two mysterious antiquated-looking arrows were found by the police, one on the roof of a construction site on East 45th, and one in Abraham Seligman, furrier. Seligman had been standing at a fourth floor window at the back of his Fifth Avenue store when an arrow pierced his chest. He was taken to Flower Hospital up in Harlem, and then sent home to Yonkers, where he later received a visit from Fairbanks's lawyer. The papers didn't say if he was offered cash or tickets to the *Robin Hood* premiere or anything else for his trouble, but I imagine so, given the way what could have been a major scandal dropped quietly to nothing. Without the papers lingering on it, too, it was left for a footnote in biographies and a misremembered anecdote.

All of which brings me around one more time to the Ritz-Carlton rooftop. Here's what I remember: the sun was warm, but the breeze bit at us in our exposed position above the surrounding buildings. Fairbanks and his poses, and then a single arrow loosed into the sky.

None of us expected him to actually shoot, I don't think. I'm not even sure if he meant to let the first arrow fly. The whole crowd went from relaxed and joking to tense in those seconds after his fingers flexed. None of us were quick enough to follow where it went.

He gave a satisfied nod, as if it had gone where he meant to send it, though I have no idea if that was the case.

He was shooting arrows off a windy roof in Manhattan, and we were all too scared or surprised to venture that it wasn't a good idea. If we were real reporters we could hide behind journalistic integrity, some obligation to observe rather than become part of the story. None of us stopped him.

With the second arrow I noticed the precision of his stance: the relaxed shoulder of his bow arm, the line created from the arrowhead to his drawn elbow. He looked like an athlete, even in his fine suit.

I tried to follow his gaze. West, toward Fifth Avenue, toward some invisible target. What does one use as a target in Manhattan? The *Tribune* article the next day said he'd aimed at the ventilators on the roof of a nearby church; I cannot for the life of me recall the actor saying where he was aiming, nor can I recall a church in that direction. St. Patrick's Cathedral loomed large at our backs, a few blocks off.

In the moment before the arrow flew, his bow arm elbow overextended slightly and his shoulder dipped. I don't know why I had this thought, but because I was watching him so closely, because I had seen the perfect line of his arm and then the broken line, it flitted through my mind that the arrow was not going to go where he intended.

I saw it in slow motion. Cinematic; that strange moment in a disaster where everything feels at once preventable and inevitable. The arrow left the bow, traveling west, and from my position near the edge, New York teemed with people, ant-sized people on the street and in the windows below, people who had no idea there was an arrow flying in their direction.

We have choices, sometimes. Moments when we can do one thing or do another. If I stayed an observer, wrote down what I saw and called it in, I would have a genuine story on my hands. Not only the arrow's flight, as everyone saw it, but perhaps a note about the actor's archery form. A story of my own, not just a news bit. A career as a newspaperman, my own byline, my words in print.

Almost in slow motion. These are thoughts I've stuffed into the moment in retrospect. I can say what I think I was thinking, but I don't remember thinking at all, or choosing, though in my action I did close the shutter on my journalistic aspirations. Maybe I thought of the fairy stories our parents had read us, and the way that a curse might be mitigated if not lifted entirely. An edit, not a new line. The arrow was already flying, had perhaps already hit.

I decided. I had been his voice so many times. I had no megaphone, no theater, no title cards, no sister to play against. I wasn't even supposed to speak in his presence, Lenny had made that clear, but in my best projecting voice, as if I had a megaphone in hand, as if reading a title card, I shouted, "What a relief! The arrow caused no lasting damage."

Everyone on the roof looked at me, then. I'd exposed myself as a fake among fakes, the only impostor to announce himself, and in such a strange way. I didn't know if any of them had noticed the dangerous trajectory of that second arrow, or had tracked it down from the roof and through the open window. Fairbanks stared like he was trying to figure me out, like I was the problem and not his arrow; his press man started in my direction, even as the others returned to ignoring me and cheering the actor for his prowess. If a third arrow flew I wasn't there to see it.

I made it to the stairs before the agent. Nobody tried to apprehend me as I descended from the roof and exited the building. I didn't stop until I stood on the opposite side of Madison, half a block south of the hotel.

When I looked at my right hand, it was smudged with graphite. The graphite reminded me of my notebook, but when I reached for it, my pocket was empty. I'd had it on the roof. An arrow loosed into the sky, a sentence uttered, my notebook fluttering from my hand. I looked up at the cornice then, half-expecting to spot Fairbanks and his bow, but there was no sign of anyone who had been on the roof, up there or down below. I told you how I walked home and went to the theater and bought the newspapers to learn where the arrows had landed.

And that's the story. You know the part about how the mysterious arrow that hit Seligman and the marksman who shot it were put together, and how none of the reporters on the roof said anything about what they'd seen that day. I've mentioned Golde and her acting, and Bess, and my career as a script doctor for the talking pictures, later, though perhaps I left that part out.

It was a good job; I can say I loved it, though I never got to put my name to anything of my own. It even put me in the same room as Doug Fairbanks again a few years later. I told him about shouting his lines as a kid and he joked about hiring me to voice him again for the talkies. He looked at me like I was familiar, though he couldn't place me. He didn't know what we had shared and I didn't need him to know; I didn't do it for him. I did it because it wasn't right for a man to die of an actor's publicity arrow while taking a moment's break from work to admire a perfect October sky.

I suppose all of that's a story for another day too, how I made it to the movies for real, fixing bad lines and bad scenes more legitimately than I had as a boy. Mainly, I wanted to say that I briefly knew magic, real magic if small, and just once I got to use it to do a small, real, good thing in the world. Or at least I tell myself so.

Remember This for Me

Words were elusive; they came and went. People, too, and events. Bonnie was glad the Muse had always spoken in vivid, vibrant, fully formed images, even if they crowded the other stuff out. That was the trade-off, though she'd never agreed to it as such, and these days it seemed to take more and more. Still. All she had to do was get the images out of her head and onto the canvas intact.

This one flowed from a dream. An anxious dream, in which she saw someone she knew, and chased that person down a crowded street. She didn't know who it was, just that she had to reach them. She woke with the image in her mind, a blur of almost-recognition.

She didn't need to look to know where her notebook was, on the bedside table. She reached out and it was there. Flipping to the first blank page, she drew a rough sketch, just a blocking, a placeholder, to help her remember until she coaxed it out of canvas.

A pair of paint-splattered overalls hung over a chair beside the bed, along with a heather gray t-shirt. She put them on, then her slippers. She tucked the notebook into her overalls' hip pocket and went to put on some tea.

The range had no dials. Her rooster's comb kettle was missing from the burner, too, but after a moment she noticed an electric kettle plugged in beside the stove. She pressed a button and it hummed and lit up, electric blue. The mugs and teas were where they were supposed to be, so the weirdness ended there. She leaned against the counter and pulled her notebook from her pocket.

On the first empty page after her sketch, she wrote, "WHERE ARE THE KNOBS FOR THE RANGE?"

She flipped two pages back. There was a page labeled "Things to Remember" but that wasn't what she was looking for right now. On the third page back there was a list of questions and answers. The first one, in her own handwriting: "WHERE ARE THE KNOBS FOR THE RANGE?"

An answer, in the same hand: *"They took them away for my safety. I left the kettle whistling until all the water boiled away."*

That explained why her beautiful old kettle was gone, though she couldn't imagine having done something so irresponsible. Maybe she'd been painting and gotten distracted; when her Muse wanted attention, everything else tended to slip away.

The electric kettle didn't even whistle. It gave a soft click, but Bonnie's ears were still good, and the blue glow had disappeared too, so she poured water over her teabag, added cream and sugar, and sat down at the table.

A woman walked into the kitchen, a tall Black woman with a cloud of natural hair framing a kind face. She wore a plush dressing robe, forest green. Nobody broke into a house in a dressing robe, so Bonnie decided to give her the benefit of the doubt and play it cool.

"Good morning," Bonnie said. "There's hot water if you want tea."

"Morning, Bonnie. Thanks. Read the first page of your notebook."

Bonnie flipped back to the first page. The first question, again in her own handwriting, was, "WHO IS THE WOMAN IN MY HOUSE?"

The answer below was, *"Her name is Patty. She helps me. She lives here with me."*

Interesting. She looked up at the woman—Patty—and watched her bustle around the kitchen. She knew her way around. Knew about the notebook, too. Bonnie looked down at it again. "HOW LONG HAS SHE BEEN HERE?"

Answer, in her same spindly hand: "*Two years.*" (But how long ago had she written this note to herself? So, two years and then some.)

"WHERE DID SHE COME FROM?"

"*An agency that matches people who need homes with older folks who need somebody in the house to maintain independence.*"

Below, in someone else's handwriting: "*KEEP HER HAPPY. You can stay in the house as long as you don't drive her away.*"

Who else would be writing in her notebook? She'd been using this method of remembering things since she was a kid, since the first memory had disappeared. Nobody else was supposed to know about it, let alone use it.

And "Keep her happy." What was that supposed to mean? Sure, she'd gotten mad at people before, but only when they deserved it. She remembered chasing her agent from the house, flinging brushes and palette knives like javelins. She'd never do that to a stranger.

Why had he deserved it? She tried to remember. He'd told her a painting was done, when it wasn't. It was still missing something. He'd arrived with the packers to take her work to a show, and she was still working on the final piece. It couldn't be rushed. He'd deserved to be chased.

A giggle escaped her mouth, and the woman in the kitchen—what was her name again?—glanced over. "What's so funny?"

"Nothing. A memory. Someone I never liked very much, getting what he deserved."

The woman appeared beside her with hot cereal, a syrup swirl and a constellation of raisins garnishing the bowl. She hadn't even thought about breakfast yet. She supposed it was helpful to have someone in the house making sure she ate. She'd always forgotten to eat. Too much to do.

Keep the woman happy. "Thank you."

Bonnie tried to mix the syrup into the cereal, but it was a little too liquidy and the swirl kept swirling. She dragged the spoon in circles. Like storms across the surface of a gas giant, she thought, then wondered where that thought had come from. She'd never been much for astronomy, but the image in her mind's eye was a marbled planet, and now the marbled planet and the figure from her dream melded together, and she knew it was from her Muse. Just like her Muse, to give her something she hadn't had in her head to begin with. What had it replaced? More than anything she wanted to get up and get to work, but she forced herself to eat a few bites so she wouldn't look ungrateful.

She smiled as she walked into her studio space, warm and bright. It had been a sunroom in the apartment's previous life. Staged at the showing with a rainforest's worth of greenery. She looked straight through the plants to the windows, the sun, the inviting light. Plants were a distraction. The realtor had asked where her husband was, and she'd taken great pleasure in saying no husband, this is for me, have you heard of women's lib? She'd paid in cash, with the money she'd made from her first big show.

There was a canvas already on her easel. It looked finished. She didn't remember painting it, but she knew her own style. A shoulder that was not a shoulder, a face that was not a face, paint scalloped and layered inches thick. She touched the figure in the painting, the figure that was not a figure: her Muse. So close, but still so indistinct. Had she been satisfied with this painting when she'd walked away from it? It was maddeningly wrong.

She fought the urge to throw it on the ground and put a foot through it. Looking around, there were only three stretched and prepped canvases in the corner, and there was no reason to ruin this one even if it was wrong, wrong, wrong. Who knew how easy it was to get new ones these days? (She wrote the question in her notebook, to ask and answer later). Sand it down, prep it again. The colors were good, anyway.

The canvas wasn't heavy, but it slipped from between her fingers as Bonnie shifted it to the floor. It landed corner-first on her middle left toe and she yelped in pain.

"Are you okay in there?" asked someone from the other room.

"I'm fine," she said. Her slipper felt warm inside, but the pain had been one brief bright flash and gone. She'd deal with the toe later.

She set a fresh canvas on the easel, then turned her back on it. She'd never minded a blank canvas, not even in her thirties, when she'd worked on pieces as big as a bus's broadside. A blank wasn't a challenge or a taunt, as she'd heard some people describe. The piece was already done by the time she conceived it. Frustration, when it came, came in the end stages, if the physical manifestation didn't match the image she'd envisioned, if the skills she'd honed over her lifetime still weren't enough. Those occasions were blessedly rare.

Those giant pieces were the best she'd ever done, according to the critics. The combination of skill and talent and training and her Muse's vision had culminated in the Voyages series. Those were the ones people discussed when they talked about a Bonnie Sweetlove.

She remembered the retrospective at the Whitney, where they'd collected four giant Voyages and several smaller pieces from before and after. Standing in the center of it all, before the doors opened and the views were obstructed by people. Standing in the center, spinning slowly, and the Muse in her head radiating almost-happiness, telling her yes, this is close, this is almost it. Wrong, but close. It didn't blame her for the wrongness. She was on the right track.

That was what she strove for, always. That feeling that the thing she'd made had made her Muse happy. It created a joyous feedback loop, a pleasant buzz that spread through her whole body. Sometimes it struck as she made her last fine adjustments and stood back; sometimes she didn't feel it until several pieces were placed in a room together, resonating, forming something close to the whole they were been meant to be.

She closed her eyes and spun, seeing her paintings radiate out from the place where she stood. She looked for the gap, the place where the new one belonged, the missing piece in the larger puzzle.

"Aunt Bonnie?" asked a familiar voice. It didn't make sense for her niece Lori to be here. She was in college.

Bonnie opened her eyes, but there was nobody to be seen. No—a woman in the doorway, hesitating like she was prepared to duck if something was thrown at her. The woman had Lori's voice but looked much too old to be Lori. Bonnie glared, willing away the interruption.

"I'm sorry to bother you while you're painting"—at least she was smart enough to recognize that this, too, was painting—"but I came to check on you and—oh, jeez, what did you do to your foot?"

Bonnie looked down to see a crimson flower blooming on her pepto-pink slipper. What had caused it?

The person calling her Aunt Bonnie was pushing stuff off a chair buried underneath her paint counter, and pushing her into the chair, and pulling her slipper off her foot. The skin of her middle toe had split below the nail, and that toe and the ones beside it were sticky with blood. The nail itself was a thin veneer, nacre over a beautiful purple-black swirl. Broken? Maybe. She tried to wiggle it and pain flashed through her along with something else, something she couldn't quite say but she knew she needed to paint now, before she lost it. Purple-blacks, a stormy swirl, a gas giant.

"Does it hurt?"

"Not really, no." She didn't know why it was bleeding, so she was glad that question went unasked.

"Hang on, I'll clean it up. I think it looks worse than it is."

Things always looked worse than they were. Her niece Lori, who had the same voice as this person, had once sliced her forehead on a low-hanging branch on a rainy walk in the woods. She hadn't even known she'd hurt herself, had come running to show Bonnie something she had found, her face a bloody curtain. What was the thing she had found? A frog, maybe? Nothing like the thing Bonnie had found as a child and carried home in her head. Lori's cut had only been a thin slice by her hairline.

Bonnie looked down at the woman kneeling before her, dabbing at her toe with a wet paper towel. "You have the same scar as my niece, Lori," she said, touching the woman's forehead.

"I am Lori, Aunt Bonnie," said the woman who was too old to be Lori, with a combination of exasperation and patience.

Fair enough. This could be Lori. Stranger things had happened. Memories played tricks, and muses took memories. Years compressed into nothingness. People changed faces. Some kids walked into the woods and came out holding frogs; some kids walked into the woods and came out with a Muse in their head.

She'd been on a thousand panels about creativity and never heard anyone else say they had breathed in a Muse, so she never said it either. Came up with a thousand silly answers to the question "where do you get your ideas" to avoid the true one. It obviously wasn't something you mentioned in polite company. She wouldn't even have said that a second before, and she'd probably lose it again in another second. Not the Muse, just that curious moment when something crumbled and the air changed and she had breathed in and felt its presence inside her, making itself a new home, remaking her from that first moment.

It had been something else before it was a Muse. It had remade itself, too. That was a thing she'd figured out recently. A thing she'd avoided thinking her whole life, because you don't look a gift horse in the mouth, or question a Muse when it has chosen to work through you. Or maybe she'd known it forever, and only gotten around to remembering it now, along with Lori's frog and the cut forehead, along with the thing in the woods, its colors, its spores, the way it had crumbled when she'd touched it, the way she'd breathed it in.

"All better," said the woman kneeling in front of her, and Bonnie looked to see if she was trying on shoes, but there was a bandage on her toe, and no shoe at all.

"This store has terrible service," she told the saleswoman.

"This isn't a store, Aunt Bonnie. I'm your niece, Lori. I'm going to put your slippers back on. Are you going to paint some more?"

She looked at the woman, and it was Lori, but since when was Lori a shoe saleswoman? Lori was in college. No. Lori worked for a college. Lori had two children and a wife who looked like Paul Newman.

"How are the kids, Lori?" She couldn't remember their names, but she had formed their faces in her mind. Six and nine, maybe?

Lori looked pleased. "Leo's frustrated with his committee, but he's slogging away. Rachel is enjoying the Peace Corps now that she's settled in. We're hoping to go over there once she's allowed visitors."

"How lovely," Bonnie said. She had follow-up questions but they'd make her look ignorant, so she didn't ask them.

"Do you want lunch?"

Had she lost the whole morning already? She glanced at the clock. No, it was only eleven. "Not yet. I have work to do."

Lori gathered a handful of something off the floor, and gave Bonnie a kiss on the head as she left. "I'll hang out for a while. We can eat and chat when you're ready. I have something I want to talk to you about."

Bonnie had already had enough chatting, but that would probably be a rude thing to say out loud. Her painting wasn't going to paint itself. And now that she was alone, she couldn't actually remember what her project was for today.

She stuck out her tongue in frustration, fought the urge to kick something. Before, she would have chased interruptions out of her studio. Nobody would have dared to walk in while she was working. That was part of why she'd always lived alone. Too much to do.

The canvas was still blank. Blank canvases didn't intimidate her, but she'd lost the thread. She pulled her notebook from her hip pocket and leafed through it, looking for a reminder, for something to wake her Muse. There were pages and pages of questions in her own handwriting. Some had answers, some didn't.

On the second-to-last page, she found what she was looking for. The sketch was rough, basic. Nothing to it but a shape, but the second she looked at it she remembered the dream, the almost-figure, the colors. "Thank you," she whispered to her Muse. The picture in her mind brightened and threw itself onto the canvas. She followed it with her palette knife.

She lost herself in the piece. First, a layer blocking out the shapes. After that, she knew what she was doing and the sketch was no longer a necessary reminder. On a lark, she tore it from her notebook and stuck it to the painting, in the middle of the back-that-was-not-a-back of the figure-that-was-not-a-figure. Nobody would know it was there, not after she covered it with a thick midnight blue, blended midnight and sky and space, coaxed waves forward with her palette knife, tendrils, licks of flame, fingers, teeth, reaching forward out of the flatness.

The deeper she went, the closer the painting and the image in her mind got to each other. The trick was to shut everything else out. Ignore the cramping fingers, the pain in her shoulder, the fatigue in her legs. Her Muse ignored all those things; it didn't remember them anymore.

She stepped back to look at her work, waiting for her Muse to tell her she had gotten it right, to feed her joy. She got it, paired with a shock of recognition. She bent down to look for the canvas she'd discarded earlier in the morning, now buried under the materials that had been on the chair.

They weren't identical. Same subject, same blocking, same shoulder that was not a shoulder, same face that was not a face, same deliberately unfocused figure. What was different? Today's gave her the sense of rightness that the previous one didn't. She'd used the colors a little better today, perhaps, and the paint's textures. And was the figure a little closer? Yes, perhaps it was. Variations on a theme.

The exhaustion that came with a work completed nudged its way forward in her mind. She was hungry, too, and she had to pee, and she was covered in paint. She headed for the bathroom to wash up.

When she returned to the living room, a middle-aged white woman sat on her couch with a sheaf of paperwork, and a tall Black woman stood in the kitchen mixing something in a bowl. She ducked back into the bathroom and pulled out her notebook. Leafed back through page after page of questions in her own handwriting, looking for something to explain who they were.

WHO IS THE WOMAN IN MY HOUSE?

Her name is Patty. She helps me. She lives here with me.

That was presumably the woman in the kitchen. The other looked familiar.

"Bonnie, would you like some lunch?" called the woman named Patty. "I heard you go to wash up so I started putting something together for you."

It was considerate, really. Bonnie dropped her notebook back in her pocket and ventured out. The table was set with three place settings, her everyday dishes. There was a plate in the center piled with toast, cut diagonally, a salad bowl, and a bowl of chicken or tuna salad.

The woman named Patty sat down at the table, bypassing Bonnie's favorite spot, even though it was the closest to the kitchen. Bonnie had always preferred that seat because it put her close to the radiator but still let her see out the window. The sky today wore a frigid blue, streaked with wispy clouds.

The other woman came and joined them in the third seat. She looked like Bonnie's mother, but she wasn't.

"Sandwich or salad?" asked Patty.

"Salad, please," Bonnie said, and took the bowls as they were passed in her direction.

"Aunt Bonnie, I have some good news for you," said the woman who was not Bonnie's mother, and she must be Lori, though she looked much older than Lori. Lori was the only one who called her "aunt."

"I'd love to hear some good news."

"The Forward Museum wants to do a retrospective of your work."

Bonnie smiled. "The Whitney did a retrospective once. It was almost right."

"I remember." Lori heaped chicken salad onto bread. "You were disappointed for some reason, but the critics loved it. Anyway, the Forward has a huge special exhibits space, and they read an article somebody wrote about patterns in your work, and they want to try to gather everything mentioned in the article and more."

Interesting. "What did the article mention?"

"The Voyages series, of course, but then some more recent stuff, too. Transformations, Evolutions."

Transformations! The Transformations paintings had been some of her Muse's favorites. Tiny self-portraits of a Muse: the pathways it had carved to make room for itself; the places it hid; synapses firing, synapses at rest; endorphins wearing love's cloak. Most of them had sold to private buyers and they'd never been collected in one place.

An image blazed through her brain: a room full of paintings, large and small. Not the Whitney. Something more right, a flaw corrected. "Would I have any input?"

A patient look on Lori's face, like she had answered this before. "The author of the article is guest curating, but we can definitely arrange something. I guess it might depend on if he thinks you'll agree or disagree with his thesis."

"Which is?"

"A pattern."

Another image, this one a shoulder that wasn't a shoulder, a face that wasn't a face, a figure in a crowd, a hand reaching out, a figure that wasn't a figure dissolving into constellations of spores, purple-black swirls like oil on water.

"How soon?"

"September. It's January now."

"That isn't enough time. How could they possibly do it with that short a lead time?"

"Look at the third page of your notebook, Aunt Bonnie."

The third page:

THINGS TO REMEMBER:

The woman who looks like Mom is Lori.

The woman who lives in the house is Patty. Don't throw things at her.

There is a retrospective coming up of my work.

Bonnie looked up. "It's already happening?"

"You've been working on it for a year already."

Bonnie's mind reeled. How had she forgotten something this significant? If she'd forgotten this, who knew what else she was forgetting?

She tried to paper over the gap. "Why did you pretend you were telling me about it for the first time? I'm not stupid. I don't need to be manipulated."

"I'm not manipulating you," Lori said. "But if I start from the assumption you remember it we usually have to backtrack."

"So I already have input?"

"Every step of the way, Aunt Bonnie."

Bonnie bit her lip. "What museum?"

"The Forward. I'm not sure you've ever been there. It's pretty new, but they've been doing some really interesting exhibits. I've got some layouts here if you want to look at them? And some other stuff for you to sign."

"Yes. I'll have to ask my agent about the show, but yes."

The woman across from her sighed. "You fired your agent again. Right now it's you and me."

"Oh! You're my new agent? I'm glad that other dolt is gone. Have we met before?"

The woman across from her sighed again.

―――

THINGS TO REMEMBER:
The woman who looks like Mom is Lori.
There is a retrospective coming up of my work.

WHY DOES THAT WOMAN KEEP ASKING ME QUESTIONS?

The woman is Lori, even though she looks different. The questions are from the guest curator, to help him write text for an exhibit.

WILL THEY INCLUDE THE NEW SERIES IN THE RETROSPECTIVE?

Yes! Lori sent pictures to the guest curator and he thought they fit the show.

THINGS TO REMEMBER:
If he asks me about patterns, say they were intentional.

WHAT ARTICLE IS THIS MAN TALKING ABOUT?

It's called "Inner Journeys, Outer Journeys, and the Radical Geographies of Self in the Works of Bonnie Sweetlove." A guy named Levy Reznik wrote it. It's equal parts genius and crap. I've read it. If I ask to read it again, Lori will get frustrated.

THINGS TO REMEMBER:
If he asks me about patterns, say they were intentional. If he asks me why I said they weren't the last time, why I said he was barking up the wrong tree, swallow my pride and tell him I don't remember.
Tell him yes, the constellations hidden in the Voyages paintings are accurate. Tell him yes, viewed edge-on, Evolutions #7 is a relief map of the Guiana Highlands, impasto as sculpture.

IMPORTANT: WILL THEY INCLUDE THE NEW SERIES IN THE RETROSPECTIVE?
Yes.

WILL THEY LET ME ARRANGE THE PIECES THEY'VE CHOSEN?
They did. Lori and I drew it out together. Months ago, she says. The curator said it was an innovative design and the museum added it to the press kit as a selling point.

"Are you sure this is the right way?" Bonnie asked the driver. "This is a terrible neighborhood."

"It's been a while since you were down here, Aunt Bonnie. It's different than you remember. The museum built down here, then artists started moving into warehouse spaces in the neighborhood."

Another woman, in the backseat, said, "I grew up not far from here. The whole block was flattened to make way for condos. Everyone getting priced out, pushed out."

The driver had called her "aunt," so this must be her niece, Lori, though she looked too old. Bonnie wasn't sure who the other woman was. She watched the buildings go by. Maybe the driver was right. There were more people on the streets than she remembered, and the warehouses weren't boarded up anymore. When had that happened? She picked at the delicate beading on her skirt. Not out of nerves, but because her hands liked having something to do.

The driver pulled the car up to the museum entrance.

"You don't need to drop me at the door. I can walk, you know."

"I know! I figured you'd be on your feet all evening and I'd save you a few steps."

That made sense, but once she'd complained, Bonnie didn't feel like apologizing, so she didn't say a word on the walk up from the parking lot. Good thing she'd worn sensible shoes, and it was still light out. She kept one hand in her pocketbook, fingers clasped around her notebook. When the second woman offered an arm, she accepted the support.

The museum door said gallery hours ended at five, but the door swung open without protest. The lobby had a sleek design, like it remembered the neighborhood's industrial roots without owing them anything. Brick and steel, mottled cement floors, open spaces and floating walls. She followed the driver—it was her niece, Lori, she saw that now—down the empty hallway.

They came to a glass door. A gallery. They must be here for a party, since she was dressed up. Bonnie pulled her notebook from her pocket.

"We're here for your opening reception, Bonnie," said the woman whose arm she was leaning on.

"Come on, Aunt Bonnie." Another woman held the door for her, and it must be her niece Lori, because who else would call her "aunt," though she looked older than Bonnie could account for.

She stepped into a brightly lit room. A bar had been set up to the left of the entrance, and two young bartenders were setting up cobalt wine bottles and strings of tiny bulbs in a pattern that caught the light and sent it dancing. A party with no partiers. She pulled her notebook out and wrote "WHERE ARE ALL THE PEOPLE?" then tucked it back in her pocket.

"We're here an hour early," a woman beside her said, as if she had seen the question Bonnie had written down. "You asked to come in before anybody else to see your paintings without any people in the way."

Spying wasn't polite, but the answer was useful. "Thank you."

She wrote, "I'm here early to see the paintings without any people in the way." It was nice when questions and answers lined up so neatly.

Bonnie walked closer to see what the art was, and her Muse kicked a memory her way. This was her exhibit. They had listened to her suggestions for the exhibit. She could tell even before she stepped past the bar. Paintings suspended from the ceiling at different heights within the larger space. Walls overlapping walls, paintings overlapping paintings. Like rose petals. She hoped it had the effect she'd envisioned.

It had been decades since she'd seen most of these paintings, but the Voyages that formed the outer walls were as familiar as her own home. Huge swaths of scalloped blackness, colors in the undersides of the sculpted paint waves. Secrets she'd forgotten but remembered now: the things her Muse used to be, the places it had traveled. Secrets her Muse had been bursting to tell to someone through all the endless time before it chose her.

She picked a random didactic to read.

Voyages #6
Bonnie Sweetlove
Oil on canvas
1956

Sweetlove's Voyages series can be looked at through many lenses. They explore form, style, and color in a way that is both playful and technically masterful. They also conceal secrets from the average viewer. Astronomical charts, geographic features, physiological pathways. Viewed from eight feet back and two feet to the right, Voyages #6 reveals the tracks of the 1944 Atlantic hurricane season.

Secrets her Muse hadn't even told her, apparently. She was only the conduit. No—that wasn't fair. A conduit without talent or skill or work ethic couldn't have made this work. It was a collaboration, even if she didn't know the meaning of every detail of what the Muse asked her to do.

1944 would have been the Great Atlantic Hurricane. Bonnie remembered her father boarding up the windows and telling her and her sister and mother to sit in the windowless pantry. She'd lived through worse hurricanes since, but that was the first one she remembered. It had taken down trees, created ponds where there were none, altered the familiar landscape. It hadn't been long after that she'd walked into the woods on her own and out of the woods with a Muse in her head.

If she read all the captions, she'd learn all kinds of things about her art. The curator had done his homework. If he ever asked her, she'd say yes, it was purposeful, of course. The safer lie. Safe like accepting a diagnosis of dementia when nobody would understand the true reason you couldn't remember things. Protect the Muse, protect yourself; those were two things she'd never forgotten no matter how much else had slipped away.

"Are you okay, Aunt Bonnie?" someone asked, and she waved aside the question. No distractions. Not here, wherever here was, in the place where someone had finally put her work together in the right way.

She wandered past Voyages and into Evolutions, where she learned she had hidden topographical maps, some for geographic features yet to be located, and a series of unusual MRIs, and a partial genome of something unidentified. Those weren't the things she saw when she looked at the Evolutions: she saw her Muse, cloaked in golden light, too bright to be seen.

After Evolutions came Transformations, tiny hyper-detailed works that begged the viewer to come closer, to look inside, to look inside her to where the Muse nestled, where it made its home, at the ways she could no longer tell where it ended and she began. Twenty-seven of them, three cubed, grouped on one wall in a fractal pattern.

And finally, at the center, the new works. Glimpses, twelve numbered Glimpses out of however many she'd made. Painted not-figures, expertly unfocused. Bodies of light, celestial bodies, things that had bodies once but didn't anymore.

She came to the center, the center she'd created, and looked outward. From this vantage she saw parts of everything: an incomplete

Voyage, an Evolution in progress, a series of Transformations, Glimpses of something that was so close now she could almost touch it, almost know it for what it truly was, or what it had been. Her Muse glowed. It radiated happiness, telling her through images that reflected back what she saw in front of her that yes, this is how it was, this is right, remember this for me.

Remember this for me. Her Muse suffused her with joy, and she thought that if she could just remember long enough to get home to her paints, she might, just once, capture the true face of it, the thing it remembered being, far from here, long before it was a Muse. Her hand closed around her notebook, but she couldn't possibly block this with paper and pen. Lines would confine it.

Remember this for me, it said, and she knew she'd remember until she forgot, until she breathed out her Muse and it found someone new to infect, to inspire, to tell its long story, to tell and be retold in a new medium. Remember this for me, it said, and she promised to remember until she forgot.

The Mountains His Crown

The Royal Surveyors drove their machine through my fields at midday; it took six hours to put all the fires out.

They didn't stop. A flag depicting the new Emperor's crest, depicting his own face in profile, whipped and snapped in the wind. They came from the direction of our farm's northern border, from Ommen Birku's land, at the same plodding pace as my two-horse plough, but taller, wider, spitting fire like a storybook dragon, armored like a beetle.

Catastrophe can happen at any speed. I thought of that as I watched the machine cut its slow ten-meter swath through my sunflowers. A horse could trample someone quickly, but that person might take weeks or years to die. A swarm can descend overnight and leave nothing for the harvest come morning.

This was a slow catastrophe. I had time to estimate the rows. Time to check which way the wind was blowing, if it would spread in the direction of our home. Time to spare a thought for Birku, to wonder if his own cover crop had met the same fate. Time to be thankful that this was the season of soil nourishment, of secondary crops. Twenty-five rows of sunflowers was a smaller catastrophe than twenty-five rows of hay or redwheat. Burning enriched soil too.

I stood at the kitchen window, clutching the mug of mint tea I had put to steeping just before my eye caught movement in the field. The mug cooled in my hands.

"What are you watching?" Lara asked me, coming into the room. When I didn't answer, she followed my gaze. "What is that?

What are you standing here for? We need to put out the fires before they spread!"

I shook my head, pointed to the banner. "Better not to get in their way. Wait until they're gone."

"Then at least we could prepare buckets. Take the horses somewhere."

She was right. Those were the words needed to break the window's spell. We set the children to fetching water.

"Go out the front door," I told them. "Don't let the machine see you."

"The people in the machine," Lara said, giving me a look. Right again. No need to scare them with invented monsters.

I went out the front door with them. There was no way to stay hidden and get to the barn, but the monster was already past the barn and the house. No way to know if anyone was watching from the machine's side or back.

The horses greeted me with agitation, stomping feet and swishing tails. They smelled fire. Star was the cleanest, so I saddled him and haltered the others. Leading three horses while mounting a fourth wasn't easy in the best of times; I was glad I had taken the time for a saddle instead of trying it bareback. They were all half-draft beasts, all calm by nature, but the fire and my own clumsy distraction added to their restlessness. It would all have been made easier if I had brought one of the kids. I wasn't thinking. My mind wasn't on the fire but on the crest that flew atop the machine.

The road was wide enough to perhaps act as a firebreak if we didn't keep the flames under control, if the wind picked up. If we needed to, we could send the children across. That was what I told myself as I led the string up our drive, then across the way to the Maris place.

We'd never gotten on with the Maris family, but Ellum took one look at me and opened the gate to an empty corral.

"What's burning?" Ellum asked as I unsaddled Star and dumped the saddle beside the gate.

"My sunflowers, but I don't think only mine. Big machine, flying the royal crest."

He nodded. "Boys!" he called back toward his house. The door opened and his oldest, Ianno, leaned out. "Get your shoes on. Fire at Kae's place. She's going to need us all."

The air behind our house was thick with smoke. We hurried back together, saying nothing. It didn't matter that we disliked each other's farming methods, or that he still resented our refusal to sell him our land. An unchecked fire at my place could destroy his as well.

By the time we had the hose unwound and pumping from the pond, the machine was at our property's southern end. It took six hours to put out the main fire, even with all of the Marises and all of our family working on it. We drained half the pond, a problem we'd have to deal with later. We were lucky; the fire didn't want to spread.

"Thank you," I said to the Marises, knowing they would feed and water our horses from their own stores when they returned home. "I'll get them in the morning."

"Nothing you wouldn't do for us."

All that was left to do was spend the night walking the burned swath, putting out any embers that flared. Darkness made the chore easier, despite the exhaustion creeping in around the edges. Lara took the children indoors to put them to bed; she was better at settling them.

She came back out after a short while. "They were both asleep on their feet before we got in the door."

We walked down to the southern perimeter, the great stones of the ancient border broken and scattered like pebbles. To the south, the sky was lit with flame.

"What are they doing?" Lara asked as we turned north again.

"I don't know," I said.

"It was so precise." She kicked a burning stalk we had missed, ground it into the soil with her boot. "Did you notice that nothing has burned outside these rows? If we hadn't put the fire out, I think it would have burned out on its own. Taken these rows but none of the others."

"You're saying we wasted all our effort?"

"Not necessarily. I might be wrong. And they might have a way to keep the adjacent rows from burning, but if they can't control the wind, we're still better off being careful."

We walked, kicking divots, grinding embers. My feet ached, my back, my shoulders. Not the familiar aches I went to bed with most nights; these were the kind that would have me waking sore.

The fires were the only subject of conversation at the next market day. At the first stall, Shin Davi caught my wrist in her firm grip as I reached to scoop from her barrel of dried brownbeans.

"Is it true?" she asked. Her knuckles stood out like mountain peaks, bones visible beneath paper-thin skin. "The Conqueror's troops, here again?"

I pried her fingers loose one by one, squeezed her hand and put it down. Even after fifteen years here, the people always touched a little too easily for my northern comforts.

"They flew his crest, but I don't know if they were his soldiers or his magicians or his dogs run loose. They set fires, they kept moving. They didn't stop to talk."

"Tsk. Dogs."

"Have you spoken with any of the others? Do you know how many lost crops?"

"Birku, as you know, and the next three farms to the north. At least four to the south of you as well. All in a row." She drew a line in the air, north to south.

"Beyond that?"

She shrugged. "Who knows? Information only carries so far."

"They never wavered?"

"Not on the path they took through this area. If they turned somewhere, or stopped to eat or piss or sleep, it wasn't here. Kae, remind me, you're not from the same place he came from, right?"

He. The Emperor, the Conqueror. "No. He came from somewhere to the west, over the sea. He came to us in the mountains first, though. Sixteen years ago, long before he came here the first time. Built his fortress there."

"He's why you left?"

"He's why I left when I did, yes. But I was twenty-five and antsy, and I likely would have gone anyway, sooner than later. I'd always wanted to live somewhere it would be easier to farm. Not that it's ever easy, but the soil is better here, and the winter isn't as cold."

She dumped an extra scoop of beans into my sack and waved away the payment I offered.

I walked through the market, wondering as I always did at how the offerings here differed from those of my childhood. Back then there had been stalls full of electronics now no longer permitted outside the emperor's own walls. In the north our markets had been full of dried goods, anything that traveled well; when someone arrived from the sea with salted fish or from the south with fresh fruit or vegetables, their wares would be gone in minutes.

Here, people grew their own produce, but the rows were lined with a different sort of practical. Anything someone might find it easier to buy than to make, we could find here. Textiles and clothing, jewelry, pots and pans, bits and bridles. Lara and I made our own clothing, but we understood how hands that ached from shelling might not want to knit or churn or stitch leather at the end of the day.

At every stall, the vendors wanted to speak to those of us who had lost crops. Some of the interest was prurient, some practical: if the machine had come once, it could come back. They all put extra portions in my bags, and I revised my feelings about southerners for the hundredth hundredth time. They stood too close when they talked, but nobody wanting was left to struggle, nor even to ask for help.

"I didn't buy extra," I said when I returned home, dropping my overladen saddlebags on the kitchen floor. "Everyone wanted to give something."

"I remember when you would have been too proud to let them give." Lara hefted the beans. "When I met you, you would have refused anything that might be construed as charity."

I put my arms around her, buried my face in her thick hair. It smelled like sweetgrain. "When you met me, I didn't have a family to feed."

"I should hope not!"

Her teasing always lifted me. I let her swat me, and we set to putting the food away.

"Anyway," I said after a moment, "I was too young to understand that sometimes people need to give."

Lara and I were working in the kitchen garden when they arrived the second time, a month later. We both had our heads down, our knees in the dirt, and the ground was soft from recent rains. We didn't even hear them until they were nearly upon us, their horses' hooves churning up the rows between the sunflowers.

The lead horse reached out and broke off an entire stalk as they reached the field's edge. That's how they approached us: three riders, three black horses, one dragging an enormous yellow flower.

We stood, dropping our tools in the soil so we wouldn't look aggressive. Not that they looked aggressive either. No banner, no machines, but their saddlecloths and jackets bore a crowned head in profile, red on gold. This ruler didn't waste time on symbolic representation. He was his own lion, his own castle, his own symbol of power.

"Are these your fields?"

Lara nodded.

"You are to keep the burn barren and free of weeds, by order of the Emperor."

I fixated on the sunflower. The horse was still chewing the stalk, the flower bobbing up and down, up and down. It made the soldiers less intimidating. "How do we survive without the revenue those fields would have brought? This is a small farm. Twenty-five rows are not insignificant."

The soldier shrugged. His look was almost sympathetic. "I can't say. But I wouldn't defy the order if I were you. Better to pretend that land is gone than to waste time and money planting only to have it burnt again."

They turned back toward the fields. I would have liked to tell them to take the road, to stop trampling our remaining crops, but I knew better than to rile them. The speaker's horse dropped his flower as they disappeared back between the rows.

"What possible reason could they have to do this?" Lara asked when they were out of earshot. "Is it to be a new road? We already have a road."

"I don't know. Better to do what they say than have them come back with machines and magicians, I suppose."

She knelt and picked up a spade, attacking the roots of a weed that had sprung up among the winter greens.

"Can we do it?" I asked, still looking at the abandoned flower. "Can we afford to leave that much land unplanted in the spring?"

"We can if we don't lose anything at all to blight or weather or insects. The margins will be thinner, and none of that is within our control. But I guess it could be worse."

With soldiers, with emperors, it could always be worse. After a moment I knelt beside her.

The Marises came to dinner that night. We'd tried to be friendlier with them since the night of the fire had brought us together, and it seemed to be working, mostly. Ellum had baked redwheat loaf, sour and sweet, and we all tore hunks to dip in my bean soup.

"I don't understand what they're doing," Tari Maris said. "Why don't they simply take the land?"

"It's smart," Lara said. "If they take the land, they have to find people to maintain it. This way they leave us to do the maintenance, and they still collect taxes from us as the owners."

I hadn't even thought about the taxes. "Can they do that? Tax us at the same rate we were paying when it was considered arable land?"

"They can do anything they want." Ianno Maris made faces at our twins, who giggled. He spoke like an adult now, even if he still acted the child when he was with the younger ones.

"I'm just glad they came through our land, not yours," Lara said. "You have so many more mouths to feed. And with less to plant, maybe we'll have more time to help you when you start to need it."

Tari smiled and rested her hand on her belly, where she was just beginning to show. "We'll help each other."

The third visit came in the dead of winter. I was in the barn oiling harnesses when the twins came running.

"It's a THING," said Ash.

"In the SKY," said Sable.

I took another swipe at a dried sweat spot on the girth I'd been cleaning. "A bird?"

"A thing," Ash repeated. "It's shaped like a fat fish. And it flies different from a bird."

"How big is it?"

Sable held up her fingers. "But it's in the sky. A greathawk far away looks like a sparrow, and then it comes close and . . ." She spread her fingers wide until they were greathawk wings.

"Smart girl. Show me the thing in the sky."

I dropped my rag and followed them out into the gray daylight. We hadn't seen sun in a week. It was cold enough we'd had to break ice to water the horses, but no snow had fallen.

"See?" Sable asked. Something large and fish-bellied was sinking below the tree line to the north. I caught a glimpse of a red-on-gold profile.

"You're both clever to have called me. That's an airship."

"An airship." Ash tested the word. "Why have we never seen one before? Can you ride on it?"

"In it," I said. "You've never seen one because the Emperor keeps technologies for himself. He has airships and all kinds of things that he's taken away from us, some of which are quite useful. Some of them are good things and some are very bad things. And what I need you both to do is run across to the Maris house, and stay there until I come and fetch you. Run now, extra fast. Tell them I was testing to see how fast you could run together. Stay with each other!" I added the last bit as they took off.

I knew they would tell Ellum and Tari about the airship, and the two of them would figure out I had sent the children for safe-keeping. I went to clean myself up for the visitors.

They took several hours to arrive. The Emperor's party came from the road this time, by hovercar. I hadn't seen a hovercar in years, not since the annexation, just after I had come south.

We were outside waiting when they arrived; better to meet them there than to let them in the house when we didn't know their intentions. There were six in their party, three women and three men, one small and dark, from my region or near it. Another woman wore the Emperor's red and gold, though it wasn't the infantry uniform we had seen in past years. She alone among them stood with military bearing, and she alone had a visible sidearm.

The man who spoke was stooped and angular, with a long narrow jaw that left his teeth crowded and his speech slightly forced. "The Emperor requests your assistance."

"Requests or requires?" I asked.

Lara shifted her weight to step on my toe. I stood my ground. I knew better than to goad them; this was clarification, not goading.

Narrow-Jaw folded his arms. "Requires, yes. The Emperor requires your assistance. He has sent his Royal Surveyors up in his airship, and—"

I couldn't help it. "That's you? The Royal Surveyors?"

"Yes."

"Love, why don't you stop interrupting His Majesty's emissary, so he can explain his purpose?" Lara had given up on subtlety.

"Sorry," I said. "I won't interrupt again."

He started over. "The Emperor requires your assistance. He has sent his Royal Surveyors up in his airship, and determined that your lands must be kept in sunflowers in all seasons possible."

"All of our lands? What reason could he have for that?" I couldn't help it. "And does he know that isn't even possible? Crops have seasons."

"All seasons possible," he repeated.

Lara tried to be more diplomatic. "I think what my partner is trying to ask is whether the Emperor understands that the flowers will naturally follow cycles of growth and decay? Or that they won't grow in winter, even here?"

"The Emperor understands. You'll still be able to grow a kitchen garden, and you won't be expected to raise flowers in winter. The Royal Agriculturists will provide a schedule so that you and your neighbors achieve peak bloom simultaneously and repeatedly."

"Repeatedly. We're not allowed to grow redwheat or grasses for hay at all? How are we supposed to survive on sunflower income alone? Or feed our animals? We can't feed horses on a kitchen garden or sunflowers." I tried to match Lara's calm tone, but my questions felt shrill even to my own ears.

Narrow-Jaw held up his hands and shrugged. He looked uncomfortable. How many farms had he been to already that his own message still made him uncomfortable?

I continued. "For that matter, how are those of you in the mountains going to eat without our farms producing redwheat and beans for your markets?"

"Not everyone will be growing sunflowers. There will be a large group of redwheat growers to the west of your stripe."

Lara's turn to be incredulous. "Our stripe? And are they expected to grow redwheat all year long, while we grow sunflowers? Your Royal Agriculturists know that soil can't sustain more than one crop of redwheat a year, right? That without cover crops or burning in between, the nutrients in the soil will disappear and future growth will be stunted?"

"Our Royal Agriculturists are working on the answers to all of these questions."

"Why?" I asked. "What's the point of all of this? We're the Emperor's farmers. There's been no sedition. We don't need to be broken or proven."

Narrow-Jaw had done all of the speaking until then, but now one of the women in the group stepped forward. She held out her hand to reveal a small button, which flowered into a map projection.

"This is a view of the Emperor's lands from his airship. He was traveling in late summer last year with his children, when his daughter pointed out that a particular stretch of rocky coastline in the north looked rather like his nose. See, here?"

She zoomed the map in on an outcropping that did indeed look like a nose. "And then both children began to expand the idea. A mountain lake, his blue eye. The northern mountains themselves, his crown. Once they showed him the resemblance, he was delighted. 'You see, these lands were meant to be mine,' he said.

"He insisted on touring the whole continent to see how far the resemblance carried. Here in the south, the areas that would be the edges of his robe were lined with gold—your sunflowers—as is his favorite robe. He determined that everything would stay just so: red cloak with gold lining, for as much of the year as will grow."

Neither Lara nor I spoke. We stared at the map, dumbfounded. The rocky nose and chin, the eye, the mountains his crown, the fields his robes. Our family's ruin laid out in gold. A question grew in me throughout the surveyor's explanation, but I couldn't quite bear to ask it. I didn't want to know the answer, even if I needed to.

Lara had apparently been thinking the same thing, and gave it voice. "You say we're the outer lining of the robe. What happens to those outside the border? There are further lands within his empire to the east. Neighbors in our community." She traced a line down the map.

The woman shook her head. "The Emperor isn't interested in maintaining lands outside of his image. Those places no longer exist as part of his empire."

"No longer exist?" I asked.

"Their land is not part of his empire. Those people are no longer citizens. There aren't many. The border is remarkably clean."

"Clean," I repeated, thinking of our own fields east of the line, and our neighbors beyond that. "And is there any risk that the Emperor will choose to, um, cleanse those lands further? If their crops interfere with his colors or lines?"

Another woman in the group, the slight one, spoke. Dark skinned as me, dark eyeglasses, and with an accent I hadn't heard for years, not that distant from my own. "Would you doubt it for a second?"

The military woman gave her a jab in the ribs, and she amended her comments. "Our new Emperor is a master of consistency. We should all commend him for this brilliant idea, which will bring glory to all of his people." She didn't sound like she believed it.

"We'll be the planet's largest work of art," said one of the men. "Glory to the Empire."

"Glory to the Empire," I said drily.

Lara shook her head. "Please convey our thanks to the Emperor for this opportunity. You'll be going now?"

Narrow-Jaw nodded.

"When will you be back?" I asked. "Do we have time to harvest the redwheat we've already planted?"

"Depends on when you harvest. The Emperor has given us seven more months to create the complete tapestry. As long as your fields are gold by the time we survey again . . ."

As they turned to go back to their vehicle, the small woman stepped toward Lara and clasped her hands. "Good luck too, yes," she said, as if we had made the same wish to her.

The military woman had waited and took her arm. It wasn't a gentle gesture, and I couldn't quite tell whether she was guiding a woman who couldn't see well or escorting a prisoner. "You know you can't do that," I heard her say as they walked away.

We watched them drive down the road and turn toward the Maris house.

"Ellum will be taken by surprise," I said. "Everyone's assumed only the farms on the burn line would be affected."

"I wonder if she has the same good wishes for everyone she encounters," Lara said.

"Who? What?"

She glanced toward the road, then opened her hand to reveal a handful of small seeds. "The woman with the glasses. She slipped them into my hand. Do you recognize them?"

I took the seeds from her and rolled one between my thumb and palm. Nodded. "They're from a northern plant. Lavaflower. We grew it all over the sides of mountains where nothing else took root. Why would that woman give the seeds to you?"

"She may have guessed—correctly—that you'd have withdrawn your hands if she had grabbed them."

"Okay, yes, that's true. But why lavaflower?"

"What color are its blooms?"

"Blood red, red-orange, red-gold, gold," I said. "Hence the name. It looks like rivers of lava. It's hardy as anything—it'd probably grow down here too—but it only blooms every eighteen years."

"And? You're a farmer now, Kae. How's it useful?"

I sighed and thought back. "I saw it bloom twice before I left home, once when I was a small child, and once just after I'd reached adulthood. My mother took me up into the mountains to harvest it by the armload."

"For?"

"For my father to turn the fibers into cloth. It makes lovely cloth. Smooth as a horse's summer coat. And then my mother boiled the flowers for dye. If the dye was made right, it took on all the colors of the blooms. Our Queen herself bought cloth from my family before the Emperor drove her away."

"Why would that woman give us seeds that flower red if we're not allowed to grow red?"

I shrugged. "Her own small rebellion?"

"She picked the wrong people if that's the case. We have children to look after. And we're too old to cause trouble."

"She didn't know we have children."

She gestured at the swing hanging from the tree.

Fair point. "All right. She knew we had children."

"Maybe she saw in you a fellow northerner."

Lara walked toward the house, and I followed. In the kitchen, I placed the seeds in a bowl. Looked out the window at the winter growth of our redwheat, scrubby and green still.

"I wonder," she said. "How fast does your lavaflower grow, did you say?"

"Sixty days? Ninety days? Quickly, I think. The bloom comes in the first days of summer in its first season, but then doesn't return again for eighteen years."

"And it can grow beneath the crops? Between the aisles, or beneath the wheat or the sunflowers? Would it interfere?"

"Interfere with what, love?"

"Will it choke the crops? If we introduce it here?"

"What do you have in mind?"

"We could make him a new cloak, out of your lava plant. A fine cloak with all those colors mixed in . . ."

I considered. "I think there's a serious risk it could take over, but if we planted and harvested it before we plowed the whole field under, and cleared all the individual roots by hand, we might be able to kill it again after a single season. Or—wait."

"Wait?"

I sat down at the table, closed my eyes. Tapped my fingers on my forehead.

"Love, what are you doing?"

"Math, Lara." I kept my eyes closed a minute longer, double checking my figures. Looked up, grinned. "She didn't say 'good luck too, yes'. She said 'good luck, two years.' Two years. In two years the lavaflowers in the mountains will bloom for the first time since his arrival."

"And?"

"If she's giving seeds to other northerners scattered from their homes, I think she wants everyone to plant for a bloom in two years' time, to coincide with the bloom in the mountains."

I closed my eyes, picturing the bloodstains rising everywhere on the map-portrait, spots blooming on his majestic nose, his golden hem.

Opened my eyes again to Lara's frown. "And what if he punishes those who do it? Or misses the bloom? What you're talking about is a symbolic action, like your tomatoes. If he doesn't understand the significance, it will all be for nothing."

She was right. The other idea appealed to me, but hers held promise too. "You're right, love. We'll plant the seeds now. We'll make the emperor a cloak."

The lavaflower seeds took well. By the time they bloomed, our last redwheat had grown tall enough to conceal them. I taught Ash and Sable how to harvest the stalks and flowers, as I had for my mother when I was a child. We saved the seeds in case we would need them again.

The Marises made a brocade, trading at the winter market to get silver thread and black dye. They came over often to help with the tedious process of converting fiber to textile.

We had just enough to make a cloak worthy of an Emperor. If we couldn't get him to change his plan, perhaps we could get him to change his taste in clothing. Our gifts, not only to the Emperor but to all of our neighbors as well.

The Emperor's festival fell at the beginning of autumn, in the season of peak sunflowers. We were all sick of sunflowers by then.

We curried our horses until they looked palace-kept. I put Ash and Sable to work shining the harness and sweeping the wagon. Lara wrapped the cloak in a blanket to keep it free of road dust. Tari Maris was ready to birth her baby at any moment, so she and Ellum stayed home, sending only their son Ianno with us.

For the last ten years, since he had instituted this tradition, the Emperor had arrived in a fine horse-drawn carriage, to show he was a man of the people. This time, we saw his airship tethered in a field near the festival.

"To inspect his artistry from above, no doubt," Lara said with no small trace of bitterness. The horses pulling us were grass-fat and sleek now, but we both wondered how they would survive winter without stored summer grains and hay.

"Can we go closer?" Sable asked, leaning out of the cart. "I want to see it!"

I grabbed her collar and pulled her back into her seat. "Not now. Enjoy it from this distance. We have to get in line."

We left Ianno to watch the horses and ventured into the market square, made over with garlands and banners for the Emperor's visit. The line for giving tribute was already long.

"Why aren't we leaving the cloak in the gift depository?" asked Ash. In the past, we had always left our gifts there, since we hadn't wanted or needed an audience. I'd never had any desire to meet the Emperor face to face.

"We've never made anything worthy of giving him in person before," Lara said, a far more diplomatic answer than mine would have been. Better not to give the children the idea we were ever less than happy with the Emperor, lest they turn around and say as much. When they were old enough to have discretion, we could explain. Assuming the thing we were about to do didn't get us all killed.

When we took our place in line, we let the children run off to play in the market aisles. We stood behind Shin Davi and her grandson, who were holding a basket of sunflower seeds between them. The type of gift we had given every year in the past: seeds, oils, hulled redwheat for the Emperor's winter stores.

There wasn't much point to standing in line with such a gift, unless you wanted to catch a glimpse of the Emperor himself. Or maybe it was a better gift than I thought: the grandson shifted it in his arms at one point, and I saw that the basket itself was adorned with the words "He Who Is The Land And The Land Is He." Grammar aside, it was decent flattery.

"What do you have there?" the old woman asked, leaning over me to catch a glimpse of what I had wrapped in my arms.

"A cloak, Shin Davi," Lara told her.

The day was hotter than usual for this time of year, and the insides of my elbows sweated under the blanket and cloak. I held it away from my body so I wouldn't soak it.

Another hour passed, and we reached the last straightaway. The line ended at a table of inspectors. Beyond that, the tent in which the Emperor sat, waiting to receive those who were chosen to present their tributes in person. Lara kissed me on the cheek and left me to deliver our gift on my own. That was what we had decided, that we wouldn't risk both of our lives to deliver the message. She had offered to be the one—"You aren't the most tactful person, Kae"—but I insisted on doing it myself.

One more hour, and I reached the inspectors' table.

"Name?" asked my inspector.

"Kae Bakari. I carry a gift from my family and the family Maris. We made it together."

I unfolded the blanket and shook our tribute free. A red and gold cloak, soft as a horse in summer, with colors intermingled. A red and gold cloak with silver and black brocade, colors we could never duplicate in the land. A red and gold cloak with a shape that billowed to encompass all the farms cleaved and set loose by the narrow cut of a gold-trimmed robe.

The inspector rocked back in his seat. "That's a fine garment," he said, his tone suggesting surprise. "You may deliver it to the Emperor in person."

I nodded, swallowing back my fear.

I was ushered past the table and into another, much shorter line, just outside the Emperor's tent. I took my place behind a woman carrying a thirteen-strand braided bread in the shape of a sunflower. There were only two people ahead of her, then one, and then I stood alone before the closed tent, staring at a frowning guard.

The tent flaps parted, and the guard nodded to me. Inside, the tent was both cooler and brighter than I had expected. I knelt, careful not to let the cloak touch the ground.

"Rise, and let me see what you've brought."

I rose, and lifted my eyes. The Emperor sat on a golden throne, on a dais. My first thought was how heavy that throne must be, to be carried around from town to town. Electric lights in the corners lit the space. Fan machines pushed air past him, rustling his hair beneath his crown.

The years had been kind to him. I had last seen him riding a hovercar through city streets, a glimpse long enough to take aim at him. He'd been young and haggard then, a warrior with a warrior's concerns. I still recalled the look on his face when the first tomato hit his head, fear and fury and embarrassment.

His face was softer now. The profile on his banner made him look taller and leaner than he actually was. I supposed nobody could live up to the frozen perfection of a portrait at every moment of their life, even an Emperor.

Two children sat at his feet, playing with mechanical horses that galloped on their own when released. They were about the same age

as Ash and Sable; I tried to imagine how an offhand remark by children of that age could be allowed to dictate the fates of thousands
of farmers.

I pushed the thought from my mind and unfolded the cloak
again, setting the blanket down. With my arms stretched wide, I
held it aloft. The electric lights shone through the lavaflower reds
and golds and oranges. I couldn't see past the cloak, but I heard his
intake of breath, and when the tiny horses stopped galloping, they
weren't wound again.

"Look, Father!" one of the children said. "It's like stained glass."

"It's beautiful, Father!" said the other. "You'll take it, won't you?
You should take it. It's nicer than the one you have now."

My arms shook, but I didn't dare lower them.

"Thank you," the Emperor finally said, and someone arrived to
take the cloak from me. I was left standing empty-handed. "That
is a tribute of remarkable quality. I've never seen anything like it.
I shall wear it with pride, and remember your region with favor.
Thank you."

He lifted one soft hand and flicked two fingers. A guard
appeared beside me and took my elbow.

I gathered my nerve. The cloak itself might be enough, even
without me saying anything else. It might be enough to convince
him to decree different colors the next year, allowing us to rotate our
crops and harvest enough to survive, but how could we rely on that?

"Your Royal Highness," I said. "If I may."

His hand still hung in the air in front of him, as if he'd forgotten to return it to his lap. The guard tugged at my elbow again.

"Please," I said.

The Emperor's daughter paused in winding her mechanical
horse and looked up. "Nobody ever stays—"

"—after Father does that finger thing." Her brother got to his
feet as well, looking at me like a toy that had done something unexpected. "Why are you still here?"

"I . . . I have twins too, about your age," I said. "They sometimes finish each other's sentences like you do. I'm worried they're going to starve."

"What's starve?" asked the girl.

I risked a glance at the Emperor. His hand no longer floated in midair, which I took as a good sign. I took another deep breath and began.

"This idea of turning your whole Empire into a portrait of yourself. I've seen the coastline myself, in my youth, and I think the resemblance is remarkable. But if you accept that you are the land, or the land is you, you'll have to accept the ravages of bad seasons as well as the beauty of the good ones."

He looked angry for a moment, but didn't speak. I continued.

"There will come winter, and a corner of your cloak will grow ragged. A year of drought or locusts, and your robe will look threadbare. A bad storm might change the coastline and disfigure your chin, or cause the lake of your eye to flood your entire face. And the mountains, your crown, the mountains have secrets. I come from the mountains, and I can tell you that there are things there that can't be tamed.

"This idea to carve your Empire in your image is a wonderful one"—I glanced at his children—"but wouldn't it be truly special to say that this land was briefly a portrait, and to draw maps and paintings to celebrate your likeness, but then to allow the land to do what land does, and to let farmers plant according to their needs, according to the needs of your citizens? Something fleeting is often more valuable than something lasting."

I knelt again, begging leave, then fled before he could say anything. I realized when the flap had closed behind me that I had left our blanket inside. I wasn't going back for it. The expression on his face had suggested he was considering my words; it was all I could ask.

If the cloak didn't convince the Emperor to let us return to our proper crops, in two years the lavaflowers in the mountains would bloom for the first time since he had arrived from across the sea. In two years, the mountains would run red, a bloody crown to shame him, and the surveyor's flowers would stain his robes. If he hadn't changed his mind by then, or abandoned the idea altogether, perhaps that would change it. That was the seed I had come to plant; now we just had to wait for it to take root.

Where Oaken Hearts Do Gather

<u>About "Where Oaken Hearts Do Gather"</u> (5 contributors, 5 notes, 7 comments)

→"Where Oaken Hearts Do Gather" (Roud 423, Child 313) is a traditional English folk ballad. Like many traditional songs, the lyrics are unattributed. Child transcribed twenty verses, and a twenty-first got added later (and is included here for some unknown reason—I keep writing to the Lyricsplainer mods to get someone to delete it or include it as a separate entry, but nobody responds, and all they've done is put brackets around it. Sometimes I hate this site). Most modern recordings pick and choose verses and include far fewer than the full twenty. There are several variant titles, and the characters' names shift through the various broadsides and folk and rock versions.—*BonnieLass67* (<u>11 upvotes</u>)

›The song has also been passed down as "Fair Ellen," "Ellen and William," and "Sweet William's Heart." There's a distant cousin in the ballad "Robin Hood and the Waking Wood," which changes William to Robin Hood and gives him a revenge arc; that one has always struck me as a derivative corruption, though it wasn't the first to steal someone else's narrative and give it to Robin Hood.—*BonnieLass67* (<u>7 upvotes</u>)

→It was documented in John and Alan Lomax's 1934 book *American Ballads and Folk Songs* as "While Oaken Sisters Watched," with a number of changes and Americanizations. In modern times, the ballad (or its variants) has been recorded or played live by artists as varied as Joan Baez, the Grateful Dead, the Kingston Trio, Windhollow Faire, Dolly Parton, Jack White, and Metallica. The verses each chose, and the order they chose to sing them, change the meaning of the song.—*BonnieLass67* (6 upvotes)

>Have you heard the abomination that was on Idol? Some finalist butchered it as "Where Broken Hearts Do Gather."—*HolyGreil*

>If we don't speak of that I can pretend it doesn't exist.—*BonnieLass67*

→This song, included among the famous ballads documented by Francis James Child, is an allegorical tale of a tryst between two lovers and its aftermath.—*Dynamum* (2 upvotes, 1 downvote)

>That's awfully reductive, and I'm not sure what allegory you're seeing. There's a murder and a hanging and something monstrous in the woods. Sets it apart from the average lovers' tryst.—*BarrowBoy*

>Fine. I just thought somebody should summarize it here a little, since "about the song" means more than just how many verses it has. Most people come here to discuss how to interpret a song, not where to find it in the Child Ballads' table of contents.—*Dynamum*

→Dr. Mark Rydell's 2002 article "A Forensic Analysis of 'Where

Oaken Hearts Do Gather,'" published in *Folklore*, explored the major differences and commonalities and their implications. In *The Rose and the Briar*, Wendy Lesser writes about how if a trad song leaves gaps in its story, it's because the audience was expected to know what information filled those gaps. The audience that knew this song is gone, and took the gap information with them. Rydell attempted to fill in the blanks.—*HolyGreil* (1 upvote)

>I've found my people! That's the first time somebody has ever beaten me to mentioning Rydell's work in a conversation before. I got a state grant this year to make a documentary about him and his work and his disappearance. It's going to be called *Looking for Love in All the Lost Places*. I named it after his blog. Have you read his blog? It's a deeper dive into the stuff in his article. More personal, in the way an academic article isn't supposed to be.—*HenryMartyn*

>No, only the article. Didn't know he disappeared either. I'll check it out!—*HolyGreil*

>@HenryMartyn it's been two years since your last post on this tune. I keep hoping to get news about your documentary.—*HolyGreil*

Listen to the Kingston Trio: "Where Oaken Hearts Do Gather"

Listen to Joan Baez: "Where Oaken Hearts Do Gather"

Listen to Windhollow Faire: "Where Oaken Hearts Do Gather"

Listen to Steeleye Span: "Where Oaken Hearts Do Gather"

Listen to the Grateful Dead: "Where Oaken Hearts Do Gather"

Listen to Metallica: "Where Oaken Hearts Do Gather"

Listen to Moby K. Dick: "Where Oaken Hearts Do Gather"

Listen to Jack White: "Where Oaken Hearts Do Gather"

Listen to the Decemberists: "Where Oaken Hearts Do Gather"

Listen to Cyrus Matheson: "Where Broken Hearts Do Gather" [FLAGGED by BonnieLass67][UNFLAGGED by Lyric-Splainer ModeratorBot]

Full Lyrics for "Where Oaken Hearts Do Gather" (traditional) (7 contributors, 95 notes, 68 comments, 19 reactions) (see disambiguation for other versions)

(see related songs)

One[1] autumn[2,3] as the wind blew cold

and stripped red leaves[4] from branches

Fair[5] Ellen[6] ran to meet her love

Where oaken hearts do gather[7,8]

[1] Some versions begin "In autumn . . ." One early broadside notably began with "each autumn."—*BonnieLass67*

[2] Like the more famous "Barbara Allen," this ballad begins by setting the season. In "Barbara Allen," of course, the season is spring, the season of new love.—*HolyGreil*

[3] "Barbara Allen's" "merry month of May/when green buds all were swelling" is also echoed in the 1880 hit "The Fountain in the Park," also known as "While Strolling in the Park":

"I was strolling in the park one day/in the merry merry month of May/I was taken by surprise by a pair of roguish eyes/in a moment my poor heart was stole away." I wouldn't mention that except for the literal heart getting stolen away Temple-of-Doom-style in this song.—*Dynamum*

[4] trees that have red leaves in autumn include black cherry, flowering dogwood, hornbeam, sourwood, red oak, white oak, winged sumac, sweet gum, and red maple. it's reasonable to assume this is referring to red or white oak trees given the title.—*HangThaDJ*

>*White and red oak aren't native to Britain.—BarrowBoy*

> *What if it was originally "rowan hearts" not oaken hearts? Rowan berries could leave a red carpet, plus there's all that great mythology around rowan trees.—Dynamum*

>*A) there's no record of a rowan version (check me if I'm wrong, @BonnieLass67, you seem to be the version expert) B) rowan leaves turn more yellow than red, C) the line says red leaves, not berries.—BarrowBoy*

[5] It's interesting that the woman in the song is referred to in almost all versions as "fair," despite her actions.—*Rhiannononymous*

> *She could just be fair as in blond?—Dynamum*

—*BarrowBoy marked this as a stretch*—

[6] Alternate versions feature the usual gang of "Maggie," "Polly," "Molly," "Jenny," and "Peggy," etc. as seen in countless other songs, and also "Elswyth," which I haven't seen in other ballads. I've looked to see if there's a version of the song with willow trees, given the derivation of that name, but haven't found one.—*BonnieLass67*

[7] the woods, presumably.—*HangThaDJ*

[8] In his 2002 paper, "A Forensic Analysis of 'Where Oaken Hearts Do Gather,'" and subsequently in his blog, the University of Pennsylvania professor Dr. Mark Rydell attempted to track down the exact provenance of the ballad. He said that not every ballad can be traced to a specific incident or location, but this one had a couple of markers that made him think it was possible. He pointed out that of the two common British species, English oak tree leaves turn coppery brown, not red, in autumn, and sessile oak leaves turn yellow. While it's true that the song doesn't specifically say the red leaves are from oaks, it's the only tree mentioned specifically, and it's right in the oldest known name of the song, so presumably it means oak trees when it says oak trees. North American oaks might more specifically meet the red leaf missive, Rydell pointed out. In that case, the song would have had to make its way to British lore from America, when songs moved more commonly in the other direction, or else somebody would have to have brought North American trees to Britain early enough that they'd be mature for this song. (Why mature? Nobody pictures skinny little saplings when they're talking about oak trees. And there's a "gnarled and knotted ancient" in a later verse.) In his initial research, Rydell attempted unsuccessfully to locate a village with a bridge and a steep embankment and a stand of imported oak trees somewhere nearby. Later, after consultation with a botanist, Rydell came to understand that American oaks planted in Britain don't necessarily have the same bright color there that they have in their native country; anthocyanin, the main red pigment, needs bright, crisp autumn days to kick into high gear. It just isn't the same in overcast, damp climates. He concluded that he would not be able to

use tree species alone to trace the ballad, but he still had other clues to pursue.—*HenryMartyn*

—BonnieLass67 marked this as cool stuff—

Sweet William robbed the butcher's son[9,10,11,12]

He turned her heart to fancy

And bade her meet him 'neath the[13,14] bridge[15,16]

Where oaken hearts do gather

[9] This line sets William up as a robber, thus deserving of his fate, and the next line makes you think that Ellen is as fair and innocent as the first stanza implies.—*Rhiannononymous*

[10] The Kingston Trio's version changes this to "Sweet William WAS the butcher's son/ WHO turned her heart to fancy."—*BonnieLass67*

[11] Sweet William was supporters' nickname for Prince William, Duke of Cumberland, known as Butcher Cumberland to his Tory enemies! He died relatively young, with no children. Possible link?—*Dynamum*

—BonnieLass67 marked this as a stretch—

—BarrowBoy marked this as a stretch—

> *There's absolutely nothing to connect this with Prince William, Duke of Cumberland. You're barking up the wrong oak tree.—BarrowBoy*

[12] Dr. Mark Rydell, in attempting to pinpoint the origin of the song, posited a theory that the line should actually read "Sweet William, Robert Butcher's son."—*HenryMartyn*

> there was a robert butcher born in liverpool who became an australian politician! he had three sons and five daughters, but he was probably born too late to be referenced in this ballad.—HangThaDJ

> Yeah, Rydell dismissed him. There's nothing connecting this song's path with Australia. It didn't need to be a famous Robert Butcher, just one who was locally famous enough to be worth putting in the song, so Rydell tried looking for any Robert Butcher whose son named William might have died under unusual circumstances. Rydell found what he was looking for: an aging solicitor named Robert Butcher, living in a village called Gall, had written a strangely passionate pro-hanging letter in the 1770s, right around the time that its prohibition became a popular cause, saying "there are circumstances for which, tragically, hanging is the only proportionate response." Not "crimes" but "circumstances." Rydell said in his blog that he was going to England to check Gall out for himself. He made one more post from something called an internet café—this was pre-smartphone, so I guess that was the only place he could get online?— anyway, one more short update and then he never posted again. (Did I mention I'm making a documentary about him? I'm planning on visiting Gall this October. I've got an appointment lined up with the woman who runs their town historical society too. Hopefully I can get some answers.)—HenryMartyn

> What a fascinating story! Your documentary should be really interesting.—HolyGreil

>You should check out Rydell's blog Looking For Love in All the Lost Places too— it's like a folksier, less academic version of his research. You can still find it on the wayback machine even though he and his host site are both long gone.—HenryMartyn

> did this robt butcher have a son who was hanged? what was he hanged for?—HangThaDJ

>I've messaged with the town historian, like I said, Jenny Kirk. She said Butcher's

letter is in their museum. She warned me that it's just a one-room museum-and-gift-shop, because nothing much ever happened there, but because of that, its publication in London was one of the bigger things that happened to anyone from Gall. He had four sons, one of whom was named William. His William did die by hanging, but there's no mention anywhere of a crime or a trial. I can see why Rydell thought this was a good lead.—HenryMartyn

>*Did you ask her if Rydell ever got there?—HolyGreil*

>*First thing I asked! She said that would've been back when she was a kid, and they don't keep a visitor log.—HenryMartyn*

>*i always think of historical society ladies as old biddies.—HangThaDJ*

>*Can confirm she is definitely not an old biddy.—HenryMartyn*

[13] Variously, "the bridge," and "Toll Bridge," in the British versions. "Tall Bridge" in one early American version, "Fall's Bridge" in Dolly Parton's. Unclear whether "Fall's Bridge" means a bridge belonging to someone named Falls, or a more poetic version involving autumn.—*BonnieLass67*

[14] If it's a toll bridge, maybe the toll is what William pays in the end.—*Rhiannononymous*

—*BarrowBoy marked this as a stretch*—

[15] The fact that William asked her to meet him under the bridge goes well with the robber line, since we're told he's sweet but then immediately told that he's both a robber and someone who would lure a young woman under a bridge. Maybe it's an ironic sweet, like an ugly mobster called Prettyboy or something.—*Rhiannononymous*

[16] Guys! I'm here! In Gall! It has almost everything mentioned in the song: a village, a woods, a stone bridge with a steep

embankment. No red carpet of leaves, even though it's October, but everything else seems to check out.—*HenryMartyn*

—*HolyGreil marked this as cool stuff*—

"Don't go," said Ellen's sisters two.[17,18,19,20]

"There's no good that can follow

A man met moonlit 'neath the bridge[21]

Where oaken hearts do gather"[22]

[17] the sisters function as a sort of greek chorus here.—*HangThaDJ*

—*BonnieLass67 marked this as a stretch*—

[18] Ellen and her sisters represent the three Fates.—*Dynamum*

—*BarrowBoy marked this as a stretch*—

[19] I've always thought the sisters were just sisters, trying to warn Ellen, like a good sister would. There are lots of songs where family tries to warn a woman that her man is no good.—*Rhiannononymous*

[20] It's worth noting again that the American version documented by the Lomaxes was "While Oaken Sisters Watched."—*BonnieLass67*

[21] Okay, but if you take the whole verse as the warning, "There's no good that can follow a man met moonlit 'neath the bridge," it can either be a warning telling Ellen not to go because there's danger for her, or it could be a warning that there's going to be trouble for <u>him</u>, in which case they might also be saying Ellen herself is no good for William.

They seem to know an awful lot about this very specific thing—not just that no good can follow meeting a man at night under a bridge, but also specifically meeting a man at night under that particular bridge, where oaken hearts do gather.—*Rhiannononymous*

> *Or oaken sisters watch—BonnieLass67*

[22] The quotation marks are obviously not part of the song as passed down orally, but they're in all the sheet music and broadsides I've ever seen. In this stanza the chorus really does sound like it's part of a quote from the sisters, like they know this place by its reputation.—*BonnieLass67*

Fair Ellen turned her eyes from them

For she had long decided[23]

To meet him while the village slept[24,25]

Where oaken hearts do gather

[23] This plays like you would expect in this kind of song. Young woman rejects advice from her wise elders and chooses love, and then discovers too late that her family was right and she's set herself up for tragedy. This ballad later twists that expectation. (Though that leads to the question of why her sisters don't want this, if they don't mean the usual 'it will lead you astray.')—*Rhiannononymous*

[24] I used to think this meant that the village itself slept where oaken hearts do gather.—*Dynamum*

> *That's just stupid.—BarrowBoy*

>*Hey! I said "used to." And anyway, there were trees there before people, probably, so technically I'm right either way.—Dynamum*

[25] The village that Rydell located, Gall, was adjacent to a small, dense woodland that would have been larger back then. The main road went north/south, with south heading through the woods and over an old stone bridge.—*HenryMartyn*

>*I'm here now! Bus took ages. Gall was bypassed by the major motorways, so the village is pretty isolated. But that means the woods are still woods! It's a bit of a walk to the bridge, and very dark at night, but doable. I'll admit I was hoping there'd be graffiti carved into the bridge saying "William was here" or "El and Will" or something.—HenryMartyn*

Fair Ellen's steps did lightly fall

On autumn's red-stained blanket[26,27,28]

As off she ran to meet her love[29]

Where oaken hearts do gather

[26] Could be blood!—*Dynamum*

[27] This brings us around to what was previewed at the beginning—there the leaves were being stripped by autumn wind, here they're already on the ground, but she's off to meet her guy.—*Rhiannononymous*

[28] Hear me out: if you go with the "in autumn" opening variant that the Dead used instead of "one autumn," this is something that happens every year. The leaves turn red, and off sweet Ellen goes again. That would explain the different-but-repeated nature of the opening and this stanza. That's what always happens; what happens

to William specifically is what happens **this** time.—*HolyGreil*

—HenryMartyn marked this as cool stuff—

[29] Her light steps and "her love" here tell us that from the narrator's perspective she is in love and has no intent to deceive. That makes what happens all the more surprising to the listener.—*Rhiannononymous*

Young William stood in moonlight's glow

When Ellen came[30] upon him

And kissed him as she stole his heart[31]

Where oaken hearts do gather

[30] Some versions use "fell upon him" instead of "came upon him" but that definitely changes the nature of the meeting.—*BonnieLass67*

[31] Still playing with expectations here. We expect "stole his heart" as in fell in love, but the next stanzas makes it grossly literal.—*Rhiannononymous*

She begged sweet Will to show her how[32]

He differed from the others[33]

And prove to her his love was true[34]

Where oaken hearts do gather

[32] This verse is placed interestingly since if the previous one is to

be believed, she's already fallen on him/come to him and stolen his heart, literally or figuratively. Why this demand?—*Rhiannononymous*

>*Some versions do move this verse earlier. Some move it to before the previous verse (usually matched with "fell upon him" instead of "came upon him" since in that case they've already arrived at the same place). The other variant places it third, just after the invitation to the bridge, as if it's her response.*—*BonnieLass67*

> *Huh! Either of those would make more sense, since it seems like otherwise this verse interrupts action with a plea. She's making the demand after she's already set things in motion. Unless they had already talked it over, and this is her hoping that he does what he's promised.*—*Rhiannononymous*

[33] This implies that this has happened before. It's sort of melancholy. Men . . .—*Dynamum*

[34] There's no answer given to her request that he prove himself, or else the verse that follows is the test where he's supposed to prove himself.—*Rhiannononymous*

His beating heart[35] she placed inside[36]

A[37] gnarled and knotted ancient[38]

to quicken[39] come the springtime thaw[40]

Where oaken hearts do gather

[35] There's really no figurative way to take this. And ew, why is it still beating?—*Dynamum*

[36] ironic that she places the heart so delicately after ripping it out of his chest.—*HangThaDJ*

[37] Some early variants say "*her* gnarled and knotted

ancient."—*BonnieLass67*

[38] Gnarled and knotted ancient what? That's a weird description.—*Dynamum*

> *"A gnarled and knotted ancient"* = *presumably a very old tree.*—*Rhiannononymous*

>*Hey @HenryMartyn, did you or Rydell find a tree like this?*—*HolyGreil*

>*All the trees I've seen are new growth.*—*HenryMartyn*

[39] Maybe she thinks his heart in the tree will beat faster when she visits—*Dynamum*

—*BarrowBoy marked this as a stretch*—

[40] I think this is the other meaning of "quicken," like "to enter into a phase of active growth and development" per dictionary (example is seeds quickening in soil).—*BarrowBoy*

> *But then why place it in an old tree instead of in the ground?*—*Dynamum*

> *How would I know?*—*BarrowBoy*

And in his chest she built with care[41]

A nest of twigs and leaf-fall[42]

An acorn[43,44] cushioned there to grow

Where oaken hearts do gather

[41] Again, it goes out of its way to say how much care she took with this part of the operation.—*Dynamum*

[42] In his blog, Dr. Rydell said, "The true nature of the exchange

made by Ellen and seemingly agreed to by William is perhaps the greatest mystery remaining in this ballad." Jenny Kirk is helping me do research into Gall's local folklore. She was telling the truth that their museum is crap, but she's great.—*HenryMartyn*

[43] Maybe this acorn becomes the sapling at his grave?—*Dynamum*

[44] fun fact: only one in ten thousand acorns becomes an oak tree.—*HangThaDJ*

And turned he then to look at her

With eyes still seeking answers[45,46]

She kissed him twice[47] and left him there[48]

Where oaken hearts do gather

[45] I think this line goes out of its way to make clear that he's not vegetative at this point, pardon the pun. He's aware enough to ask questions, though you'd think he would have looked at her before now, and asked questions before now, like "Hey, do you mind putting my heart back? I'm using that."—*Rhiannononymous*

[46] Maybe he was under some kind of spell?—*Dynamum*

—*BarrowBoy marked this as a stretch*—

> *Stop marking me down! A few lines later he has literally no voice, so a spell isn't unreasonable. He's trying to use his eyes to ask questions.*—*Dynamum*

>*@BarrowBoy all you ever do is mark stretches and shoot down other people's theories without ever offering any yourself. Do you care about this ballad at all?*—*Dynamum*

>*I don't even like this song. The melody's okay, but it needs a*

bridge.—*BarrowBoy*

>*technically it has a bridge. old, made of stone . . .*—*HangThaDJ*

>*Argh. If you don't like the song, why are you here?*—*Dynamum*

>*For those sweet sweet LyricSplainer level badges. U?*—*BarrowBoy*

>*I love the song, but also it's fascinating! A lot of songs are straightforward, but I love the ones like this that develop a sort of detective team. We've got BonnieLass with all the background/history stuff, and Henry the dashing young field work expert, and DJ with random facts and Greil with musicology and Rhiannononymous on language details.*—*Dynamum*

>*What does that make you? Comic relief?*—*BarrowBoy*

>*Better than you, the one everyone hates but has to put up with.*—*Dynamum*

>*If @HenryMartyn's our field researcher, can I point out that he's stopped responding? His last response here was on the last verse, over a year ago, and he hasn't posted on any other songs either. I keep checking in hoping he'll tell us more about his film. I wish I knew his real name.*—*HolyGreil*

>*Hmm. I searched "state arts grant" and "Mark Rydell" and "Looking For Love in All the Lost Places" and got a hit in Pennsylvania. Looks like he's a Henry from a city called Williamsport (William's Port? coincidence?) who was a senior at the University of Pennsylvania when he got the grant. I'm not going to post his actual surname here. It seems rude.*—*Dynamum*

>*Look at you with the real detective work! Thanks for the lead. Hmm. He was part of the grant announcement, but not the end of year presentation.*—*HolyGreil*

[47] Is twice significant? She'd already kissed him once (as she stole his heart) but it's unclear if this is a second kiss, or two more kisses.—*Rhiannononymous*

> *Maybe the second kiss takes his voice.*—*Dynamum*

> *It's true that he's already using his eyes to ask.*—*HolyGreil*

> *I said he was under a spell and got mocked for it! It's not like this all has to have exact basis in truth. Maybe they just like kissing.*—*Dynamum*

[48] Where did she go? This song never quite makes her and her sisters seem like part of the village.—*Rhiannononymous*

Young William to the village went

His feet still knew the pathways[49]

He knew he'd left his years[50,51] behind[52]

Where oaken hearts do gather

[49] He'd made this trip so many times he knew it automatically. (I almost said "by heart")—*Dynamum*

[50] "His years" = the rest of his days? Living on borrowed time now?—*Rhiannononymous*

[51] Some variants say "his fears" instead of his years; others say he left "something."—*BonnieLass67*

[52] this does make it seem like some kind of spell, like he's stumbling back without knowing what he's doing or what has happened.—*HangThaDJ*

> *THANK YOU. I TOLD YOU.*—*Dynamum*

["Wake up," he cried, though no one heard[53,54,55]

"And find the wicked woman[56,57]

Who stole my life and voice away

Where oaken hearts do gather"]

[53] It doesn't say anything about her taking his voice before this.—*BarrowBoy*

[54] @Moderator can we delete this verse or add it at the bottom? It's only in a handful of the twentieth century versions and nothing earlier. Not part of the original ballad.—*BonnieLass67*

—*Lyricsplainer ModeratorBot has received this comment and will bring it to a moderator's attention*—

[55] It changes a lot, doesn't it? "Wicked woman" sounds like it was written by someone else entirely. Without this verse, William just goes along with what's happening.—*Rhiannononymous*

[56] Interesting that he doesn't know where to find her. There's no verse where the villagers show up at her house, either, even when they spring into action.—*Rhiannononymous*

[57] i feel bad for him, but he's kind of a jerk here, trying to shout in the town square in the middle of the night or whatever for everyone to come listen to his problems. i mean, not that any of this is his fault, except he did tell a woman to meet him under the bridge without any regard for the trouble he could get her in. and it does seem like he consented to her test?—*HangThaDJ*

And when the village came to him[58]

He could[59] not tell his story

Or say what fate befell their son[60]

Where oaken hearts do gather

[58] Does anyone else think it's strange that "the village came to him"? Where was he? I mean, I guess it means the villagers, not the village, and they came to him at his house?—*Dynamum*

[59] "Would not" instead of "could not" in some early variations.—*BonnieLass67*

> *Ha! Would not = wood knot! Get it?—Dynamum*

—*BarrowBoy marked this as a stretch*—

>*@Dynamum I like that pun no matter if it's a stretch. Don't let him get you down.—Rhiannononymous*

[60] This collective "their son" is fascinating considering what they do next. This song has some messed up families, y'all.—*Rhiannononymous*

>*Wait, it's collective? Like "the son of the village?" I thought it meant "their son" like William and Ellen's son!—Dynamum*

> *I never thought of that, but that works too! Especially with the whole quickening thing!*

We talked about quickening a seed, but not quickening a womb.—Rhiannononymous

—*Rhiannonymous marked this as cool stuff*—

—*BonnieLass67 marked this as cool stuff*—

—*HangThaDJ marked this as cool stuff*—

They looked at him with mournful eyes[61]

Then listened for his heartbeat[62,63,64]

Then hung him from the gallows pole[65]

Where oaken hearts do gather[66]

[61] The mournful eyes have always made me think they've seen this before.—*Dynamum*

[62] It's unclear whether they listened for his heartbeat because they'd seen something like this before that his tale reminded them of, or because he looks unwell.—*Rhiannononymous*

[63] And, y'know, he wasn't speaking—*BarrowBoy*

[64] Did people know about heartbeats by the time this song was written?—*Dynamum*

> *OMG have you heard of Wikipedia?—BarrowBoy*

[65] This has always horrified me, that they just went and hung him. I guess it's understandable if they were freaked out that he didn't have a heartbeat, but still . . .—*Dynamum*

[66] Out of all the stanzas, this is the one that makes the least sense with "where oaken hearts do gather" as opposed to "while oaken sisters watch."—*BonnieLass67*

> *Yeah, the town gallows pole was likely not in the same place where oaken hearts do gather, unless you count that a gallows made of oak might contain oaken hearts, whatever they are.—Rhiannononymous*

> *As you might guess, Gall took down their gallows pole like two hundred years ago.—HenryMartyn*

And in the woods[67] fair Ellen wept[68]

For she had truly loved him[69]

And tried to claim[70] him in her way[71,72]

Where oaken hearts do gather

[67] It's interesting that she's in the woods again here, since she had left him there? Didn't she go home?—*Dynamum*

[68] How is she still being called fair?—*BarrowBoy*

[69] It's interesting that the song tells us this, since otherwise you'd think she's monstrous. I mean, her actions are still monstrous, but somehow it's better if they're done out of love?—*Rhiannononymous*

[70] Some versions say "keep" instead of claim.—*BonnieLass67*

[71] This "in her way" does a lot of work.—*Rhiannononymous*

[72] Some versions say "and hoped he'd prove his love to her," which would harken back to whatever proof she was demanding of him earlier.—*BonnieLass67*

And Ellen's sisters bowed their heads[73]

"There's no good that can follow

A man met moonlight 'neath the bridge

Where oaken hearts do gather"

[73] greek chorus back for an encore of their greatest hit, "i told you so."—*HangThaDJ*

The villagers with torches went[74,75]

To rid their woods of danger[76,77]

There to avenge the boy they'd hung[78]

Where oaken hearts do gather

[74] This verse and the two above it and one below it are often sung in a different order.—*BonnieLass67*

[75] i'm anti-villagers with torches and pitchforks generally. —*HangThaDJ*

[76] They're going to burn the oak trees. William must have given good directions before they hung him, if they think they know which specific trees to burn.—*Rhiannononymous*

> *Spoiler: for real, they chopped and burned ALL the oak trees they could find. Jenny's older sisters say it was barbarous, and I've seen the result myself. Everything is new growth from the past forty years since they stopped that practice, but you can see the damage done.—HenryMartyn*

[77] I wonder what the actual danger is that they think they're protecting against. Have they had other men stolen this way? I guess if you let it happen once, it could happen more . . .—*Dynamum*

—*BarrowBoy marked this as a stretch*—

> *Argh Go stretch someone else. I'm just saying we've all got our eyes on Ellen, but what do her sisters do all day other than watch? And @HenryMartyn, what do their town records say about stolen people?—Dynamum*

>*Jenny says they lost all their old birth and death records in a fire they lost control of.—HenryMartyn*

[78] so they felt like they had to hang poor william, but then they go out and avenge him for the wrong ellen did him? there's some misdirected anger here.—*HangThaDJ*

But 'neath the bridge they saw no trace[79]

Nor down the steep embankment[80]

And none could ever find the place[81]

Where oaken hearts do gather[82]

[79] Beneath the bridge they saw no trees or they couldn't find Ellen? It's unclear.—*Rhiannononymous*

[80] The steep embankment was another specific geographic clue that Dr. Rydell had hoped to find.—*HenryMartyn*

>*Can confirm: it's here! The bridge goes over what's now a sort of dry gully, but the banks are steep. And, cool thing! I don't know whether it's the stone or the moss or some mineral or what, but I guess something's leaching into the ground here that's tinting the leaves red near the bridge. I wonder if Dr. Rydell ever got to see this.*—*HenryMartyn*

[81] The only rhyme in the whole ballad, for what it's worth.—*Rhiannononymous*

>*Some early variants have the third line as "and none could find poor William's heart." It's possible that the line was original and this change came later, since it's odd to have a single rhyming line.*—*BonnieLass67*

>*If they couldn't find William's heart, does that mean there was one old tree that the villagers didn't manage to find?*—*Dynamum*

>*I don't think @HenryMartyn can search the whole forest.*—*BarrowBoy*

>*fun fact! a forest has a traditional legal definition as land owned by the sovereign and set aside as a hunting ground.*—*HangThaDJ*

>*He can't search the whole woods, then.*—*BarrowBoy*

[82] I don't know why I'm only thinking of this like fifteen verses in, but if you frame a song around oaks gathering, isn't the opposite of that to disperse? Maybe they couldn't find them because they sometimes go elsewhere. Maybe this whole song exists to tell you what to do if this particular thing starts happening to the oaks near you. That could be why it's tall bridge and fall's bridge etc too, and different names=different aliases. Maybe there's a rotation and this town tried harder to get the warning out and protect themselves.—*Dynamum*

—*BarrowBoy marked this as a stretch*—

Long winter passed then came the thaw[83,84]

That set springtime a-budding

A sapling grew from William's grave[85]

Where oaken hearts do gather

[83] The Dead turned this verse to major instead of minor.—*HolyGreil*

[84] The Kingston Trio ended with this verse.—*BonnieLass67*

[85] Are we not even going to talk about this sapling thing?—*Dynamum*

>*I found a grave that I think is William Butcher's, though the stone is very worn and it's hard to tell. There's no tree, but I took the next verse to mean that the sapling that grew at the grave was cut down too.*—*HenryMartyn*

And every spring[86] the villagers

To the woods bring torch and axe

To cut short every sapling grown[87,88]

Where oaken hearts do gather

[86] And this verse holds Dr. Rydell's last two big clues! "Every spring" suggested that they might have some sort of village tradition that was still passed down, even if they didn't know why anymore. On his blog he said the village he found, Gall, had an annual spring festival with a parade and bonfire.—*HenryMartyn*

[87] Rydell had speculated that the village he was looking for would be near a woods full of mature oaks (keeping in mind that there are plenty of places where woods have been cut back over the centuries, so it wasn't necessarily there to find at all; he looked at places that had been forested in earlier times as well). Then he realized what this verse implied. Instead of looking for a woods full of oaks, he wanted to go looking for a woods that was, unusually, missing its oaks, under the assumption that the village had kept cutting them down. So now I can personally confirm the woods near Gall is full of old hornbeams and ash trees and the like, but almost no oaks at all. The oaks that are here are younger, which matches up with recent changes to the village's festival. It used to involve cutting down all the oaks at the end of the spring and burning them in a bonfire, but conservationists argued that was wasteful and poor management, and they stopped doing it in the 1970s. I got here too late for this year's fest, but apparently now they just do a symbolic burning of a single tree they've chopped down for the purpose.—*HenryMartyn*

—*BonnieLass67 marked this as cool stuff*—

[88] Interesting that this accounts for the saplings in the woods,

but not the one at William's grave. Did they cut that one down or leave it?—*Rhiannononymous*

>I was asking about that sapling too!—*Dynamum*

>There's one broadside that includes a verse that may answer your question. "And when that day the villagers/uprooted William's sapling/a keening cry was heard by all/where oaken hearts do gather"—*BonnieLass67*

>Why wasn't that one generally included? That's great.—*Rhiannononymous*

> Child may not have liked the sourcing. In that one version, it replaced the big Revenge On the Trees verse, which was definitely original.—*BonnieLass67*

Still sometimes[89] when the wind blow cold

And strips red leaves[90] from branches

Fair Ellen takes[91] another love[92]

Where oaken hearts do gather[93]

[89] Some early versions say "somewhere" instead of "sometimes." Somewhere doesn't make as much sense, since presumably the where is known, even if the trees weren't found.—*BonnieLass67*

> *That "somewhere" was something Dr. Rydell speculated about in his final blog post. That post was published widely after his disappearance and derided as sentimental and unmoored from fact by many of the same people who had praised his original forensic work. He had worked so hard to find this village, only to start musing about whether a stray "somewhere" might mean this had happened in more than one place. It undercut everything except the song's extensive travels.—HenryMartyn*

> *You haven't told us anything about his disappearance! What's up with that?—HolyGreil*

>*After that last post saying he'd landed in London and was heading to Gall, he stopped posting and all his known emails bounced. He never returned to his professorship. Nobody here remembers him, and there's nothing in the police records (I was trying to be thorough). Unsolved mystery.—HenryMartyn*

⁹⁰ I'd just like to point out you've discussed stealing voices and oaken hearts but you'll only accept accurate botanical explanations for the red leaves. Not every line has to be perfectly based in truth. Magic? A portent? Some weather pattern that changes the amount of anthocyanin in certain years? A poetically resonant image? (@BarrowBoy, I'm going to beat you to the punch.)—*Dynamum*

—Dynamum marked this as a stretch—

⁹¹ I love the present tense in this verse, like it's still going on. And the multiple meanings of "take" here: take a lover, take a life, or the whole sentence "takes another love where oaken hearts do gather" like she's bringing him home to meet the family.—*Rhiannononymous*

⁹² And this reminder again from a narrator that we have no reason to disbelieve, saying that it's a love she takes, not a victim.—*Rhiannononymous*

⁹³ In his last blog post, Rydell wrote, "One of the strange things about this ballad is that we're never quite sure what kind of story it is. Is it a warning about monstrous trees or monstrous lovers? A cautionary tale about forest management? Are we meant to laud the villagers as heroic for their actions? The Gall festival would suggest so, but then why is Ellen portrayed so ambiguously? Maybe we are meant to sing it as the love story of sweet William and fair Ellen. If you ignore the incongruous 'wicked woman' verse, neither lover betrays the other's expectations, and it's only because of the villagers that their story turns tragic."—*HenryMartyn*

>*Having been here a while and listened to Jenny and her sisters, I've come to think it's a little of all the above. Maybe Rydell is right that it's a love story with a message that love involves give and take, and some ask for more than others. That's not always such a bad thing, if you're willing to give.*—*HenryMartyn*

>*@HenryMartyn can you ask your friend Jenny if there are any old oaks that escaped the festival? Like in the "none could ever find the place/none could find poor William's heart" verse?*—*Dynamum*

>*Thanks for that suggestion! Jenny says she thinks she knows of one. We're taking another walk in the woods tonight. I'm still looking for the right ending for my film, but I think I'm close. It feels funny to be searching for traces of Rydell where he was searching for traces of truth in this ballad, like we're all chasing each other. Anyway, thanks for your continued help on this, friends. If nothing else, maybe we're part of the cycle, bringing an old song to new listeners.*—*HenryMartyn*

Science Facts!

We all made it down the mountain. That's the first thing to tell, because otherwise you'll jump to certain conclusions. You'll think you know our story: that we went feral, turned on each other. The prurient details you add will depend on the type of media you devour, on your desire for human triumph or nature's retribution, on your own base assumptions about what must have happened if this doesn't start with telling you eight of us went into the woods, and eight came out.

So here's what happened: It was five AM, and we were loading the van for the trip, and everyone was some combination of under-slept and undercaffeinated and underfed, because our dream team counselors Killerwhale and Godzilla, Killa and 'Zilla, had promised we'd snack on the road. Then 'Zilla loaded the last pack into the van, and closed the back door, and stepped back into a hole, and snapped her ankle. We heard it go, a sound like a dry twig cracking underfoot, immediately followed by "Fudge." Godzilla was such a consummate camp professional she didn't even swear in front of her campers in this situation.

Commotion ensued. Killa radioed to wake the nurse and the camp director, and the nurse called an ambulance, and then Killa took six up-too-early twelve-year-olds back over to the dining hall where we'd slept the night before since you don't get a cabin unit when you're only at camp a single night before heading out on your trip. The kitchen staff were the only other ones awake, but they were sympathetic to our cause and plated us scrambled eggs and toast and oatmeal from enormous pots while we waited to hear the fate of our trip, and even let those of us who wanted it have some of their secret stash of good kitchen-staff coffee. A couple of us moaned about how much we'd been looking forward to this trip, and the others just looked quietly disappointed. Killerwhale tried to keep everyone distracted, first with going over plans for the week, and then with a game she called Science Facts.

"How are science facts a game?" asked Lucia. "They're just facts."

"Here's how the game part works," Killa said. "Your fact has to be connected to the previous fact in some way, like how in a card game you can match the suit or the number. You get extra points for weird things, and extra points for things I don't know."

"How can you tell if we're telling the truth?" That was Justina.

Killa pulled her phone out of her pocket. "Honor system. I'm allowed to look it up and verify at any point, but there are a million games where you invent answers, and this is not those games. I'll go first: female elephants in Mozambique are evolving to have no tusks."

"I thought evolution was a really long-term thing?"

"It's a response to poaching, I think. If the elephants with tusks are killed, the tuskless ones are the ones around to have babies."

"Good for them," said Andrea. "So, the next fact has to do with elephants or tusks?"

Katie counted off on her fingers. "Or evolution, or Mozambique, or female animals, or babies, or poaching."

Killa nodded in approval and the game began. Lucia offered up the fact that baby porcupines are called porcupettes, and then Justina said baby hedgehogs are called hoglets, and Nicky said hedgehogs are immune to some poisonous plants, so they chew them and then lick poison-filled saliva onto their spines, and anything that tries to eat them gets an even worse surprise than the spines alone. From there the game devolved into a semantic argument about poisonous versus toxic, until the camp director finally made it to the dining hall to brief us.

The sun had started its rise by then, though the dining hall's large west-facing windows were still night-black. The camp director looked weary and stressed, which was pretty much her usual state. We were convinced the trip was doomed, since Killa wouldn't be allowed to take us on her own, even though she'd been looking forward to it as much as we had, she'd said so. She'd been a trips counselor for four years now, and this particular backpacking trip was always the highlight of her summer.

The director walked over to the hot drinks station and dispensed a cup of carafe coffee into a travel mug, then made a face like it was left over from the night before, which it probably was, since nobody from the kitchen had come out to change it yet. She took a few sips before walking over to us. "Thanks for your patience, girls. Godzilla made it to the hospital. She's waiting on x-rays but they think it's a clean break."

Katie and Andrea, who had been on last year's canoe camping trip with Zilla, made relieved sounds.

"And I have good news for you," she continued. "We found someone else to go in her place, so your trip can still happen."

Killa tried to catch her eye, clearly surprised. She looked away. "There's no dedicated drama program this week, so Diva was scheduled as a third counselor on junior arts and crafts. She said she'd be willing to go."

"Crap," Killa said. We looked at her, and she tried to save herself. "I mean 'crepuscular.' That means 'related to twilight,' but I like twilight, so I use it to mean 'great.'"

"Crepuscular!" said Justina with enthusiasm.

The camp director sipped her coffee, winced, and continued. "Godzilla said Diva could use her gear, so she's down at the van right now repacking 'Zilla's pack with her own clothes. You should be able to leave soon."

"Crepuscular!" Katie and Andrea said. Andrea might have said "Crap-pustular," which was closer to Killa's opinion.

She turned to us. "Why don't you all use the bathroom one more time before we hit the road? You have my special permission to use the indoor instead of the outhouse." The indoor was usually reserved for counselors.

We headed toward the foyer, and Killa turned to her boss. She wasn't quiet. "You couldn't find anyone else?"

She shook her head. "I'm sorry. I know you two don't get along."

"Has she ever camped a night in her life? She chose the nickname 'Diva.' She runs the drama tent." Killa could go on. Diva had only applied to work there because she was between apartments. She didn't like kids. She was a clean freak who avoided touching the costumes in her own drama tent. She disappeared at the end of every week when it was time to clean. Saying any of that also served as an indictment of the director for hiring her, though, so Killa stopped.

"Okay, so you want me to cancel the trip? Do you want to tell those girls? It's Diva or nothing. No trip. Disappointment City. And who knows if their parents are around to take them back, or went away themselves. Not to mention we can't afford refunds on an entire program; this is the minimum damage option. Please say you can deal?"

A week with the counselor she hated most. A week managing someone who probably needed more maintenance than any of the campers. Or no trip, and knowing she was the one who had disappointed us.

She sighed. "I can deal."

So we all walked back to the parking lot, where the van still waited for us, only now Diva was there doing some kind of yoga pose, her tall, rail-thin frame bent toward the passenger-side door like a windblown sapling.

She smiled when she spotted us. "Hi, girls! Thanks for letting me join your trip. I'm Diva. Should we do an introduction game?"

Killa shook her head. "We're hours late already. We need to get going. They can introduce themselves once we're on the road. Also—" She moved closer, so we had to work to hear her. "—you can't wear those."

Diva looked at her manicured and flip-flopped feet and slapped her forehead dramatically. Sandals actually weren't allowed in camp except in the shower house and the waterfront, but the drama tent was her own fiefdom, with its own rules. "Oh, I meant to change those. My head isn't on straight yet, everything's been moving so fast. I'll only be a minute."

"Do you have hiking boots? I've seen those Uggs you wear around. You'll ruin those boots and your feet if you hike in them." Diva frowned and Killa took it as a no. "How about sneakers, then?"

She ran off in the direction of her cabin, flips flopping. Killerwhale felt bad wishing Diva would hurt herself too, after what happened to 'Zilla, but her joy in this trip was fast being replaced by dread. She had headed off the fashion boots at least, which was either an act of kindness or an attempt to spare herself the otherwise inevitable whining about blisters.

We got into the van and arranged ourselves according to the unspoken hierarchy: Lucia and Justina in the back row, away from the counselors and the indignity of being clambered over; the quiet girls behind the counselors; Katie and Andrea wedged in between. Killa climbed into the driver's seat and scooted it forward—'Zilla had driven it last, and she had six inches on Killa. By the time she had fixed the mirrors and plugged in her phone and programmed the address, then gone over the packing list one more time, Diva was back, in blessedly functional-looking running shoes.

Once we'd made the highway, Diva twisted around in her seat and insisted we all introduce ourselves to her, using a game she called "world's greatest sandwich," wherein each of us gave our name and the ingredient we'd include in the aforementioned world's greatest sandwich. Katie chose falafel, which Lucia said was definitional to the sandwich and not a fair first choice, and Andrea chose Nutella, and Meghan didn't say anything so Diva chose turkey for her, and Lucia made puking noises and said she was vegetarian, and science fact, domestic turkeys can't even mate, and then she picked pickled carrots, and Justina picked pickled pickles, which she said like that, "I pick pickled pickles," which led to a debate about whether something could be re-pickled, pickled again, or if a thing once pickled was at the pinnacle of its pickling metamorphosis. Nicky had her nose in a novel through the whole game, and when her turn came around she looked annoyed to be interrupted and said she didn't like sandwiches. Diva pushed her until she admitted she liked ice cream sandwiches, which brought another argument about whether the ingredient was ice cream on its own or the whole, in which case it was an ice cream sandwich within a sandwich. A sub-sandwich, Killa ventured from behind the wheel, but everyone ignored her.

Diva tried to build a dramatic arc into unveiling our falafel-turkey-Nutella-pickled vegetable-ice cream sandwich, which probably would have been more dramatic if there were more than six of us. What had she learned from this game that wasn't on our allergy sheets? That we hadn't already figured out in putting the menu together the night before? Not much, beyond Justina's desire to audition as Lucia's shadow. We were in good spirits, at least. After Diva finished her game, Killa tuned the radio to a pop station, and everyone but the quiet two sang along for a while, Justina enthusiastically off-key.

We stopped at the three-hour mark for gas and one last indoor bathroom. Killa considered catching Diva for a heart-to-heart in the truck stop, telling her what was expected of her on this trip, but then she saw her in line with the girls, each picking a candy bar on her dime, and decided it wasn't worth the confrontation. The thing was, everybody else liked her. It was irritating.

We turned off the state highway at the sign for Dramis Heaths Forest and Wilderness Preserve, entry by permit lottery only. "That's bad branding," said Diva. "How do you fit a name that long on a hat?" The turnoff lulled us into thinking our destination was near, but there was still another hour's travel at fifteen miles per hour down an unpaved road to the interior.

There were no other vehicles at the trailhead. Diva went around to the trunk for the lunch the kitchen had packed us, while Killa checked in with the ranger's office. Except the ranger was out, and a sign at the desk said it was honor system: complete the information sheet and waiver and leave both in the slotted box. She unsheathed the emergency packet from its waterproof sleeve and copied off our info, then added her own. She'd told us her real name—Tamara Hunt—the night before, under promise of secrecy, in case we needed it out here in the real world. She had files on everyone except Diva. First name Amanda, she knew that much, but she couldn't remember a surname. "Amanda Diva" she put down, then added the camp director's name and number for an emergency contact.

The form ended with a few waiver statements. *I understand that everybody in my party hikes at their own risk or, if minors, with the permission of a parent or guardian. I understand this is a designated wilderness area and the park is not responsible for anything that might occur within its bounds. I understand wild animals should not be approached. I attest that nobody in my party will hunt or fish in the wilderness area. I attest that we will not damage any living trees. I attest that we will not make any fires if the fire risk sign is at orange or higher. I attest we will only build fires in designated fire circles. I attest that nobody in my party will knowingly carry out materials from the wilderness area. I attest that nobody in my party has ever been in this wilderness area before.* We had gone over all of these rules in our conversation the night before, and our parents had all signed off on them before that; she dutifully initialed all the lines.

The box was full, but she managed to fold the form enough times to wedge it in. She took a handful of maps and our permit, which was in a labeled folder on the desk with the camp name on it. The system seemed really lax, but probably nobody drove an hour down that rutted road to this trailhead without a permit. This area was so protected it only opened to backpackers via a hotly contested annual lottery system; some camp alum had won and donated her spot this year, so the back country trip could go somewhere new. Yet another amazing perk of the best job ever as far as Killa was concerned.

A weather radio blared minute by minute updates from the far desk, and Killa lingered a moment listening as it confirmed clear skies, seventy-degree days, sixties at night. While she listened she scanned the posters on the walls, looking for any info she didn't have. What to do if you met a mountain goat or a bear, don't forget to purify your water, pack out your trash, et cetera, et cetera. Nothing she didn't already know; she prided herself on doing her research. She was sorry the ranger wasn't there, since her favorite camping trick was to ask, "What should I know that I wouldn't think to ask." In her experience, you got all kinds of cool answers, like secret vistas and places to avoid. Not because rangers were in a habit of withholding, but because you sometimes got cool intel by leaving the question open-ended. Maybe they'd run into the ranger during the week and get a chance to inquire.

We ate our lunch and threw the basket back into the van, then began sorting out the packs and gear. We'd tested and weighed and adjusted straps the night before. Everyone had expected Lucia to sport a brand-new bag, but hers was blue and gray and weathered like a hand-me-down; Justina was the only one with a monogram. We'd taken a short hike around camp before dinner to practice walking with them. Andrea's little sister had been in one of the units we passed, and waved like we were a queen's procession, so we all gave little queen waves back.

The packs dwarfed all of us except for Meghan, who was tall and sturdy, and Justina, who was wide and sturdy. Nicky had her grandmother's old-school frame pack, and it looked like it might pull her over backward, but she said it was comfortable enough. The counselors had tried to make everyone's loads as light as possible, which meant putting more communal stuff into their own packs. Killa's own gear was broken in and fitted to her; Diva staggered when she picked hers up, but tried not to show it.

We checked every cranny of the van to make sure nothing important had rolled away under the seats, and Killa locked it up and made a show of exactly which zipped pocket she was putting the key in, in case she forgot, and then put a reminder in her phone, too, before also making a show of putting away her phone. By the time we'd done all this, it was already 4 PM; we were supposed to have been on the trail at 12:30.

"Let's call today a warm-up," Killa said. "We'll hike for an hour or so and start looking for a place to camp. That way if anything is rubbing or too heavy or whatever, you can tell me now, and we can double-check all the tents again. Tomorrow we can get an early start and make up the time." We all nodded in agreement. "Who did we say is leading first?"

We'd chosen that the night before too. If Killa and Zilla had made their own plan, they did a good job of hiding it beneath questions for us, making it seem like we were the ones making the decisions. A few of us had orienteering badges already. We were ready.

Andrea hadn't asked to be first, but we'd chosen her the night before, and she had tried to play it cool, though secretly she was pleased. Orienteering was her favorite part of scouting. She always sought out those opportunities, even when they were hidden under silly program names like "Zombie Escape" and "Survival Games." Katie was quick to sign up for those sessions too, and they'd long ago made a pact to be each other's apocalypse buddies, since they were both so good at it.

Katie took the monsters seriously, though, the external forces, and Andrea was more worried about the geography of survival. She'd watched every episode *of Off Course,* and she always knew exactly where the contestants had gone wrong. Even when her dads took her and her sister to the mall or the movies, she practiced looking for the escape routes, the high places, the hiding places. They'd sent her to therapy when they realized what she was doing, but the therapist had agreed it wasn't harmful as long as it was a game, not an obsession. It wasn't, she swore. She just liked knowing where she was in relation to everything and everyone.

She held out her hand for the map. Killa passed it over, and she examined it again, even though we'd plotted our whole route the night before and the beginning was pretty straightforward. Wooden signs pointed to three different entrances to the forest, with three different shapes blazed and painted alongside the trail names. She scanned the signs, then the trees around us, for blue diamond-shaped trail markings. She pulled out her compass, looked seriously at the trees then back at the map, evened her pack, and set off marching, everyone else at her heels.

The first hour took us through rainforest. An easy start, with only a slight incline. Thick, ferny underbrush surrounded the trail, like an Ewok forest; mosses made Victorian ghosts of the massive conifers and bigleaf maples. Unseen birds called to each other in a half-dozen bird languages, high overhead. Everything was green, a thousand shades of green; even the air smelled green, which we wouldn't have known was possible until we smelled it. The sun filtered down between the trees to warm us as we walked. Andrea sent up a silent prayer for the fires on the eastern side of the mountains never to find this place.

When we came to a river, Killa called for Andrea to stop. "What do you see?"

Everyone was quiet for a second; nobody wanted to go first, in case they said something that wasn't what Killa was looking for.

Andrea was impatient, and she didn't think there was a wrong answer. "A river?" She looked back and forth between her map and the actual river, even though she didn't need confirmation.

"A water source?" Katie figured maybe the question was about utility.

Lucia followed with "A designated fire circle?"

"An outhouse?" That was Justina.

Killa gave them all thumbs up. "Yes, yes, yes, and yes. Why don't we stop here for the night?"

The tents were pretty easy to put up, especially with two-person teams. Andrea and Katie had theirs ready in three minutes flat—they were the only ones who timed themselves. Meghan and Nicky communicated well despite their silence. Lucia made Justina do most of the work on theirs, but Justina proved surprisingly adept. Killa went around between them all helping and encouraging. Diva disappeared.

Killa put up the tent she and Diva would be sharing, then turned to us and said, "Tonight's the only night we'll be in a place we can have a fire, so why don't you girls buddy up and gather firewood? Only dry and dead stuff."

Easy enough. Andrea and Katie looked at each other and moved off in the direction we'd come from—there'd been a pile of deadfall behind the outhouse. That turned out to be the direction Killa walked a minute later to look for Diva, who sat on a log a few yards off the trail, rubbing her bare foot and chatting on her phone.

"You've got to be kidding me," Killa said.

Diva looked up. "Gotta go, girl. I'll text you later tonight."

"She won't," Killa said, raising her voice like she wanted it to carry to the person on the line. "She's busy all week."

"What are you doing?" Diva looked at her with annoyance.

"We told the girls no phones all week. It's hypocritical of us to use phones except in an emergency. Put it away."

"That's not fair. I wasn't even supposed to be on this trip; you can't expect me to give up my life for a week."

Killa stared at her until she sighed and slipped her phone into her backpack. "Fiiiinne."

As Killa turned her back to return to the campsite, Diva muttered "... bitch orders me around like a child when this trip wouldn't even be happening if I hadn't agreed to come ..." Andrea and Katie exchanged another glance at the language. They knew they should carry the wood back to the campsite, but they wanted to hear how Killa responded.

"I'm grateful you agreed to come, and I don't mean to treat you like a child. You can call me names, hate me, I don't care; I don't think much of you, either. But you will not do anything that detracts from the experience for these girls. This is the one chance they get in the year to get away from their families and be who they want to be without judgment. I don't want them thinking about their phones, or the bullies at their schools—or the kids they bully, who knows?—and I don't want them thinking about how lousy people can be to each other in the real world. Let's rise above this, for them. Otherwise it doesn't matter if you agreed to come, and we might as well turn around. Please."

Killa faced Diva squarely, like she dared her to call the bluff. Hopefully it was a bluff; Andrea couldn't imagine leaving now. Wind rustled the trees, and, up the path, she heard the clatter of branches being dropped on other branches. Diva shrugged and nodded, and followed Killa back toward the campsite.

Killerwhale had said to collect firewood, and then she'd walked away like we didn't need supervision. Which we didn't, as far as Lucia was concerned. Had we not over twenty-five wilderness patches between us? Were we not all between the ages of twelve and fourteen, an age when one could babysit a younger sibling, or even stay home alone? We could be trusted to collect firewood.

The others went into the woods, and Lucia picked her way down to the riverbank. Justina followed a few paces behind her. There was a fir tree that had fallen across the water like a bad-idea bridge. They examined the tangled, tentacular roots and everything that had upended with them, imagining what it was like to be torn from your place in a larger whole.

The fir had died long enough ago that it was dry inside and out. Its branches snapped easily, and Lucia collected a few for kindling, leaving them in a pile on the bank. One poked her between the first knuckle of two fingers, a tiny puncture that welled a dark drop of blood, too small for her to bother Killa about. She prided herself on being tough. She'd wash it out herself once they'd gotten everything done, rather than make someone fuss over her.

People at camp sometimes thought she was an attention hog, but that wasn't it; she got no attention at home, and that was fine. Her family ran an animal rescue. They had nine dogs, and eight horses, and three elderly donkeys, and one mule, and seven cats, and seven goats, and five kids, and a vague and variable number of rabbits, chickens, hamsters, et cetera. If there was one thing she knew about, it was pecking order. When you found yourself part of a new herd, you needed to establish your place before someone else decided it for you.

Lucia balanced on the log and took a couple of steps out toward the fallen crown on the far bank, then retreated when Justina climbed on. Lucia once got a fortune cookie that read "Nobody can be exactly like you," but nobody had ever told Justina. She trailed when Lucia walked back to the campsite too, even though she didn't yet have an armful.

Lucia preferred having the entire group's attention, not only her Justina-shaped shadow. The others had found larger branches and moved out in different directions. She considered. We could be trusted to collect firewood; that didn't mean we shouldn't have fun doing it.

"I have a game," she said, when we were all near the campsite, and we all reoriented to face her. "Each of us has to pick a tree for herself. You have to be able to identify it again later, but without damaging it, because we are tree stewards. Then when we pass here again on our way back in a few days, we'll try to guess which one is whose."

"I think the aspens might be clones," said Justina. "They all look the same."

Lucia rolled her eyes dramatically, then allowed the point. "Each of us has to pick a trunk, then. Or don't pick an aspen. Memorize the things that make your trunk different, if there's anything, so you can recognize it again. Or leave something to pick up later, where nobody else can see it, or mark it somehow, without hurting it."

"How do you know we won't cheat and say a different one was ours if someone picks right?" That was Justina again.

"We won't cheat because we're scouts, and there's no honor in cheating. What's the point? It's not like there's a prize for winning."

Everyone nodded as if that made sense, the rules were accepted, game on, except Meghan, who looked scared. She always looked scared, but then she did everything anyway. She and Nicky were quiet in different ways; Nicky's quiet held menace, like she didn't have time for you, but Meghan was inscrutable. Fear, maybe? Insecurity? Lucia found animals way easier to read than people.

We all wandered off in different directions this time, even though technically we were supposed to be in pairs, we were always supposed to be in pairs, it was exhausting. Lucia walked upstream past the fallen fir, to a big-leafed tree she didn't recognize; some kind of maple, maybe. Its trunk had bent out over the river, like it had its chest puffed out about something. The bend allowed it to make use of the empty space above the river and get some sun for its crown. She appreciated the effort this tree had gone to for itself.

Lucia had made the rules, but now she wondered how to mark her tree. She was anti–bark damage. She could put a little cairn of rocks near its roots, or an arrangement of leaves, or smear some mud on its trunk. Yes, that made sense, her initials in mud. She made her way down the bank and scooped mud in her hands. Her hand still oozed blood, and it mixed with the mud as she smeared LT onto the roots in small letters, where nobody else would see.

Satisfied, she gathered a few more dead branches for the campsite. Four of the others were back, but not Justina. Great; she'd probably get in trouble if her shadow got lost. She found Justina a little ways up the trail we'd come in on, squatting behind a hemlock tree.

"Don't look!"

"Sorry," Lucia said. "I didn't know you were peeing. I wanted to make sure you weren't lost. You do know there's an outhouse near where we're camping, right?"

"I know! But now you know which tree is mine!" Justina said.

"You're marking it with pee?"

"What else was I supposed to use?"

She didn't want to explain her mud initials, since then Justina would know what to look for, even though she'd have to check a lot of trees to find the right one. She also didn't bother pointing out that pee wasn't really a good marking system if you had a human sense of smell.

"Come on," Lucia said. "We're the last ones out here. We don't want to worry them. I promise I won't tell which is yours."

Justina shimmied her pants up and came around the hemlock. "Thank you—and thanks for coming to look for me! You're the best."

Lucia didn't really think she was the best, but she'd worked pretty hard to make everyone else think so in the short time they'd been together, and it gratified her that at least one person had fallen for it.

We all convened on the campsite again. Someone had dragged a thick branch from the river, too wet for firewood, but the rest looked like an appropriate mix of logs, branches, and kindling.

"Nice job, girls," Killa said, and a couple of us smiled to show we appreciated the encouragement, even though we were scouts and obviously we were doing it for the good of the team, not her approval.

After dinner, we sang songs around the fire. We could have cooked over our little gas burner, and it was warm enough that the fire was superfluous, but Killa liked to sing around a fire the first night as a bonding thing. Don't think about how many nights you're away from your family, or the darkness, or anything it contains.

We were at the age where everyone at school was telling us what was cool and who was cool, and some of us were maybe starting to believe it, but right now, for a few more nights or a few more minutes, we sang earnestly. Even Meghan sang along, though she shook her head when it was her turn to pick a song.

This was what Killerwhale loved most about leading these trips; this and the views. This and the chance to teach kids it was possible to step away from their devices for a minute. To teach us to look up and look around. To be somewhere and just be. All of which was why she was so pissed off when she looked over to see that Diva had her phone by her thigh, typing with one thumb, her neck craned at an unsubtle angle.

"Hey, Diva," she said. "Do you want to lead a song?"

The other counselor startled and slipped her phone back into her jacket pocket. The illuminated screen shone through.

"I, uh, I don't really sing, but I can tell a story. Do you girls want a story?"

"Is it scary?" asked Katie.

Diva grinned. "You can tell me after you hear it."

Killa opened her mouth to say "no scary stories on the first night," but there wasn't a good way to say it in front of the girls. It was another thing her usual trips partner, Godzilla, knew implicitly. Anyway, we had all reoriented ourselves toward Diva, with looks ranging from excitement to trepidation on our faces.

"Once upon a time," Diva started, and Killerwhale remembered that Diva was the drama counselor for a reason. She'd shifted into a narrator's voice. What was her background again? A local theater troupe, and she'd been up to Vancouver to act in a couple of TV series, bit parts, but even Killerwhale had to admit she wasn't bad.

"Once upon a time, a beautiful young actor got invited to spend the summer working with kids at a scouting camp. She was excited about it. A chance to live in a cabin in the woods, rustic but not without basic amenities, a chance to impart a love of acting to the campers. She took the time to research activities for kids, and she catalogued and disinfected every item in the costume tent, because she wanted to do a good job.

"She had three mostly good weeks, doing all the things she was supposed to, and then something unusual happened. Another counselor injured herself, someone whose job was to take advanced campers backpacking, and the actor was told she was needed on the trip.

"She asked if there were any other options—she wasn't really much for camping, though she'd done it a few times as a kid—but her boss called this "other duties as assigned" and made it clear it was non-negotiable.

"So she went. She hiked and she camped and she ate bad tacos over a fire. She did her best, even though the campers all knew more about backpacking than she did. She made up for it by telling them stories."

"Are you just telling us what's happening right now?" interrupted Lucia. "This isn't a story."

"Sssh," said Diva. "This is where it changes."

"At the end of the trip, the group made their way back toward the parking lot where they'd left the van. They emerged from the woods at the spot where they'd gone in, but for a second they thought they must have made a wrong turn. The parking lot had become overgrown in the week they'd been gone, the gravel erupting with young conifers and deer ferns and bushes heavy with ripe salmonberries in red and orange and gold. 'Maybe we took a wrong turn,' said the actor."

"'This is definitely the right place,' said the other counselor, who thought she was always right. 'I'm never wrong.' 'Somebody is wrong,' said the most loudmouthed camper."

"Hey," said Lucia. "Is that supposed to be me?"

"Ssh," said Diva. "Names have been changed to protect the innocent. Where was I? A young forest had grown up where the parking lot should have been. The ranger station had a hole in the roof with a cedar tree growing through it, and it looked like one of those old barns by the side of the highway, that nobody has kept up, so it kind of falls in on itself."

"Was the van still there?" Katie's voice was only a whisper.

"It was! The insufferable counselor was correct that they were in the right place, but the van was barely recognizable, and surrounded by baby trees. Its tires had rotted away, so it was standing on four rusted rims. It had moss growing on top of it, and broken windows, and mice had made nests in the seat upholstery."

"How did they know it was their van?"

"At first they didn't, but when they opened the back door, there was a blue plastic cooler right where they had left their lunch cooler the week before. Plastic takes ages to decay."

"Also, the keys fit," said Andrea. "They opened the trunk, so the keys must have fit."

"Good point," said Diva. "What do you think they did next?"

"Checked their phones? If they'd turned off their phones like they were supposed to, or had extra batteries or solar power, maybe they still had battery."

"Oh, yes! They tried that. Nobody answered, and they didn't have any signal at all."

"They should go into the ranger station."

"Yes, that's what they did next. The actor went in, because she didn't want the campers to get injured if the rest of the roof fell in. And do you know what she found?"

No, nobody did. Meghan looked ready to cry.

"The building didn't even have a door anymore. The actor walked in. On the wall inside, she found a rain-ruined poster that read 'Have you seen these people?' But it had torn, so she couldn't see who was on it. There was a rain-rotted wooden desk, and on it was a National Parks calendar, but it said 'July 2044' which made no sense to her. It must have been a joke calendar. Except when she went outside, she found one of those bulletin boards that stand at the start of trails, and on it there was another 'Have you seen these people' poster, but this one was laminated. And the picture on the poster . . . was a picture of her and her campers!"

"We didn't take a picture. It's not us. We didn't take a picture."

"Maybe it was Photoshopped? Or our parents gave our pictures?"

"This isn't about us, obviously."

"But it is! You heard her! Our van! Twenty years passed!"

"No it didn't," said Katie morosely. "More than twenty years passed. 2044 was what was on the calendar, but that calendar was obviously from the last month when the station was still in use and had a roof and everything. Then there was more time, after it wasn't kept up anymore. That was when they let the roof rot and fall in. We've been missing way longer."

"Not we," Killerwhale said sharply. "That wasn't a story about us, remember? Tell them, Diva."

"No, of course not. It's just a story."

"I want to call my mom."

"Better not to. What if she doesn't answer because time passes differently here and it's already been a hundred years?" Lucia said in a helpful tone.

Half the girls looked ready to cry. Killerwhale glared at Diva, who looked delighted.

"Show them," Killa said.

"Show them what?"

"Take out your phone and show them the date."

"What phone?" asked Diva innocently. Killerwhale summoned her most lethal glare.

Diva did as she was told, then responded to an incoming message before putting away the phone. "See? It still sends. You can ask me to show you my phone anytime. And I bet Killa has a solar battery she'll let me use to make sure my phone doesn't run out of charge, so we can keep checking all week." She looked pleased with her generosity; Killa looked murderous. "Satisfied? It was just a scary story."

"It wasn't much of a story," said Nicky. Everyone looked over. Was it the first time Nicky had spoken voluntarily? It might have been. "That isn't an ending. It's a plot twist. That's where the story begins. A good story would go on from there to tell us what they all did next."

"Okay, fine," said Diva. "What do they do next?"

Nicky folded her arms across her chest. "It's your story, not mine. You figure it out. It's not even like one of those urban legends where the helpful stranger has some identifying feature exactly like the murderer's, or the woman places the final puzzle piece and realizes it's her house, with somebody staring in through the window. You know in those stories what happens next is the murderer murders her. If that wasn't going to happen, you'd have to tell the rest of the story, since that's the obvious conclusion your imagination fills in. As it is, you just said all that to scare us, which is not a nice thing to do to a bunch of kids you're supposed to be looking out for."

Everyone looked at Nicky like she had grown a second head. "What? I read. In case you hadn't noticed."

"And we're all glad you do," said Killerwhale. "That's a really good point. Now that we've listened to Diva's disturbing and entirely fictional story, how about one more song and then we head to bed? We have a long day ahead tomorrow. Nicky, you can choose the song."

Nicky chose the song the counselors usually sang to serenade the campers at the end of a campfire, and looked at Killerwhale and Diva expectantly. Killerwhale, in turn, looked at Diva to make sure she understood that she was expected to join in. She did.

Killerwhale waited until we had all brushed our teeth and settled into our tents before climbing into the tent she and Diva were sharing. Diva lay in her sleeping bag with her eyes closed, like Killa hadn't seen a screen lighting up the tent one second before she unzipped it. Not worth fighting the same battle again; she chose a different one.

"What happens at the end of your story?"

Diva shrugged. "I hadn't figured it out yet. It's something I think about every time somebody makes me go camping, ever since I was a kid. Time flows differently to a forest, so why wouldn't time flow differently in a forest?"

"Why tell these poor kids a story like that?"

"Are you kidding? They loved it."

"If anyone gets scared tonight, you're the one comforting them."

Except, of course, she wasn't. When Killerwhale heard crying in the middle of the night, she reached over to shake Diva, but Diva didn't stir. And really, who would want to be comforted by her? None of these girls. Killa sighed and went to help Katie, who was, not surprisingly, having a nightmare about the story Diva had told.

———

Katie hated that Diva had gotten to her. She'd always been easily scared by stories. She had inherited her brother's books as he outgrew them, but she made him pick through them first for anything he thought might frighten her. The ones he missed she had her mother give away; she didn't even want them in the house. She was still haunted by the one with the ribbon around the woman's neck, not to mention the poor dog in that Stephen King book. Not to mention all the times she'd crept into the living room while Antoine and his friends watched horror movies. She had thought those things would make her braver, desensitize her, but they only made her miserable. She carried them all with her forever now, and the images visited unbidden when she closed her eyes at night alone in her room. She was full of regrets.

That was what she loved about camp. You never had to be scared or alone. You always had a buddy, and they were obligated to do everything with you, even go with you when you had to pee in the middle of the night. Even when they didn't want to, they went, because they knew you'd do the same for them. Katie wasn't scared of heights, or depths, or anything that came at you in the daylight. She liked rock climbing and rafting. She wanted to swim with sharks someday. Those were scares that left you exhilarated.

She hadn't expected Diva to tell something so creepy. It had snuck up on her, like most terrifying stories did. Here's someone doing a jigsaw puzzle in their own home, unaware of the danger outside the window. Here's a group of kids doing the things groups of kids do, with no clue what they're about to unleash. She should have expected a twist; otherwise there was no story.

Nicky's comments helped. If it wasn't even a good story, it couldn't possibly be true, right? She could pretend that made sense, up until some other part of her brain said that true stories didn't have rules. Happily ever after was a fiction thing. Everyone getting what they want was a fiction thing. Even horror rules like how sex gets you killed and curiosity gets you killed had a misplaced sense of fairness about them. Real life gave you school shootings and climate change and all kinds of things where the virtuous and the polar bears don't come out with a win. Real life was weird, so who was to say Diva wasn't right and they'd never see their families again. Or you'd get home and when your brother opened the door, he'd have a strange haircut and clothes, and you'd realize it wasn't your brother at all, but your brother's son, the same age Antoine was when you left a week ago.

All of that raced through her mind as she closed her eyes, but no matter how hard she willed herself to sleep, that re-forested parking lot kept floating into her mind. The wind blowing through the hole in the ranger cabin's roof. There were no monsters in the story, and it still terrified her. She tried breathing deep, smelling the wonderful smoky campfire scent that had permeated her hair and clothes. She thought she hadn't even fallen asleep, hadn't even known she was making sounds out loud until Lucia in the next tent said, "Shut up!" And then she was awake in the dark for real, and still terrified, like everyone else in the world had disappeared except these four tents.

Then Killerwhale was there to try to make it better, a steadying hand on her shoulder through the sleeping bag. "Hey, Katie. Nightmare?"

She couldn't talk yet, so she nodded.

"About that story, or something else?"

She nodded again.

"Look, I don't know why she said all that, but you don't need to worry. You heard Nicky: it wasn't even a good story. We all know it's impossible, right? She showed you her phone. If you need to, you can call home to see for yourself. Do you want to do that?"

What if nobody answered, because it was so late at night? Her mom had promised to always answer when she was away, to sleep with her phone plugged in by the bed, but what if she slept through it, or forgot? Better not to call. She shook her head and pulled her knees tight inside her sleeping bag.

It helped knowing Killa still existed. She'd keep them safe. She was the counselor everyone wanted to be when they got old enough: cool, wise, brave. There were counselors who you were pretty sure would save themselves in an emergency and counselors who you trusted to save everybody. Killa was the latter; Katie and Andrea had both agreed that she would be the first person they'd recruit for their apocalypse survival team.

And even without the apocalypse, Katie had a dream of being camp staff herself someday, of being a trips counselor when Killa was, like, thirty and too old to do it anymore, and being a role model for a new group of kids, knowing she'd learned from the best. Demonstrating how to be a functional member of a camping group, showing that survival and stewardship weren't incompatible, demonstrating what to eat and not to eat, and what to burn and where to do it, and to always, always, always put your fire out completely before you leave it. If you were a counselor cut from that cloth, maybe sometimes you had to calm yourself when you were scared.

Katie summoned up the words "I'll be okay" from somewhere in her core, and forced them through her mouth. Killa being Killa, she stayed a little longer anyway.

The first night was uneventful other than Diva's story and Katie's nightmare. We'd gone to bed not long after dark, and got up around sunrise. Everyone other than Katie and Andrea had slept well, and Katie was stoic in her exhaustion.

Because those two were tired, the map and compass somehow wound up in Justina's hands. Killa had given them to her and she had said, "Are you sure?" Then she mentally kicked herself, because she had promised her mother she'd try to be more decisive and assertive on this trip. She had spent the entire school year following Ginnifer Hand around, doing her homework, laughing when she laughed. Then one day Ginnifer was smoking in the bathroom, and Justina had been there listening to Ginnifer complain about their math teacher, and she had not been smoking herself, she had always refused, but Ginnifer had shoved the cigarette at her and ran when Mrs. Prince walked in, and somehow it was Justina who took all the heat without speaking up for herself.

We walked. The blue diamonds led us up and up, though the slope was gradual. This wasn't technical like rock climbing, just one-foot-in-front-of-the-other. We covered six miles that day, leaving the rainforest and entering the subalpine forest, where the trees gave each other a little more room and wore fewer accessories. When we got to our next campsite we all keeled over into the dirt.

"I'm never moving again," declared Justina. "Or at least until tomorrow."

"Me neither." Diva took off one of her sneakers and then peeled off her white cotton ankle sock to examine her heel. Something was wrong with it, a glimpse of something dark and pink-edged she cupped beneath her hand. To her credit, she hadn't complained.

Killa rummaged in her pack and pulled out the first aid kit, and from within it, an individually-packaged antiseptic wipe and an adhesive bandage with dinosaurs on it. "Here. But you are all still moving, because we need to put up tents and make dinner and get some water from the river to purify."

Diva groaned. "What if we didn't?"

"That's up to them, not us," Killa said. "They can explore for a few minutes without their packs, though. Maybe they can find the outhouse; I know there should be one somewhere around here."

One by one we dragged ourselves to our feet. At least we didn't need to wear the packs any longer. We rolled our shoulders out and stretched our backs as we walked around. Katie and Andrea came back with their shirts purpled and pouched full of berries, enough to share. Justina had seen the same bushes, but had been afraid to take any without someone telling her they were safe. She was afraid to stain her shirt, too.

"They're edible, right?" Katie asked. "You said not to eat anything we found without checking with you first. There were a lot, so we took some but left some for the birds, and didn't deplete any one bush, like you always say."

Killa grabbed one and popped it in her mouth. "Blackberries! Invasive around here, but safe to eat. Thanks for checking. If you see more shaped like these in this color, they should be fine. Just keep checking with me about anything else."

Justina followed Lucia back into the forest, but this time she gave herself permission to snag a blackberry when they passed a loaded bush. Juice burst between her teeth when she bit down, sweet and sour, and she felt like she was one berry closer to being the person she wanted to be. She was the one who found the outhouse, too.

We made dinner working as a team, then moved on to songs. Killa skipped Diva's turn in the song choosing and went straight to Andrea beside her, which truth be told we all were fine with, except that Justina couldn't resist pointing it out. Even as she said it, she knew she probably shouldn't have.

"Oh, my bad," Killa said, like it had been an accident and she had lost track going directly around a circle. "You didn't have a song, did you, Diva?"

"Maybe she has another story," Justina said. Katie shot her a look of pure despondence.

Diva didn't seem to notice, but Killa did. "If she wants to tell a story instead of choose a song, maybe she has a nice non-scary story for us today, after the non-scary day we had." Not exactly subtle.

"I can tell another story," Diva said. We all noticed there was no promise made.

"Once upon a time, a beautiful young actor got invited to teach a camp drama program."

"Is this the same story as last night?" Nicky was not having it.

"No, you'll see. May I go on?"

Nicky nodded.

"The drama program was going fine, and she thought that was going to be her whole summer, until she generously volunteered to take over for an injured counselor on a backpacking trip."

"You volunteered, now?" Killa couldn't stand revisionist history.

"She volunteered. The person in the story, who is not me. And actually, she was pretty good in the woods, all things considered. She didn't like camping, but that didn't mean she hadn't done it before. She'd even camped in that very park with her family as a child! And she did own decent shoes and socks, but they weren't with her at camp, because she was supposed to be running a drama program, not backpacking, and she still volunteered for the trip, even knowing she'd probably destroy her feet. And everything was going well, they were all having a great time, until—"

She stopped and sipped cocoa from her cup, a dramatic pause that continued until poor Katie whispered, "Until what?"

"—Until the day the sun set in the north."

"The sun can't set in the north. That's impossible." Andrea looked to Killa for reassurance on that point. Killa nodded.

"Of course it can't," said Diva. "Which meant something was wrong with their compass."

"They only brought one?" Lucia had no pity.

"Did I say compass? I meant compasses. Something was wrong with all their compasses. They were so prepared they had each brought two, but every single one of them pointed north toward the setting sun."

"What does that mean?" Someone whispered.

"Well, for starters, it meant they'd probably been traveling the wrong direction for a while. Since whenever they'd checked last."

"I checked," said Justina. She pointed in the direction we'd last seen the sun. "That's west. That's north. I promise, I checked. I swear."

Diva ignored her. "It meant they'd been traveling in the wrong direction. It meant they were lost."

A ragged breath escaped Justina.

Killa had enough. "We're not lost. Girls, we're not lost. This is a story. Can you tell me why we're not lost? Don't panic; think."

"Justina was doing fine at navigating. She's a surprisingly good navigator." That was Nicky, who had looked skeptical of this story throughout. Justina flashed a grateful smile.

"Blue diamonds," said Katie. "A compass isn't our only tool. We're still following the blue diamonds."

"I hadn't gotten to that part," Diva said. "They decided to sleep on it, but when they woke up, all the trees had blue diamonds on them—"

"Stop," Killa said. "This isn't funny. Girls, don't worry. There's also the terrain, the maps . . ."

Andrea pointed into the darkness. "The river! The river has been on our left this entire time we've been traveling uphill, and we know where the river goes from the map. All we'd have to do is walk back downhill with the river on our right."

Diva frowned. "You're taking the fun out of telling a story."

"You've delighted us long enough," said Nicky.

"But how does it end? We need to know!" Justina appealed to the rest of us, but we all averted our gaze.

Diva shook her head sadly. "Sorry, Pickled Pickles. The spell is broken. You'll never know."

Which is how night two ended with everyone falling exhausted into tents, and, two hours later, Katie's nightmare waking everyone except Diva, who slept through it, and Justina, who hadn't slept yet, replaying the walk in her head and wondering if we all would have been better off if she had refused to navigate.

"Ghost stories," announced Diva, after dinner on the third night, before we'd even had a chance to sing.

"No," Killa said. What was the opposite of ghost stories? "Let's play Science Facts."

Everyone eyed her; half of us relieved, half disappointed.

"Science Facts," Killa repeated. "I'll start. You don't actually breathe through both of your nostrils most of the time. You breathe through one or the other, and the dominant one changes throughout the day, so it's not like being right or left-handed."

Everyone breathed quietly for a second, testing their nostrils.

"Fine," said Lucia. "I'll give you a fact about the strap-toothed whale. They have two teeth that cross over the top of their head and as the teeth grow, they eventually keep the whale from opening its mouth more than a couple of inches. It has to suck in squid and stuff like it's drinking through a straw."

"How is that related to the nostril thing?" asked Katie.

"Nostrils are on faces. So are mouths."

Everyone looked at Killerwhale to arbitrate. She nodded; she'd had something less disturbing in mind, but this did fit the instructions, even if it was a stretch.

"Fine," said Katie. "Narwhal horns are actually their one and only tooth, only it's inside out and has like millions of exposed nerve endings, so they basically go through life with one long ice cream headache."

Killa wasn't sure that was actually a fact, but we were all making sympathetic whale noises instead of complaining, so she decided to let it slide. She wasn't taking out her phone to check.

Justina spoke. "I'll tell you a fact about elephants. Elephants evolved to only have a few molars at a time, and when those wear away, new ones come in. Six times. After the sixth set wear down, when they're old, they can't chew as well and then they die." She looked to Lucia, who nodded, approval bestowed.

"Good start," Killa said. "But why do you all have so many facts about animal teeth?"

Lucia grinned. "Our troop did the Nothing But the Tooth dental hygiene badge a couple of years ago."

"I'm glad it left an impression." Killerwhale looked around to see if anyone had gotten her pun. Nicky gave her a single thumb up, weak acknowledgment. "Does anyone have any facts about something other than teeth? Consider it a new round."

We were all silent for a minute, then Andrea spoke. "The largest clone forest is in Utah, and it's actually all one cloned tree. It's called Pando, and it's an aspen with like forty thousand trunks. It's the world's heaviest organism and one of the oldest living things in the world, but they don't know how old, because you can't count rings like a normal tree."

Katie frowned. "How can forty thousand trees be one tree?"

"One organism, with lots of trunks," said Lucia, eager to take the attention back. "Like you're one organism with lots of hairs on your head that are all part of you."

For one second, it seemed like Lucia would lean in for the kill—one of those digs that devastates you at twelve, with an implication that Katie had too much hair, or too little hair, or hair in the wrong place—but before Killa could open her mouth to interrupt, Lucia finished with "If I were one giant organism, I'd be a honey mushroom. There's one in Oregon that's the largest single living organism on earth, in acreage, not weight."

"What's a honey mushroom?" Justina asked, looking like she knew the answer; ever the dutiful henchman.

"I'm so glad you asked. Honey mushrooms sometimes look like mushrooms and sometimes look like shoelaces and sometimes look like a weird milky sap. They spread with tendrils underground, kind of like Andrea's forest. One giant organism, acres and acres big, killing all the trees around it by suffocating them, even while they try to push it out. They kill the trees really slowly, so it's twenty or fifty years before they die."

"Why would you want to be that?" Nicky spoke for the first time in hours. "Why would you want to kill trees?"

"I don't want to kill trees; I like the stealth part. Killing them slowly, traveling underground. Like a spy. No, like an assassin. Black Widow."

"Black Widow doesn't kill trees," muttered Nicky. "That's a weird thing to want to do."

"Where did you learn that one?" Killa asked, curious against her better judgment.

Lucia puffed out her chest. "Fungus Among Us badge. I can also tell you about the fungus that turns ants into zombies and good fungi that help trees and identify three local edible mushrooms that definitely don't look like any toxic mushrooms, if we need to start foraging. I have the Forest Forage badge too."

"We don't need to forage," Killerwhale said. "Please don't eat any mushrooms."

Nicky was not afraid of anything in the woods. She read nonfiction as well as fiction. She'd researched the folklore of this area as well as the flora and fauna, and found nothing particularly concerning: a few wolves, bears, mountain lions, none of which were likely to be hungry enough to go for their group at this point in the summer. No venomous snakes, no cryptids or indigenous mythological creatures, and only one spider of note, known to be shy. Snowberries and death cherries, with their gorgeous names and lethal beauty, easily avoided.

No, none of that scared her. What she didn't like was the people. That had been her argument to her grandfather when she suggested bailing on camp for this year. She and her grandparents lived a quiet life; a reading life. She didn't mind school, because sometimes there was interesting stuff to learn, and the classes were too overcrowded for the teachers to ever spend time trying to get her to socialize or make friends. At camp, there was no place to hide.

Maybe you'll make friends, her grandfather had said. Maybe you'll see something spectacular. In the end, though, her grandmother had said how much she missed camping now that her back was too bad to do it anymore, and how she missed seeing alpine flowers in bloom, and Nicky had agreed to go, if only to take pictures of alpine flowers when they reached the lake region.

The tents were cramped, even for two people not yet fully grown. Nicky wasn't one to complain, but everything woke her. Katie's nightmares in the next tent over, the counselors arguing in hushed voices, the whistle of wind through the upper branches, the crick-crack of a million billion tree frogs in deep conversation and the hoo-hoos of the spotted owls, and every single breath of her tent mate, Meghan.

Not her breaths, really; the lack thereof. Nicky was positive the girl had apnea, like her grandfather before he got that machine. She didn't snore, but she stopped breathing for what seemed like minutes at a time, before gasping, turning in her sleeping bag (its own susurrus, hard-to-ignore sound), and settling into a deeper sleep. Nicky didn't know whether to talk to Meghan about it, or the counselors, or just continue to count through the gaps between breaths. What had seemed like minutes turned out to be approximately fifteen to twenty seconds, but if she didn't count it felt like forever.

"Meghan," she whispered. "I need to pee."

For all the disturbance in her sleep patterns, Meghan didn't stir. She tried a second time, and a third, then spent a few minutes debating exactly how badly she needed to go, and if it was one of those situations where you'd eventually fall asleep and forget until morning, or the kind where you'd listen to the river flowing outside your tent and the pressure got worse and worse until it was unavoidable.

If Meghan didn't want to go with, couldn't wake up, that was fine, though then she'd be alone in the tent, and there would be nobody who knew if she stopped breathing or a branch fell on the tent or a bear decided she was a well-wrapped snack. Was that what was called acceptable risk? She hadn't been given a choice, but she hadn't given Nicky much of a choice either. Nicky kicked herself free of her sleeping bag, grabbed her headlamp, pulled on her shoes, and slipped from the tent, zipping it behind her so nothing could get in while Meghan was alone and defenseless.

Nicky didn't even particularly like Meghan. They had been buddied by external forces. Katie and Andrea made sense, since they were actually friends who coordinated their attendance together, and Justina had attached herself to Lucia like one of those birds that symbiotically plucks insects off a hippo's back. There had been some talk of tripling people up, but it would have made a tight fit tighter. Which left Meghan and Nicky. Which was fine. Nicky didn't talk much because she was too busy observing; she spoke when necessary, and she liked a good conversation when there was something worth talking about. Meghan, as far as she knew, didn't have any impediment to speech. She just didn't speak, and didn't wake up when Nicky needed her.

Nicky's headlamp illuminated the outhouse. A few years before she'd dropped her flashlight down a latrine at camp, and everyone had decided there was a ghost in the hole and refused to go in that particular privy for the rest of the session; she'd been too embarrassed to admit it was hers. Her grandfather had been angry about the flashlight, but eventually he'd come around and bought her the headlamp instead. She loved the headlamp.

When she finished peeing, she shut the door as gently as possible so she wouldn't wake anybody. She was proud of having conducted this entire maneuver on her own, and now she just had to get back to the tent and slip in beside Meghan of the Snores. Except as she neared the campsite, she saw that somebody else was awake: Diva.

The counselor tent flapped behind her, even though it was impolite to leave your tent open. Weirder still, she wasn't walking toward the outhouse, but perpendicular to the trail, away from the river, straight into the woods. She wore no socks or shoes, even though that was against camp regulations. Something looked slightly odd about her feet, but they were moving through underbrush and Nicky couldn't quite see.

"Diva?" Nicky loud-whispered, but the counselor didn't turn in her direction.

What Nicky should have done was stop at Killa's open tent to wake her, since she'd know better what to do. It made more sense for a counselor to follow into the woods instead of a camper. Except, that was why they had two counselors; so even if one went someplace, there was another to stay with everyone else. A counselor being the one in trouble wasn't built into the equation, even though it could obviously happen. They'd seen it with 'Zilla, though 'Zilla'd had the good grace to get injured before they even left, so there weren't any rescue situations that needed to be engaged.

Anyway, how far could Diva be going? Nicky followed. They'd spent their days hiking steadily uphill, following the river toward its source, but this was a different uphill, straight into the trees, with no path or markers.

"Wake up, Diva, you're sleepwalking," she tried, but Diva didn't stop.

Nicky was being stupid. What she needed was another person. No, she needed two more people. If she woke one other, and something happened and they needed to go get Killa, somebody would still be alone. She would have preferred to wake Katie and Andrea, but Katie had spent the last two days dead-eyed and dead-tired from her nightmares. Diva was walking a slow and arrow-straight line into the trees, so Nicky figured she had a few seconds. She ran back to the campsite.

"Lucia, Justina, wake up." She directed her voice through the tent's back wall, near their heads.

Lucia groaned. "No more nightmares."

"No, I need your help. This is Nicky." She added her name for urgency's sake. Even if they weren't her friends, they ought to recognize by now that she didn't ever try to get anyone's attention unless it was necessary.

The tent unzipped. Nicky ran around the front. Lucia was sitting in her sleeping bag, and Justina had her hands over her face blocking the lamp beam.

"Diva is sleepwalking," Nicky said. "I'm afraid she's going to hurt herself, but if it's just me following and something happens, I can't stay with her and go for help at the same time."

"Where's Meghan?" That was Justina. "Your tent mate is supposed to be your buddy."

"She's fast asleep. She's not alone—Killa and Katie and Andrea are still right here. Come on, hurry. We need to catch Diva before she hurts herself."

Lucia nodded and pulled on her shoes. "We're coming."

Justina, ever the loyal lieutenant, followed her lead. "Okay, but you owe us."

Nicky said, "No, I don't," at the same time as Lucia said, "No, she doesn't. There's no owing in helping people. We're scouts."

They followed Nicky as she set off straight through the trees, as Diva had done. Nobody second-guessed her, which was nice. She kept a quick pace, her headlamp illuminating a not-path, trees looming from the shadows at the fringes.

They caught up with Diva before too long. She was still plodding forward, oblivious to the branches that scratched at her face.

"Diva, wake up," Nicky said without affect. If the counselor woke on the first try, Nicky would look stupid. Diva kept walking.

"Hey, Diva," Lucia tried clapping her hands along with the syllables. She turned to the others. "Anybody know her real name? Maybe she'll answer to that."

Nicky and Justina shook their heads. Nicky imagined that Killa and Zilla were both the kind of counselors who answered to their camp names even in their sleep, but Lucia was right about Diva.

"Diva, wake up, you're going to miss your audition," Nicky tried. It was worth a shot, but no response.

Justina stopped to tie her shoe, then caught up again. "Should we try shaking her?"

Nicky shook her head. "I think you're not supposed to physically disrupt a sleepwalker, the same as you're not supposed to touch someone during some kinds of seizure." When her grandfather had his space-out seizures, she was supposed to walk with him and tell people what was happening, to try and stop him from getting in any trouble.

Lucia looked thoughtful. "Maybe we can get ahead of her and block her path so she thinks she has to turn around?"

Except they didn't need to put anything in her path, because at that moment, Diva walked face first into a chain-link fence, sending an eerie metallic rattle down the line. She didn't look hurt; she rocked back on her heels and put her left hand out to touch the lattice.

"Can sleepwalkers climb?" whispered Justina, low enough that she couldn't be accused of giving Diva the idea if she heard. The fence was maybe eight feet high, the kind they put around construction sites or mean dogs in the city. Nicky didn't know the answer, so she didn't respond. They'd find out in a second either way.

They stood for a long minute, two, three, who knew, time was endless when you stood in a dark woods with no timekeeping device. Just when Nicky was about to ask if anyone had a watch, Diva stepped back from the fence, reached into her pocket, and then flung something. It glinted in the light of Nicky's headlamp as it arced up and over the fence to land in the branches of an enormous tree on the other side. They all eyed the counselor, whose hands were both now on the fence.

"Was that the van keys?" Lucia asked. "Please tell me that wasn't the van keys."

"It was definitely a keychain," said Nicky.

Diva let out a long sigh, and said, "Memory, my dear Cecily, is the diary that we all carry about with us." She turned around, nearly colliding with Justina, who had been standing right behind her and leapt back like it was a game of blindfold tag. They followed their counselor back through the woods and back to camp, where she crawled into her tent, collapsed on top of her sleeping bag, and immediately stilled.

The three girls stared for a moment, like parents watching a sleeping newborn. A newborn with filthy feet, and something black and stringy and spongy-looking stuck to the soles.

"Should we zip their tent?" Justina asked.

"For Killa," Lucia agreed, fumbling for the zipper. "And I hate to say it, but I think we need to go back up there."

"Wait, what?" Justina looked confused. "We did what we were supposed to do. We saved our counselor from certain death. Now we get to go to sleep."

Nicky was tired too, but she understood what Lucia was saying. "We know where the keys are right now. We should get them while we're still sure of that, before a bird steals them or they fall and the wind covers them with leaves or pine needles or something. Anyway, it was weird, right? I haven't had the map much, but I don't remember seeing any fences on it."

"Maybe it's not on the map because it's not near the path, and you're not supposed to go stomping through the woods in this park."

"Maybe."

Nicky and Lucia exchanged a look.

"If you need to go back to sleep, that's okay," Lucia said. "Nicky and I can be buddies."

"That's not how buddies works! If the two of you go, I'm alone in our tent."

"You can go sleep in my tent," Nicky suggested. "Then, if Meghan wakes up, neither of you is alone."

"But what if something happens to you?" asked the loyal lieutenant. "If there are only two of you out in the woods, and somebody breaks an ankle, the other would have to leave her behind to get help."

"Good point," said Lucia. "You should come with, I guess."

"But then, if someone breaks their ankle, there's still one person running back here alone."

"How's that different from the normal buddy system?"

"One is the outhouse. One is the woods."

"What if we leave a map?"

"Or take someone else."

They argued out the merits of Katie versus Andrea for a moment, before deciding on both. At which point, they could no longer avoid waking Meghan, no matter how difficult it was. It was only fair. They all imagined what it would feel like to know everyone else had gone on an adventure and deliberately left you out, even if you were only being left out because you slept like the dead. Nikki went to wake Katie and Andrea, and Lucia and Justina went to wake Meghan. They had to actually shake her, and she woke swinging a punch that caught Lucia in the arm. Lucia shrugged it off. "We have donkeys. This is nothing."

Once everyone was up and oriented, Katie suggested marking a map and leaving it on her sleeping bag, so if the counselors woke they wouldn't panic that their campers were all gone. Well, they'd panic, of course they would, but maybe they'd panic slightly less. She took the map she'd been leading with out of its Ziploc sleeve.

"Oh, hey," she said, looking closer under the beam of Nicky's headlamp. "Is this where you went?"

She pointed at a featureless blob on the map, shaded green or blue in the washed out light. It said PROTECTED FOREST in small-font block letters along one edge.

Nicky leaned over and looked, then nodded, the light bobbing. "I guess we never really looked at that area since it wasn't on the itinerary." She took out her pen and drew a straight line up the hill to intersect the protected area. She also offered to tear a page out of her notebook to leave an accompanying note, which she thought was a generous offer since it was a good notebook, but nobody could agree on what to say, so she just wrote in the map's margin: "Don't worry. We'll be back in time for breakfast."

Lucia took the pen from Nicky's hand and changed the periods to exclamation points, then drew a smiley face to add to the don't worry vibe. It was only three AM, according to Katie's glowing wristwatch. Plenty of time to go up and back, wherever up was.

Meghan knew she was a sound sleeper. Her mother told her it was an admirable trait, and one to actively cultivate. Someday she'd have roommates, or partners, or pets. She'd live in the city and sleep through sirens, like she slept through fights and drunk voices when they spilled from the Irish bar below their apartment, which her mother said was the loudest place within twenty miles.

The only problem was that waking felt like fighting up through water, through soil, through layers of dream. Especially when she was woken by the other campers, most of whom hadn't even once tried to talk to her, and now wanted to know whether she wanted to come with them on a quest to get a set of keys that Diva had thrown, which might or might not be the van keys, because they all thought sneaking into the counselor tent to check the van key pocket was probably overstepping bounds, but keys had definitely been thrown, so keys must be retrieved. She also didn't quite understand the destination: a hill, a fence, the woods. She followed.

Nicky seemed to be leading the way, which was unusual. She had a light on her head, and a couple of others had flashlights. Meghan concentrated on putting one foot in front of the other without tripping.

They reached a tall metal fence.

"Does protected forest mean they're protecting the trees or something else inside it?" Justina eyed the fence like she hadn't been there half an hour before.

"Maybe it's archaeological."

"Or radioactive."

"Or there's a plant they're trying to protect."

"Or an animal!"

"If it was radioactive, there'd be a different type of fence and more signs," said Nicky. "If it was that or a dangerous animal, there'd be 'keep out' postings. There are plenty of dangerous animals around, anyway."

"Okay, so it's more likely they're trying to keep something safe than to keep something in. In that case, is it smart for us to go in? What if we harm a plant that's being protected?"

"We need to get those keys. We won't go far."

"And if we see any signs saying not to trespass, we won't?"

Deal.

Three of us went left one hundred steps, following the fence line, looking for an opening. Then the other three did the same in the other direction. There had to be a gate somewhere, probably, but it might be above the ridgeline, or on the other side. Not here, so we returned.

It made the most sense to climb the fence at the original spot in any case, since we had a sightline on the keys gleaming in the tree where Diva had thrown them. We'd just put that off because it seemed like the most direct admission of trespassing. Going around a fence or through a gate was exploration; going over was a breach.

"I'll climb," offered Lucia. "We have a really mean goat at home so I'm good at climbing fences fast."

"Or me? I have the headlamp."

"You could loan me your headlamp, Nicky."

Nicky put a hand on it, like she was reluctant to let it go.

"Maybe buddies should do it. We could go together," Andrea said, putting a hand on Katie's sleeve.

Katie didn't look excited about the prospect. "Does it need to be buddies, though? We can all see the person. Someone else can go in after her if they need to, or run for help, but if the area is protected two people means more feet stepping in places we might be harming something."

They'd be arguing until dawn, at that rate. Everyone was so brave about coming up here together, but nobody seemed keen to actually do it now that they were faced with it. Well, Lucia seemed ready, anyway, but she still hadn't made a move since volunteering, like she was okay with being talked out of it.

Nobody was paying attention to Meghan, as usual. She was on the other side before anyone had even seen her put a hand on the fence. They all turned to look at her like they had forgotten she was there.

"It makes sense," she said, her voice gravelly. She cleared her throat. When was the last time she had spoken? "I'm six inches taller than any of you. That's a high branch, so it doesn't matter who's the best fence climber, it matters who can reach the branch."

They all nodded gravely.

"Can somebody loan me a flashlight, though? It doesn't have to be your headlamp, Nicky. I know it's special to you."

Andrea passed a battered red mini-Maglite through the fence mesh. It was already on, and the beam cut a swath through the trees. Meghan turned it around and pointed it down so it wouldn't blind anyone. She didn't really want to say anything else—she'd already said more than she had all week—so she saluted and turned away.

Meghan walked the twenty feet between the fence and the tree carefully, the flashlight angled down to show her if she was stepping on anything that looked delicate: moss, ferns, seedlings, the roots of the young trees at the outer edge of the big tree's canopy. Her footsteps were muffled by a thick blanket of fallen needles.

The tree in question was a huge sitka spruce, big enough that we could all have joined hands and stretched wide and still only reached partway around it. Meghan looked up into the branches. The trees were the darkness, but beyond them the sky was bright, studded with a million stars.

Diva had quite the throwing arm: the keyring had gone over a branch's point like a ring onto a finger, which was a real what-are-the-odds scenario. Below it dangled a braided plastic lanyard, the kind you made in arts and crafts, and an alarm fob that said Ford on it, and a single key. Which didn't explain why Diva had thrown it, but did suggest we had been right to climb in here.

She was also right about being the only one able to reach the branch in question; even she, tallest in the group, was going to have to jump to bring it down. She was half-hearted in her first attempt, conscious that if she reached, her shirt would ride up, and she had an aversion to letting people see her belly-button, which was an outie. She missed by inches.

"You can do it, Meghan," somebody called. A feeling washed over her, a physical wave of support, letting her know we actually believed in her. She turned so her back was to the group, and this time her fingers brushed the lanyard and closed around it. The branch bent and came down with her, and when the keyring slid off, it sprang back into place, and she slipped on the needles underfoot and fell backwards.

She landed hard, on her butt and her back and her elbows. Not her head, at least. Embarrassing. Lucia would have sprung like a cat, but Meghan was not catlike; she never felt in control of herself the way it looked like everyone else was. Her back hurt. She rolled to her side and then pushed up to a sitting position, picking spruce needles out of her palms and elbows. She was only bleeding a little. She thought she heard someone calling to her, but it didn't sound like anyone from their group, and she shook her head to clear it. She hadn't hit her head.

We were there a moment later; we'd all climbed the fence and come to her rescue. We fussed over her, and examined the van keys, and one by one put our hands on the enormous spruce's trunk, then on the needle-strewn forest floor.

"Whoa," said Andrea. Someone else echoed, a softer "whoa."

"Ow," said Justina, and the rest of us touched our backs as well.

I'll be okay, Meghan thought, and we all nodded at the assurance as if she had spoken.

Whoa, thought Katie, and a feeling of *whoa* echoed in our heads.

We all thought *huh* and we all thought *whoa* again, and then Lucia said out loud, "Science Facts, ladies," and in her head, Nicky said, *no*, and then out loud, "No, a new game: Science Theories. Any theories, regardless of scientific validity."

"Mass delusion," said Andrea.

"Collective dream," said Katie.

"Zombie fungus," said Justina.

"I marked a tree with mud but I maybe got blood in it," said Lucia, all in one breath, like a confession, "and Justina peed on a tree to mark it—"

"Hey," said Justina, and we all felt the momentary wounding, but Lucia had no bad intention, only a fear that in marking trees, we had all somehow introduced ourselves into the forest, and Nicky pointed out that we'd all been peeing in the forest all week, and brushing our teeth and spitting, and breathing, so the forest already had our DNA if—

Listen, thought Meghan at the others, and we all shut up again. The six of us were loud, loud in our thoughts and in our voices, but behind the noise of us, below the noise of us, around the noise of us, there was something beyond sound: an exchange of information in a language none of us spoke. (Yet.) We all stilled ourselves and tried to hear it, whatever it was. We couldn't, we couldn't, but it carried with it a. Feeling. Of safety. Protection, because we were small, and would take centuries to reach our full heights, to touch the stars with our crowns.

We wiped our eyes with our sleeves. We knew without knowing that it wasn't mass delusion, or a collective dream, or a zombie fungus.

"We need to go back," Andrea whispered. Nobody moved. A pang of sadness passed between us, a finality, the same feeling as the end of camp when you knew the end of camp meant going back to non-camp life, where we had to be different people, where nobody serenaded us at sunset. Carried through us all, the question *will this fade?* Glances up into our branches, then down into our roots, where the loudest voices traveled mycorrhizal superhighways beneath our feet, though we didn't have those words yet either, those would come later, in our research, in our practice, in our secret and silent conversations.

The trees lit up in a strange too-bright glow, and it took us a moment to realize another flashlight was bobbing toward us, painting us blue-white, pinning us in place.

"Who's there?" called Lucia. "Diva?"

"Ranger," came a voice we didn't recognize, invisible in the beam's glare. "You *you* aren't *aren't* supposed *supposed* to *to* be *be* in *in* here *here*."

Someone said *run*, or else someone thought it loud enough for us all to hear. Katie offered a hand to help Meghan up from where she was still sitting, and we all ran for the fence, Nicky's trusty headlamp guiding us. Lucia the fastest up and over, because of her mean goat. We felt the disconnection when our feet left the ground, held collective breath with shoes shoved into metal lattice, then unspoken relief when the ground welcomed us back on the other side.

We looked back, but the flashlight didn't follow. We shared a collective image glimpsed as we ran past the ranger for the fence: a shoeless, featureless ranger-shape, with tendrils spilling from a stained and split uniform.

It was still dark when we dropped the keychain outside the counselor tent and climbed into our own. Our eyes burned with exhaustion. We took our boots off inside the tents as we were supposed to, and set them just inside the flap. Peeled off our socks and examined our fingers and toes and wondered if it was possible to change and not be changed, if we would grow roots or needles or cones or spores.

In the morning, Killa would wonder why the van keys were in the dirt, and why we were all dragging; none of us would tell. Diva would hide her feet from us as she put on socks and shoes, and we'd feel that pang of loss again, knowing we could never come back here, and something like pity that washed in her direction. She would startle as if she felt it. We would continue our hike along the river.

Later that day, we would reach the alpine meadows that were our destination, and we would trail our fingers in frigid turquoise lakes and snap pictures of mountain goats and lupine and aster and Jacob's ladder. We would cook dinner over the tiny gas burner, and sing a round of songs, and then Diva would tell a story about how an actor went up a mountain with a bunch of campers but couldn't remember how many, and the number kept changing, and Justina would interrupt and say "Memory, my dear Cecily, is the diary that we all carry about with us," and Diva would ask why she was quoting Oscar Wilde, and we'd all erupt in giggles.

Then she'd pretend to try to finish the story but Killa would stop her, and we would go to our tents to sleep, and Killa would tell

Diva it seemed like we were all getting along better, acting as a more cohesive group, and Diva would say she'd noticed it too.

Katie would wake two hours later with a nightmare, but instead of screaming, she'd reach for the rest of us. *Are you out there?* The chorus returned *yes yes yes yes yes* and then another tentative *yes,* and another that wasn't a yes at all but felt like one. We would lie in our tents for a few more minutes, and then as one drag our sleeping bags out to the clearing, and we would drift off looking up at the stars, wondering how long it would take for our crowns to reach them.

Acknowledgments

I always put off writing acknowledgements to the last possible minute. It isn't that I have nobody to thank, but the opposite. I'm so nervous I'll forget someone that I think it's probably better not to do it at all, which is silly. Better to try.

This book was edited by the wonderful Kelly Link and Gavin J. Grant, who have turned a disparate group of stories into something cohesive. P. Rebecca Maines did valiant proofreading.

The original editors of these stories deserve thanks as well: John Joseph Adams, Jason Sizemore & Lesley Conner, Cat Rambo, Ellen Datlow, Lynne & Michael Thomas, Scott Andrews, Catherine Krahe, Lila Garrott, and An Owomoyela, Monica Louzon, Wade Roush, and the rest of the editorial teams at *Strange Horizons, Lightspeed, Apex, Tor.com, Uncanny, Beneath Ceaseless Skies,* and the assorted anthologies represented herein.

Kim-Mei Kirtland is thoughtful, perceptive, and generous with her time, a great combination in an agent.

Most of these stories went through various trusted readers, and are the better for the sharp eyes of my mother, Amira, Ellie, Sherry, Rep, Kellan, the Sparkleponies, and the attendees of the Sycamore Hill workshop. Shawn Behling gave me useful plant information for both "Where Oaken Hearts Do Gather" and "Science Facts!" and also has an extremely good dog. My father, R.B. Lemberg, Matt

Kressel, the members of the Learn Yiddish group on Facebook, and the librarians of the Enoch Pratt Public Library helped me recreate the past in "A Better Way of Saying."

My family could not be more supportive. I would love them even if that weren't the case, but it's a nice perk. My dogs walk me, and walks are where my stories start, so they get thanked here as well.

A lot of people on a lot of great zoom calls kept me social and motivated through these last couple of years, and I am grateful to the hosts and the participants. I also want to acknowledge every bookseller, librarian, public radio interviewer, professor, booktuber, blogger, reviewer, and reader who gives my weird books a chance, and the talented translators who introduce my stories to new audiences. Special shout-outs to Baltimore's Atomic Books, the Ivy Bookshop, Greedy Reads, Charm City Books, Bird in Hand, and Snug Books, and to Bakka-Phoenix in Toronto, my other not-so-lost place.

Lastly, Zu: my heart, my home.

Publication History

"Two Truths and a Lie," Tor.com, 2020.

"That Our Flag Was Still There," *If This Goes On,* 2019.

"I Frequently Hear Music in the Very Heart of Noise," *Uncanny,* 2018.

"The Boy Who Will Become Court Magician," *Lightspeed,* 2018.

"Everything Is Closed Today," *Do Not Go Quietly,* 2019.

"Left the Century to Sit Unmoved," *Strange Horizons,* 2016.

"Escape from Caring Seasons," *Twelve Tomorrows,* 2018.

"A Better Way of Saying," Tor.com, 2021.

"Remember This for Me," *Explorers, Catalysts, and Secret Keepers: Women of Science Fiction,* 2017.

"The Mountains His Crown," *Beneath Ceaseless Skies,* 2016.

"Where Oaken Hearts Do Gather," *Uncanny,* 2021.

"Science Facts!" is published here for the first time.

About the Author

Sarah Pinsker is the author of over fifty works of short fiction, two novels, and two collections. Her work has won four Nebula Awards, two Hugo Awards, the Philip K. Dick Award (for her first collection, *Sooner or Later Everything Falls into the Sea*), the Locus Award, the Eugie Foster Award, and the Theodore Sturgeon Award, and been nominated for numerous Nebula, Hugo, Locus, and World Fantasy Awards.

She is also a singer/songwriter with four albums on various independent labels. She has wrangled horses, managed grants, taught writing to college and high school students, and tended bar badly. She lives in Baltimore with her wife and two rescued terriers. Find her online at sarahpinsker.com.

Reconstruction: Stories
Alaya Dawn Johnson
HURSTON/WRIGHT LEGACY AWARD FINALIST

"Haunting, not just for its vividness, but also for how Johnson writes around felt and imagined absences."
— *Chicago Review of Books*

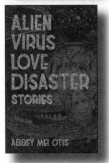

Alien Virus Love Disaster: Stories
Abbey Mei Otis
NEUKOM DEBUT LITERARY AWARD SHORTLIST
PHILIP K. DICK AWARD FINALIST
BOOKLIST TOP 10 DEBUT SF&F

"An exciting voice. . . . dreamy but with an intense physicality." — *Washington Post* Best Science Fiction & Fantasy of the year

Ambiguity Machines: Stories
Vandana Singh
PHILIP K. DICK AWARD FINALIST
LOCUS RECOMMENDED READING LIST

"Singh breathes new life into the themes of loneliness, kinship, love, curiosity, and the thirst for knowledge. *Ambiguity Machines and Other Stories* is a literary gift for us all."
— Rachel Cordasco, *World Literature Today*

In Other Lands: a novel
Sarah Rees Brennan
ALA RAINBOW BOOK LIST, JUNIOR LIBRARY GUILD SELECTION, GEORGIA PEACH & FLORIDA TEENS READ AWARD NOMINEE, MYTHOPOEIC, HUGO, & LOCUS AWARD FINALIST

"Best of all, over four years in the otherlands, Elliot grows from a defensive, furious, grieving child into a diplomatic, kind, menschy hero."
— *New York Times Book Review*